DYNAMO

What Others Are Saying about *Dynamo*

In *Dynamo*, Eleanor Gustafson weaves four threads—the man, his horse, his faith, and his God—into a tapestry of redemption. You won't need to be a lover of fine horses to care about the journey of one man and how his horse Dynamo took him on the ride of his life. You'll find wisdom in this journey.

—*Jane Kirkpatrick*
New York Times best-selling author, *All Together in One Place*

Ellie Gustafson's newest offering, *Dynamo*, is aptly named—a dynamic story, well-written and engaging, expertly carrying the reader from page to page. Highly recommended!

—*Kathi Macias*
Award-winning author of more than thirty books,
including the Extreme Devotion series

Once again, Eleanor Gustafson has woven a story that will linger in her readers' minds long after the cover is closed. It is a riveting tale, set in a world of high-stakes horse shows and stable intrigue, and an unflinching look at some of the best and worst in human relationships. Through experiences that range from the mundane to the mystical, we see and feel Jeth's struggle. Surrounded by people who are, in the extraordinary way of ordinary people, heroes and failures, victims and villains, he begins to discern the path he is to follow. As is so often the case in real life, that path leads neither where he planned nor where he feared.

—*Sally Wilkins*
Teacher and author, *Sports and Games of Medieval Cultures*

Packed with the fascinating world of show horses, *Dynamo* is a rich tale of redemption, renewal, and hope. Readers will appreciate the fast-moving plot, and root for the lifelike characters. May God "hug your soul" as you read this story.

—*Alice J. Wisler*
Author, *Rain Song, How Sweet It Is,* and *Hatteras Girl*

In typical Ellie Gustafson style, *Dynamo* is a complex interweaving of characters and relationships that wrestles with some of the central issues of life. The problem of good versus evil plays out in the world of show horses in a way that fascinated me, despite my being totally unfamiliar with that milieu. That the book held my interest speaks well of Ellie's skill as a storyteller. Please wonder with me: Will this tale get the sequel it deserves?

—*John A. Nunnikhoven*
Author, *Voices Together: A Guide to Praying the Psalms*

You'll like this book—especially if you enjoy memorable people, frustrating problems, and unexpected outcomes. Eleanor Gustafson writes a stimulating story about the fascinating world of show horses as it intersects with the life-changing world of discipleship. Her characters persuade us that even imperfect Christians can demonstrate wisdom and courage in our secular world.

—*Dr. David A. Dean*
Author, *Good Grief,* and Professor Emeritus,
Gordon-Conwell Theological Seminary, Hamilton, Massachusetts

Ellie writes you into the heart of her story, and you can't get out until it's over!

—*Lois Shaw*
Coauthor, *Today's All-Star Missions Churches* and
Missions in the Twenty-First Century

As Dick Francis brought detective fiction to the world of horse racing, Ellie Gustafson brings theology and the redemptive grace of God to the world of show horses. We find suspense and mystery, as well, as the hand of God shapes the lives of Jeth and Janni. Interludes between action sequences provide quiet moments for the reader to ponder the deeper mysteries of the Word of God.

—*Dr. George Varghese*
Principal Researcher, Microsoft Research; winner of the 2014
Koji Kobayashi Award for Computers and Communications

In this novel, you will find an engaging cast of characters (including horses), a new faith, a nonstop plot, and a satisfyingly hard-won conclusion. As well, it will leave you thinking. Go for it!

—*A. D. Ferguson*
Professor Emeritus, Gordon College, Wenham, Massachusetts

You will love this fast-moving page-turner that throws you into the competitive world of champion horses. Trainer Jeth Cavanaugh grapples with his past, his lost love, and the five-gaited Saddlebred stallion Dynamo, who is as much of a hothead as is Jeth himself. Each chapter draws you into the mighty work of the God who redeems Jeth and molds him into a new creation. While Jeth is transforming his beautiful chestnut stallion from hellion to show champion, God is shaping Jeth into a servant He can use. You will root for Jeth and Janni in their struggle to repair past relationships and change the brokenness surrounding them. As you close the book, you will cheer the new Dynamo and long for a sequel that continues God's redemptive work—in these characters and in our own lives, as well.

—*Loren Hilgenhurst Stevens*
Owner of gaited show horses; Dean of Academics,
Bradford Christian Academy
Bradford, Massachusetts

Dynamo is a horse story, but not really. The horse is almost a metaphor for the leading character, whose history, persona, and experiences bring him into contact with a spiritual dimension he could not have imagined. Ms. Gustafson writes with insight about real people who have to deal both with their own faith and the actual difficulties of life. God's interface with Jeth requires some serious thinking on the part of the reader, to analyze and compare with Scripture how God gets our attention in our busy world. Not all stories have happy endings, as is true for all of us. The reader will be drawn into the lives of those who appear on these pages. I doubt that anyone will be able to forget how it all comes together.

—*Bruce Strickland*
Retired pastor; former Bible teacher and chaplain, Keswick Christian School, St. Petersburg, Florida

DYNAMO

A NOVEL

Eleanor Gustafson

WHITAKER HOUSE

Publisher's Note:

This novel is a work of fiction. References to real events, organizations, or places are used in a fictional context. Any resemblances to actual persons, living or dead, are entirely coincidental.

Scripture quotations represent several versions: The *Holy Bible, New International Reader's Version*, nirv, © 1996, 1998 by Biblica. All rights reserved throughout the world. Used by permission of Biblica. The *Holy Bible, New International Version*, niv, © 1973, 1978, 1984 by the International Bible Society. Used by permission of Zondervan. All rights reserved. *The Message: The Bible in Contemporary Language* by Eugene H. Peterson, © 1993, 1994, 1995, 1996, 2000, 2001, 2002. Used by permission of NavPress Publishing Group. All rights reserved. The *Holy Bible, New Living Translation*, © 1996, 2004, 2007. Used by permission of Tyndale House Publishers, Inc., Carol Stream, Illinois 60188. All rights reserved. The *Holy Bible, New International Version*, niv, © 1973, 1978, 1984, 2011 by Biblica, Inc. Used by permission. All rights reserved worldwide.

The quotation from Henri Nouwen on page 11 is taken from *Show Me the Way* (New York: Crossroad Publishing, 1994), 116.

DYNAMO

Eleanor Gustafson
www.eleanorgustafson.com

ISBN: 978-1-62911-006-6
eBook ISBN: 978-1-62911-030-1
Printed in the United States of America
© 2014 by Eleanor Gustafson

Whitaker House
1030 Hunt Valley Circle
New Kensington, PA 15068
www.whitakerhouse.com

Library of Congress Cataloging-in-Publication Data

Gustafson, Eleanor.
Dynamo / by Eleanor Gustafson.
    pages cm
ISBN 978-1-62911-006-6 (alk. paper)—ISBN 978-1-62911-030-1 (eBook)
    I. Title.
    PS3557.U835D96 2014
    813'.54—dc23   2014000061

1 2 3 4 5 6 7 8 9 10 11 ⊔⊔ 20 19 18 17 16 15 14

In memory of Lydie—my horse mentor and instructor in important things, such as the birds of the air, the lilies of the field, and time spent with kids instead of housework.

PREFACE

Dynamo is a work of fiction, but you will meet characters, both Christian and not, who are caught in ugly, real-life issues such as anger, bad choices, broken marriages, tragic losses, unbearable stress, vicious behavior, and lust. But you'll also meet faith, forgiveness, trust, and love poured out to the last ounce.

Woven into this nubbly fabric are the gold threads of the God who is unpredictable, true, and faithful—the God of Ezekiel and Daniel and Maybelle; the sovereign God who pulls and shapes and lifts Jeth into the unfathomably rich fellowship of suffering servanthood.

The horse world may be new territory for you. If you need help with some of the terms, please refer to the glossary in the back of the book.

Dive in and find where you fit into this hearty mix of good and bad.

God cannot be understood; he cannot be grasped by the human mind. The truth escapes our human capacities.... We only can be faithful in our affirmation that God has not deserted us but calls us in the middle of all the unexplainable absurdities of life.... God cannot be limited by any human concept or prediction. He is greater than our mind and heart and perfectly free to reveal himself where and when he wants.

—Henri J. M. Nouwen

1

One last kiss. Simple, unadorned, passionless; two seconds, at best; and in a bottom-end motel parking lot. But kisses of any sort had been long in coming, and this one, impoverished though it was, was the last touch of love Jeth was apt to get for a long time to come.

After the quick kiss, Jeth stepped back and closed the door of Janni's powder-blue Acura. As he did, he noticed a thread of her dark hair on his sleeve. He would keep that; he'd need it to warm his emptiness. As she backed the car out, he clapped the hood and waved. His eyes hungered after her, pursued her, out of the driveway and into the stream of traffic. He looked at the hair again and shivered in a breeze that couldn't decide between winter and spring. He turned and walked slowly around the faded, scratched trunk of his own clunker. He was glad to have the heap. No money, no job, and a no-good reputation. Basic transportation, yes—along with a full gas tank and a hundred dollars that Janni had put in his pocket. Plus three pieces of cold pepperoni pizza.

"Don't call me," Janni had said. "If Daddy guessed I was even talking to you, he'd ship me to Africa, or even the South Pole."

"You're a big girl now. Somebody once took horses to the South Pole, y' know."

"Don't change the subject. Daddy can do what he wants with me, and you know it."

"I called you yesterday and got away with it. Are you sorry?"

"Of course I'm not sorry, but it's not safe."

"Why don't you do the unthinkable and get a job—get away from Daddy? Twenty-six is old enough to think and act on your own."

"Wingate women don't work. Mom buzzed off because she wanted something more satisfying than kissing the emperor's feet. If I behave myself—according to his majesty's way of thinking— I'm golden. If not... Jeth, whatever you end up doing, *don't call me.*"

Don't call. Be alone. Be cut off from everyone you know, from everything you know how to do. Horses had been his life. Horses and Janni...

He leaned his hands against the rust-pocked car and stretched his back, picking through his thoughts to determine if being with Janni once again had made him feel better or worse. He harvested the hair from his sleeve, held it up and studied it, then released it to the breeze that had suddenly become winter.

He drove almost aimlessly along the pleated ridges that marked central Pennsylvania, his eyes drawn to the long mountains that folded one into another with receding shades of green, gray, and blue. Two years deprived of that view...

He sighed and went back to considering what to do. He had hoped those few hours with Janni would help him sort things out, but he had been too distracted to think along those lines.

Early in the afternoon and a slice of pizza later, he realized he had taken a wrong turn onto a backwater road that appeared to angle across a broad valley. He didn't have a destination in mind, but he did have a direction, and across the valley wasn't it. For whatever blurry reason, he had wanted to stay on the ridge road. While looking for a place to turn around, he spotted a number of horses behind a row of new-leaved trees. Fine horses. Wingate horses, not low-grade nags. Animals worthy of white board fencing and a barn with copper-roofed cupola. But this picture was wrong. Some of the fencing was board—weathered and sagging— but far too much of it was smooth wire. Not safe. He drove slowly and came to a rutted driveway with a small, amateurish sign, "Morningstar Stables." He could turn around here, or...

On a whim and a shrug, he swung the wheel and bounced up a curved grade that opened on a large yard. Straight ahead, the open door of a sizeable though ancient barn revealed a number of stalls. To the right, more horses grazed in another pasture, with a narrow, board-fenced pass-through to the far field. To the left was a steel roundpen about sixty feet across, and behind it was a large ring enclosed by more patchwork boards—some nailed, some tied—with a number of jumps spaced around. A couple of rust-defined horse trailers slouched to the left of the barn—one a four-horse fifth-wheel, the other a more plebian two-horse rig. Far to the left, he could see an unremarkable house sheltered in a grove of trees, and around from that sat an ancient trailer, partly hidden by budded lilacs.

He parked beneath a huge, multi-trunked pine tree that over-spread an ornate bench, by far the most elegant object in sight. He uncoiled from the car and ambled to the barn, gritting his teeth against the unexpected stab of emotion that horse sounds and smells evoked within him. It had been a long time. Two hay-munching horses nickered, but he saw no person. He left the barn and was about to try the house when the door of a makeshift office on the right swung open. A man came out, gave a momentary start of surprise, and approached Jeth, his broad, open face smiling in welcome. "Sorry. I was on the phone and didn't hear you drive up. Can I help you?"

"Hello. Jeth Cavanaugh." He reached out a hand. "How you doing?"

"Rob Chilton. Welcome to Morningstar." A denim jacket, slightly less worn than his jeans, covered shoulders that match Jeth's, though his height lacked a couple of inches. He appeared a little older, perhaps early thirties, and Jeth sensed both presence and solidarity.

"I was driving by and saw some of your horses." Jeth waved toward the two pastures. "Nice stock. Thought I'd take a closer look."

"Are you looking to buy or just looking?" Rob smiled disarmingly.

Jeth shrugged. "Buying's a ways off, but is the looking free?"

Rob laughed. "Special deal. Today only. You know horses? Tell me about yourself."

Jeth didn't answer directly. His long, asymmetrical face twisted wryly. "You've got interesting, well-placed jumps in the ring. You train jumpers?"

"Yes, we do."

"For stadium jumping?" His voice edged toward incredulity.

"Yup. Getting over the jumps is all that matters. We're low-key here, me and my wife just starting up. Right now we have six promising jumpers, a couple of maybes, and two pleasure horses just for fun and a little income. Katie—my wife—gives lessons on Saturdays. She loves kids, and it's a welcome change from barn work and training. The bay to the right is Meg." He pointed toward the near pasture. "A sweetheart. Reads your soul. Won't ever take advantage. Jake—that big, broad sorrel against the trees on the left. Some draft-horse genes in him, but you'll never sit a more comfortable canter."

"Neither of them jumps, I take it."

"No. Pure pleasure. We've got a nice trail network through the woods behind the barn." Rob waved to the left. "Three, four miles, and a couple of overlooks with benches, where we can eat a sandwich and enjoy the view of Duncan ridge across the way. Our trail hooks up with another system, so we—"

"Whoa! Who's that?" Jeth exclaimed, as a small, dark horse careened around the pasture, tail up and neck kinked. Three others joined the romp, kicking and squealing.

"He's our baby, a Warmblood with sterling genes. Toogentia's Jewel, aka Toogie."

"Warmblood!"

"Yes. Mid-weight horses, between 'cold blood' draft horses on one end and 'hot bloods' like Arabians on the other. Bred more for what they do than what they look like."

"Toogie. Wow! Look at him! Turns on a dime. Quarter-horse genes along with Warmblood? Whatever, he'll fill out well. A charcoal beauty."

"He'll end up white, but a stunner, for sure. You've jumped?"

"Yes." Jeth hesitated but then went on, with a crooked smile. "I was practically born on a horse, grew up on a horse farm. My dad was one of the trainers."

"*One* of the trainers?"

"Yes." He didn't elaborate. "I've done some training, some showing, but I'm willing to do anything, even muck stalls." He grinned, seeing the question in Rob's eyes. "And, yes, I'm looking for a job."

"Well, let me see you ride." Rob turned toward the first stall. "I was just going to work Peanut. Let's saddle him and see how you do."

Rob pulled tack from a dowel-lined alcove and passed the saddle to Jeth. "He needs grooming," he said, brushing sawdust out of the sorrel mane. "But swiping him will have to do."

They led Peanut to the mounting block outside. The saddle creaked comfortably as Jeth mounted, a look of bliss softening the rugged contours of his face. "Oh, this feels good! I'm a little rusty, so cut me some slack till I get the feel of him."

"Wait! I'll get a helmet." Rob jogged to the barn and back, and after passing off the headgear, he watched as Jeth rode the ring perimeter. He trotted till the horse had finished the snort-and-cough routine, then cantered, taking his time before going at an easy fence. He moved to fences of increasing height and difficulty. The horse wavered at one. Jeth pulled him around, went back, and then took him over three more times, from various approaches.

Rob's eyes widened. While they walked the horse cool, he turned to Jeth with a touch of awe. "You're pretty amazing, you know that? Natural seat, oneness with the horse…riders like you don't drop out of the sky every day, y' know." He grinned. "What stable was it you grew up on? One around here?"

Jeth averted his eyes and ran a hand through his flyaway hair.

"Maybe I shouldn't have asked that."

"At some point, I may have to tell you, but for now…"

"For now, let me put Peanut in the pasture. Be right back."

Jeth's attention was caught by squeals of rage and a thunderous attack on the sides of a stall at the back of the stable.

"Don't mind him," said Rob, coming back inside. "That's Dynamo, a five-gaited stallion thrown in on a deal we couldn't refuse. Gorgeous animal, registered American Saddlebred, but a mean devil. We'll be lucky to live through him till I can unload him. Know anyone who wants a hunky stud?" He grinned.

"Can I see him?"

"Not easy, but we'll try." Rob grabbed a bucket and scooped a handful of grain from the feed bin. When they got close to the stall, the stallion renewed his attack. Rob raised his eyebrows and shook his head, but with a lead in one hand and grain bucket in the other, he opened the door and cautiously snapped the lead to the halter. He looped the lead chain over the stallion's nose and led him out, fighting him all the way.

Jeth whistled. Dynamo, a coppery chestnut with long, flaxen mane and tail and finely chiseled head and neck, had almost perfect conformation. The fire in his eye hinted at a raging furnace deep within his heart and bones. "Big guy! Sixteen-two hands?"

"Sixteen-three," Rob said. "He looks a mess. We don't clean him often, obviously, but he's a beauty." He pulled debris from Dynamo's mane and swiped sawdust and loose hair off his neck. "He's shedding. Needs a good grooming, but not today." He grinned.

"Yikes—those feet! How does he walk without tripping?"

"Yeah, I should have the farrier pare them back. I doubt we'll show him anytime soon, but that's how he came, so we've kept them that way. Long toes make them pick up their feet—high. That and ankle chains. But we're not training him, so no chains."

Jeth shook his head in wonder. "Saddlebreds are a way different breed. And it can't be just a matter of training. His tail..."

"That's cosmetic. They nick the tail muscle, and we've got a tail set to train it up. A horse curler." Rob grinned. "We've never put it on him. They tell me the tail nick doesn't bother the horse. If anything, helps them swish flies easier."

Jeth made a face. "Not natural, though—full, beautiful tail, forced up like that."

"I'm with you there," said Rob. "But Dynamo's got a mane and tail to die for—when it's clean. He'd be a sight in the show ring. I watched a five-gaited class last year, and they're awesome. And, to some degree it is a matter of training, though a few horses seem born with the moves. Don't know much else...except, they told me, Saddlebreds were developed on Kentucky plantations. Robert E. Lee's horse Traveller was a Saddlebred. How about that?"

"Cool! Traveller was probably friendlier than Dynamo, though. Okay, the gaits: walk, trot, canter, like other horses. Then what? The feet come down separately, like a fast walk? Can't remember what it's called."

"Slow gait. Probably like Traveller. And rack is a fast slow gait, if that makes sense." Rob laughed. "From what I've seen and heard, the faster, the better."

"Is this guy rideable?"

"I've been on him once."

"Can I try?"

"How much do you value your life?"

Jeth grinned and cocked his head. "Not enough to pass up the chance!"

They cross-tied Dynamo and got the saddle on his back, dodging kicks, bites, and foreleg strikes, but before they could cinch the girth, they had to bridle him—even more difficult. Together they managed to get all the tack in place, and again, Rob complimented Jeth on his way with horses.

Jeth mounted cautiously. "Huh! I could see this saddle was different, but sitting on it..." He started to shorten the stirrups.

"Uh-uh. Saddle seat is long stirrups. Not like jumping. Different breed, different saddle, different way of riding. Actually, the stirrups should be even longer. You've got more leg than I do." Rob adjusted one side, and Jeth the other. "That looks better. Now, sit back and push your feet forward."

"Like this?"

"Sort of. The idea, they told me, is to keep your weight off the horse's forequarters so he'll pick his feet up higher. I did what I was told but didn't ride him long enough to get used to it."

Jeth's eyebrows went up. "A lot to think about here!"

Rob led him to the ring, keeping out of mouth range. "If he dumps you in here, at least I won't have to chase all over the county to catch him."

Jeth put the horse to a slow trot. Dynamo shook kinks out of his neck, and might have done worse, but Jeth held him in check. "This is weird, sitting this way. But, man! The power underneath me! Like a jet plane on takeoff."

"Yeah—saddle seat plus power." Rob raised his eyebrows. "When you think he's ready, pull him to a walk before you canter. They're not like jumpers, cantering from a trot."

Cantering released a few more kinks, but Jeth kept his seat, pulled him down, and started over again.

"Wow!" said Rob. "What a rocker!"

"So far, so good. Okay, gears one, two, and three. How do you get into fourth?"

"They said to sit back and work the reins somehow, sort of high and out. Try whatever. I sort of got him into it, but it didn't last, and I gave up."

Jeth tried a few times from a walk, but the horse would only trot. He kept pulling him down. "All right, feet forward, sit back, reins high, and—hey! He's doing it!"

"Good show! Let him get the feel of it before you push him."

"Man, what a horse! He's Dynamo, for sure! Dynamite!"

"Looks good."

"Okay, big guy, let's see what you can do." Jeth brought his heels back ever so slightly, and the horse responded, going faster. He didn't hold for long, though, breaking into a canter.

"Not bad for a start," said Rob. "Looked *really* good!"

Jeth left the ring and dismounted, patting the horse's neck. Dynamo responded with a vicious thigh bite. Jeth swatted his mouth, and the horse swung around, half rearing. Jeth, jaw set, pulled him back and handed him to Rob. "Hold him." He gathered the reins, quickly remounted, and took the horse back into the ring. He got him into a slow gait, then rack, and held him to it till the horse was breathing heavily. Then he slowed him, patted his neck, and dismounted, patting him as he had before. This time, there was not even token retaliation.

"Whoo!" was all Rob could say.

They walked and talked until the horse was cool.

"Where do you live?" asked Rob.

Jeth scratched his head and smiled. "Wherever I need to, to work here."

Rob laughed. "Well, we've got an old trailer over there." He gestured toward it. "Not much, but the roof doesn't leak. Can't offer much in actual money, but hopefully that will improve. But before we get down to the fine points, there are some things we need to talk about."

After putting Dynamo in the stall, Rob led Jeth to the bench under the tree. "Can I get you something to drink?"

Jeth shook his head. "I'm good." He stood for a moment, admiring the cast-iron metalwork of the bench back that featured a running horse with mane and tail flying. "That's pretty fine!"

"When Katie's dad died, we got some stuff, but that was the only thing of his she really cared about. He was a horse lover all his life."

They sat. Rob studied his boots a moment, then looked up. "Katie and I are Christ followers. I don't know if that means anything to you, but it's an important issue." He eyed Jeth, who was listening intently.

Rob went on. "We do things differently than a lot of people. I won't cheat a buyer, and I give the good and the bad about every horse I try to sell. We stay away from bad language and wouldn't want it used here. We wouldn't want drinking on the job, and we'd have to talk about on the premises." He glanced toward the trailer and looked sideways again. Jeth remained silent. "Smoking, as well. Those are safety issues, as well as our own preference. Of course, drugs are out. We don't want either people or horses messed with."

This time, Jeth looked down but didn't say anything.

"How does all that sound to you?"

Jeth didn't respond right away. Then he looked off and said to the empty air, "I really want the job. There's so much going on here, so many possibilities, and maybe I could bring some things to it. I think you and I would get along fine, at least from what I've seen so far. And"—he looked at Rob, his long, crooked face grinning—"there's Dynamo."

Rob chuckled. "Let's go in the house. I want you to meet Katie—my little dynamo."

2

Jeth found Katie to be as welcoming as a bowl of soup, as practical as oatmeal, and, disturbingly, as provocative as a hot-sauced taco. She was smaller than Janni, far less suave, but equally vivacious. Her hair—short, curly, reddish blonde—put her in a different descriptive category from Janni, though Jeth couldn't quite read her label. Without apology, she tossed newspapers and magazines off the couch in the living room. "Please, sit down. Can I get you something to drink? Have you had lunch?"

Without mentioning the cold pizza, Jeth assured her that he was fine, but water would be nice. While she got it, he looked around. The house was unpretentious and hodgepodge, the furniture worn but bearing elegance akin to the bench outdoors. Horse art, some of fine quality, hung willy-nilly on the walls. Passion lived here, Jeth decided, and while money may have been part of Katie's inheritance package, the bulk of the couple's capital had been plowed into the jumpers, leaving only odd bits of monied interest to support their relaxed lifestyle.

"Jeth—cool name," she said. "As in 'Jethro'?"

Jeth fought the face he was trying not to make. "No. Not Jethro. Some people I'd rather forget used to—"

"Jeth is looking for a job," Rob cut in. "He's been around horses all his life and has trained and shown jumpers. I watched him ride, and he way outclasses me!"

Katie looked at Jeth with astonishment. "You'd actually want to work here? We're not exactly a major operation." She glanced at Rob. "We trying hard, but—"

"Hey," said Jeth, laughing, "how many jobs offer a super work environment *and* a resident devil named Dynamo?"

"Yeah," said Rob. "You should've seen him ride Dynamo. Got him to slow gait and rack. The serious rack came after Dynamo bit him. Jeth whacked him, remounted, and made him move. A fine show! I think we'd have trouble keeping Jeth's mind on jumpers."

AS THEY WENT back outside with drink refills in hand, Jeth said, "A good woman there. A keeper." He grinned.

Rob led the way back to the bench and sat down. Jeth sat beside him, hunched over his drink and some inner discomfort.

After a moment, Rob said, "How's your leg?"

Jeth grunted. "Which part of my leg do you have in mind?"

"Oh." Rob laughed. "Not just the bite, hm? Sore from riding, are we?"

"Muscles coming out of cold storage." He looked down again.

Rob sipped his drink, then looked at Jeth. "Both of us like you and are excited about the 'possibilities,' as you say, but I do need a straight answer about how you think you'd fit in with our requirements." He spoke gently.

Jeth was silent a moment. Color left his face, exposing a wash of panic. He took a series of preliminary breaths and stared straight ahead. "There's something you need to know." Long pause. "I just got out of prison. Two years of a three-year sentence." He looked down and swallowed. "I was riding in a show and badly wanted to win, for reasons that don't matter now. I shot up my horse. I'd seen it done, there and elsewhere. I knew it was going on; everyone else knew it. What I didn't know was that very day, that particular show association plugged in drug testing on winners. I got caught, along with others. I don't know for a fact, but I'm pretty sure I'm the only one who went to jail because of it. Papa Wingate saw to that."

Rob drew a sharp breath. "Wingate! You rode for *Wingate?* Or probably against him."

Jeth straightened and sighed. "For him. He nailed me—real good."

"But you said it was going on and everyone knew about it. Drugging a horse doesn't call for a three-year sentence."

"Oh, he managed! The mare came down with osteochondritis, a joint thing that could've come from just about anything, and Wingate convinced the judge that I had wrecked his best, most valuable jumper—which she wasn't. That's why she needed a little fire in her belly. I think Wingate was hoping for the firing squad, but the judge settled on three years."

Rob shook his head. "Why? A jihad against drugs?"

"A jihad against me. The juice thing was just an excuse. He had it in for me, and I handed him the gun. And I deserved it. I knew better. My father would never have done that. Huh! If my father had been alive and found out, he'd have turned me in himself." He took a drink. "In fact, being my father's son didn't help. He was too honest for Wingate's taste. But I deserved what I got and paid handsomely. Two years with a year on parole—a biggie for anyone thinking about hiring me. I have to check with a parole officer every time I breathe. The good thing is, it's bound to keep me steady. The last thing I want is to go back in there."

"Have you done drugs yourself?"

Again Jeth looked down. "I can't say never, but I can honestly say I'm not a drug user."

"Just curious—and you don't have to tell me if you don't want—what facility were you in? Here in Pennsylvania?"

"Westerly."

Rob smiled. "I've been there."

Jeth looked up sharply.

"Our church does prison ministry at two facilities, and Westerly is one of them. I went only once, but that was before your time." He stood up. "I need to talk to Katie about this. I think you understand."

Jeth put out a hand to stop him. "That's not all." He was silent a moment, and Rob sat down again. "Something else you need to know. God might tell you this is the deal breaker."

"What is it?" Again he spoke very gently.

Jeth rubbed his face. "Before all this, I got Janni—Wingate's daughter—pregnant, and she had an abortion. I'm guessing you don't like abortions."

Rob raised his eyebrows. "No, I don't, but are there degrees of sin?"

Jeth looked at him curiously, then went on. "That was the straw, I think, that Wingate was waiting for. It's not that he was against abortion. He probably would've forced Janni to have one if she hadn't already. The big deal was his daughter carrying on with the stable boy. This was his chance to get me out of there and away from Janni."

"The stable boy? I thought you were training and showing."

"Oh, yes. I was doing fine. But he had me permanently filed under 'stable boy' and didn't want his daughter connected with the likes of me in any way. She and I grew up together. I was a year or so older and had the upper hand—for a while." He grinned wryly. "But she learned fast how to handle boys. We had one pony between us and got tossed, bit, and kicked until we got a handle on him. We even got that thing to jump, and that's when my dad decided to put me on real horses. What I learned, I showed to Janni—along with fishing, catching snakes, and swimming naked. She taught me books and music, and in the rough-and-tumble of our childhood, we tumbled into each other's arms." He studied the ground a moment. "My dad, prodded by Papa W., suggested I muck stalls instead of hanging out with Janni so much. She and I still managed...just got creative." He straightened and took a big breath. "So, that's where we stand today. Still sneaking around."

Rob looked thoughtful for a moment, then put his hand on Jeth's knee.

Jeth jumped, though not overtly. In prison, you watched who you touched and who touched you. He had learned that code, and now he'd have to learn a new one.

Rob didn't appear to notice. "Let me talk with Katie." He stood again and started to walk away. "Wait." He smiled. "You still haven't given me a straight answer about what we could expect from you if you work here."

Jeth looked up and said fervently, "If you take me on, you could ask me to eat only one meal a day, and I'd do it. All I need is a roof and enough money to feed me and my car—not that I'll be driving far."

"That's right! We never did talk pay."

"Surprise me. Enough to get by is all I ask."

Rob smiled and turned toward the house.

He was gone only fifteen minutes, but it seemed an eternity to Jeth. He was back in jail, hedged by a sense of helplessness, imprisoned by bars of fear—no, terror—that Rob would come out and say, "We're sorry, but..." Jeth walked to the pasture and stared through the bars at a pair of horses dosing nose to tail for mutual fly swatting. Birds in the lime-green hedgerow brought Janni to mind. She would have named them and coupled their mating songs to their own passion. But Janni wasn't here, and birdsong couldn't ease the lump in Jeth's stomach. And besides, these birds probably hadn't decided whether to unpack their bags and hang around or push on north—like he might have to do. He went into the barn and stared through Dynamo's bars as the stallion bit and kicked his disdain.

Finally, Rob came back outside. He extended his hand. "You're on. We're trusting you, and, of course, you'll have to trust us. Is it a deal?"

The bars fell away. Jeth felt weak with relief and nearly crushed Rob's hand. "Deal!"

"We'll see you tomorrow, then. Eight o'clock?"

"I'll be earlier than that. Rob...I can't thank you enough, for—"

Rob put an arm around his shoulder. "This will be an adventure for both of us. What is God going to do through you?" He smiled broadly.

Jeth turned to go, but Rob grabbed his arm. "Wait. Do you have a place to stay tonight?"

Jeth smiled. "I'll find a place. I have enough money for that."

Rob shook his head. "Let's go look at the trailer, see what needs to be done. And supper will be on the table at six o'clock."

THAT EVENING, JETH lay in bed, not knowing when he'd ever felt so happy. Not even last night's tryst with Janni measured up to this. Two clean sheets, a soft mattress. Katie had fussed that it was old and too soft and they'd have to replace it. It felt heavenly, after two years on a practically nonexistent mattress. Even the musty smell of the trailer was better than prison stink.

Full heart, full stomach. At the dinner table, Jeth had started to pick up his fork when Rob had reached for his hand and for Katie's, and prayed over the meal and for Jeth. And before he'd left for the trailer, both had hugged him. Who in his world, apart from a hooker, would even think of hugging a stranger—one fresh out of prison, at that? Both of these acts were far out of Jeth's sphere. But those hugs felt good—really good—and tears welled up at the remembrance.

3

Next morning, Jeth was already in the barn, moving stiffly but watering the horses, when Rob came in at seven o'clock. "You take it easy today," Rob said. "I think we'll work Campion, the black gelding to the left of Meg." He gestured. "Then Gladys—short for Gladcroft—and Peanut. The others will go out to pasture. Leave Toogie. Katie can work him in the roundpen."

"Tell me about Gladys." Jeth eyed the honey-toned sorrel mare. "A bit of fire in her, maybe?"

Rob chuckled. "Fire—you got that. Think Katie. Same hair color, spunk, pizzazz… Have to watch her, though. You can't ever relax on her, but she can jump…when she wants to."

Jeth wondered if that part applied to Katie, as well.

Rob gave Jeth the routine on grain feeding and the horses that needed tendon boots and leg wraps. After learning which horses went into which pasture and which could be taken two at a time, Jeth took care of that, while Rob settled into cleaning stalls.

On his return, Jeth picked up a manure fork and joined Rob. "You do this all yourself?"

"Bennie from church comes once a week or so, but yeah, we're the donkeys. So many other things cost real money…"

Jeth reflected on this. The upkeep of even one horse was high; the cost of maintaining and training stadium jumpers was astronomical. How big *was* that inheritance? He didn't think it prudent to ask.

Katie came out when they were halfway through. "Well! I see I've been displaced."

Jeth looked up with a smile. "Mucking stalls your normal high for the day?"

She put on a mock pout. "I'm like, *yes!* My day is *ruined.*" She turned to him, pout transformed to dazzling smile. "How can I pay for your services?"

"Keep smiling. That'll do."

"Jeth can warm the horses for me today," said Rob, "but Toogie's looking for attention. Lunge him a bit and then do a little saddle work. That sound good?"

"Hey, new guy—way cool!" Katie flipped her head at Jeth and then happily turned to the task of fussing over the colt.

"How's the Dynamo damage today?" Rob asked.

Jeth laughed grimly. "The bruise is a good eight-incher. Big horse, big mouth!"

"Yeah," said Rob, "among other faults. At least you've learned right up front to keep a tight off rein. How about warming Campion while I clean Dynamo and put him in the roundpen after Katie's done with Toogie?"

"Now you're making me choose between ice cream and chocolate! I'd be happy to battle Dynamo."

"Let's stick with the plan—you, Campion; me, Dynamo—at least today."

Jeth winced as he settled into the saddle.

"Remember, no jumping!"

Jeth stopped on his way to the ring to watch Katie work Toogie. The colt was jogging counterclockwise around the perimeter of the roundpen, with Katie moving in a smaller circle, long lunge whip raised only slightly. After a bit, she raised the whip higher and urged the horse into a canter. After *pro forma* kicking and head tossing, he settled into a steady gait, until she signaled him to walk and then—with a soft "Whoa!"—to stop. She moved to him with petting and praise, and Jeth, nodding approval, pressed Campion on by.

Jeth did as he was told that morning and watched carefully as Rob put Campion and then Gladys through the jump routine.

"Okay," said Rob as he slid off Gladys. "Your turn with Peanut. When you get him warmed and I get through with him, we'll have lunch and go work on the trailer. I can warm him if you're getting too sore."

Jeth waved and went into the ring with a leisurely walk, trot, and canter, then put the sorrel gelding to a low fence. He swiveled toward Rob with a wide grin.

Rob shook his head and grinned back, and Jeth understood: Things were definitely looking up—for both of them.

LATER THAT DAY, Jeth contacted Rick Hertzog, his assigned parole officer, and told him about the job and his living arrangement. Rick replied that he wanted to see for himself, and he came by the following afternoon. Jeth was riding at the time but saw him and trotted toward the fence. Rick waved him on and watched with interest as Jeth put the horse over a series of jumps. Jeth dismounted in the ring and led the horse through the gate.

"Hey, man!" said Rick. "You're good at that! You told me you rode but didn't say nothin' about jumpin'."

"Yeah, that's what I do. Meet Campion, one of our good guys." Jeth stroked the black neck, winter hair coming off in clumps.

"Well, the guy on top knows what he's doin', too."

"A little rusty, maybe, but not as sore as yesterday!" Jeth laughed.

"Where's your boss? He around? I'd like to meet him."

"In the barn. I need to cool Campion, so you talk while I walk."

Rob met them at the door and shook hands with the short, blocky, criminal-toughened parole officer. He took Rick into the office, where they talked until Jeth had unsaddled and put the horse in his stall.

Jeth walked Rick to his car. "Super setup here, Jeth. Sweet. Don't blow it, man."

Jeth was silent a moment. "You don't know how grateful I am. Rob and Katie know where I've been and the risk of taking me on, and they're trusting me. I don't want to choke on this one!"

ROB AND KATIE insisted that the trailer needed attention, but Jeth saw it differently. If the Chiltons' house was a woman's work apron with a frill basted on, the trailer was a pair of grubby overalls, old and strictly utilitarian. It suited Jeth just fine, having had all he wanted of Wingate finery. He did agree to some general cleaning and faucet repair but couldn't have been more pleased to have his own space, right there on the property. Katie fussed over this and that, until Jeth pushed her out. "When your house looks as spiffed as this, I'll let you back in for Phase Two."

She screwed up her face and stuck out her tongue.

WHEN KATIE CAME to the barn each day, she often wore her hot-taco persona, which Jeth found both captivating and disturbing. She teased and joked and played up her role as boss lady. "Now, *somebody* didn't clean this corner over here. Knowing that my husband *always* cleans *every* corner thoroughly..." Rob grimaced, but Kate twirled away. "So Jeth, in payment for your crimes, I shall show you every corner that needs cleaning." She started off with him in tow.

"Not every corner, please," Rob called after them. "Plenty work this morning."

"Now, take this room." She led Jeth through a doorway. "Did you know this was once a chicken coop?" She shook her head mournfully. "Things were really tight after we bought the place, and we got down to just one chicken. One day, she laid a giant egg, then plopped over dead. We ate her, of course, but kept the egg warm. After only six days, it hatched, and out came this teeny-tiny horse." Her hands shaped a six-inch square. And that"—a dimple played on her cheek—"was the modest start of our horse farm." She laughed.

Jeth came right back. "Don't tell me—Peanut, right?"

He found it hard to concentrate on Pixie that morning.

4

On Jeth's first Sunday at the farm, he did the early chores and got ready to ride. Rob came out and saw him with saddle on arm. "Not today, Jeth. It's Sunday. All the horses go out to pasture, and—"

"You're kidding!"

"No. We work hard all week and need a day to rest, and soon enough, you'll see that, too." He laughed. "Katie and I are going to church. You can come if you want, or go back to bed, or go out on Meg, but no jumping—and no Dynamo!"

"Huh! Can I take Dynamo on the trail?"

"Right. With those long hooves, he'd trip over a dandelion!"

Jeth scratched his head. "Well, what about Sunday horse shows? They're either Sunday only, or they run over into Sunday."

"Yeah, there are those, and it can't be helped, but every chance we get, we rest."

After a couple of Sundays of banging around the place alone, Jeth decided to go to church with Rob and Katie to observe. Near the center of Oakley and nestled against the regional hospital, a modest church building dismantled Jeth's image of a traditional, steepled structure. Rob pulled into the parking lot. "Huh!" said Jeth. "Cool arrangement. Roll out of church into the hospital, then back to church for the funeral. Sweet." He looked around. "Too bad no graveyard attached."

They made their way inside, Rob and Katie introducing Jeth and chatting briefly with several people before leading him to a seat at the back of the church. "Not my week for childcare," Katie told him, "but I sit near the door in case they get overwhelmed downstairs." Her cheek dimpled. "Always on tap for baby care!"

Jeth stood and sat as directed, fished out a couple of bucks for the offering, but mostly looked around and studied what was going on.

On the way out afterward, Rob asked him, "How did you do? I saw you talking with folks."

"Yeah. You've been telling on me; that was plain. Some even knew my name. One white-hair told me, 'Jeth, I'm going to give you my mother's hymnal. I'll bring it some Sunday.' I told her I didn't do hymnals, but she seemed bent on it."

"Must have been Maybelle," said Katie. "She's always giving stuff away." She grunted wryly. "To the point of being a nuisance. Not everybody wants her 'sweetmeats.' But she says she needs to get her affairs in order."

"Huh!" Jeth shook his head. "An old gray mare, maybe, but from the twinkle in her eye and the starch in her back, still good to go. Besides, I probably look like I need something. Another guy asked about my background, where I grew up and all. I told him I was born in a horse stall, was an ex-con, and was planning to take you for a ride."

"You didn't!" said Katie.

"Well, those ladies of yours…maybe even May—what's her name?—if they get too friendly, that might set 'em back." He grinned.

They got into the car, and Jeth asked, "When a person decides to take on church, is the first order of business learning to hug properly?"

Rob roared, but Katie said from the backseat, "Absolutely! We offer Theology of Hugging 101, 201, 301, and 401. And if you can't do it right after that, it's out the door with you."

Jeth thought she was only half joking.

"Besides the interrogation, what did you think of church?" Rob asked him.

"It was different from what I expected, even the building. They're friendly enough. But the music...not what I'd picture coming out of a church."

"Did you like it?"

Jeth shrugged. "I guess so. Somewhere between your average pop concert and Janni's music."

"Did you feel comfortable?"

Jeth thought a moment. "I guess...as comfortable as a stranger can be in a foreign land."

Rob hooted. "Foreign land. I like that! Heavenly territory."

Katie leaned forward. "Were there services in prison, with chaplains or outside people leading? We have guys who do prison ministry."

Jeth smiled at Rob, remembering his Westerly connection. "Yeah, there were, but I never went. The Jesus guys always seemed to be fighting over something, and I didn't want to get caught in the middle."

Rob laughed wryly. "Fighting is all some fellows know, and turning the other cheek is not their language."

"I could hear their singing, though," Jeth said.

"What kind of music was it?" Katie asked.

"Oh, opera, of course. Puccini was their favorite." Janni had loved opera, and he had pulled out the only name he could remember, working hard on a straight face.

Katie looked at him, puzzled.

"The fat lady was singing, so I figured..." Jeth looked over at Rob.

"Fat lady!" Katie screwed up her face. "If you weren't in there, how would you know...?" She saw Jeth's mouth twitch. "Oh, you!" She beat on Jeth, who hunched out of her way.

"Rob, save me!" he cried. But it felt good.

HE DIDN'T GO along every Sunday, but at home, he began measuring Rob and Katie against people in the horse world he had grown up in. For one thing, Rob wanted no part in the cutthroat competition or social whirl of moneyed horse people. And though Jeth understood honesty, he had to adjust his idea of acceptable business dealings, which, for him, had always included maneuvering for personal advantage. Rob wouldn't do that. "The Bible tells us to steer clear of deception," he had said once, with a disarming shrug. "Be straight. Life's easier that way."

Jeth noticed that Rob did throw money around—a lot of it—just not on himself or Katie or the farm. "You gave money to that boozer this morning, and I don't think you were buying his horse."

"Charlie? Yeah, he was one of my muckers awhile back. He needed a loan."

"Right. And you expect to get it back?"

"No, probably won't. I do what I can and let God take care of the rest."

"You're enabling him. He's a drunk."

"Maybe. Or maybe that's a few bucks that will keep his head above water."

"Yeah! Maybe not, too."

"Caring for down-and-outers is my business. Getting anything back is God's business. A pretty easy way to live."

Jeth didn't see it that way, but he shrugged and let it go.

THE DAYS WORKED into a rhythm of chores and training and the occasional customer looking to buy or sell. There was seldom time for Dynamo, though Jeth tried each day to make a positive statement with bits of carrot or apple. Show season was coming, and Jeth's arrival had raised the bar of readiness. "This guy here—" Jeth thumped Pixie, a rich, tea-colored bay, and swung his leg to dismount. "He's your best horse."

"You think so? I'd say Campion."

"He's good, but he doesn't have Pixie's focus. Pixie's tight and athletic. An honest horse, a good learner. He wants to better himself and works at it. He's got heart and drive. You wait—he'll win some ribbons before we're done."

THAT SAME DAY, on their way to the house, Rob and Katie stopped by the ring to watch Jeth on Gladys. Rob shook his head in amazement. "Look at him on that mare," he said. "As soon as he mounts, he knows just what she's thinking, what she liked about breakfast, what she doesn't like in the ring. His first day on the job, I told him that Gladys tends toward jittery. Before he rode her the first time, he told me he listens to a horse breathe, feels how it moves; and, sure enough, within five minutes, he had her number. She doesn't exactly take naps between jumps, but he's made that energy more productive."

Katie nodded with a touch of awe. "And to think, he just appeared on our doorstep."

"Huh—even that was a mistake. He told me he was headed somewhere else and missed his turn." He stared silently at horse and rider. "God dumped him on our doorstep, and that scares me."

He rested both elbows on the fence and watched Gladys rise to a triple jump with an air of joy and a flip of her tail. "He makes her seem—whoops!" He caught the end of a board that had come loose. "Better fix that before Jeth sees it. He's been on me from day one about fencing, but he's tighter with our money than we are. At Big Lumber the other day, he pointed to the markdown pile. 'Warped boards,' he said. 'Not pretty, but they're cheap, they work, and they're safer than wire for horses.' Yeah, I know." He grinned at his wife. "You say that, too."

"At least you're listening to somebody. You don't get mad at Jeth."

"Well, we bump once in a while. His temper is quick, but it settles fast. He never loses patience with the animals, though. Maybe if we had horse names, he wouldn't get mad. Me, Dobbin; you, Maud." Rob smiled, then sobered and studied Jeth again. "What a gift God has given us." He put his arm around Katie, and the smile returned. "Maybe we should pay attention to what Jeth eats for breakfast!"

ON A BLUSTERY day in mid-May, Jeth and Rob went to an auction across the state line into Maryland, small trailer in tow. They looked over the horses and tried out two or three. "This one," Jeth said, of a handsome gelding the color of ground coffee. "He's got a huge stride, and I think there's something deep inside."

"Really deep, I'd say," said Rob. "Doesn't exactly go at a fence with confidence. Of course, he's young. What's his name—Woodbine? His blood line...?" They studied the posted sheet. "He's got some Irish Sport in him. A good line, but the courage factor seems to be down around zero. I dunno..."

"Let me take him out once more and see what I can do."

This time, Woodbine refused even the first modest jump. Rob shook his head but, at Jeth's direction, set the bar very low, and Jeth gradually worked the horse up to a respectable height. Even Rob was impressed by the verve in his final jump. "Well, friend, if you think you can make gravy out of sawdust..."

"Hey, due diligence!" Jeth smiled. "Y'just never know."

Their final bid was lower than even they had expected. Evidently, no one else had seen that buried spark.

5

One afternoon, while Jeth was working a rangy, dappled-gray mare called Nightshade, a young man climbed from a well-seasoned car and moved softly, gently, toward the ring. Jeth saw him and waved. "Be with you in a minute."

"Mind if I watch?"

"Watching's free today!" He grinned and finished his routine. When he was done, he came out of the ring and dismounted. "Jeth Cavanaugh," he said, shaking the young man's hand and sizing him up. Shorter than Rob, he seemed spare and unprepossessing—a person one might easily overlook in a crowd. His short-cropped hair framed eyes the color of filberts and an open, kind face that was cinnamon-hued and guileless.

"Cecil Berry." His voice, too, was soft and gentle. Jeth liked him immediately.

"Walk with me while I cool Nightshade. I take it you like horses. Do you ride?"

He shrugged. "Some."

Rob came over and introduced himself. There was an awkward pause as Cecil traced a line in the dust with his foot, as though stalling to draw courage. "Do you give lessons? I want to learn to jump."

Rob shook his head, but Jeth raised his eyebrows. "How much have you ridden?"

He shrugged again. "My friend has a horse. Mostly just trail riding. But we made sort of a ring in a pasture. My friend got good enough to ride in a show once. The old guy next door helped us."

"English or Western?"

"English."

"How old are you?"

"Seventeen."

"Let me see you ride." Jeth glanced at Rob and saw no objection. "Think you can handle Nightshade, here? She's had a workout; shouldn't give you trouble."

Cecil's eyes widened. "I'll try," he said uncertainly.

Rob sent Jeth a look of misgiving, but Jeth flicked his eyebrows and turned to the boy. "Come on, then. I'll give you a leg up. And here—take my helmet."

The boy's hands shook as he collected the reins, mounted, and shortened the stirrups.

"Take your time. Walk all the way around, then try a trot."

Cecil gained confidence visibly as he rode through all three gaits.

"Well done!" Jeth said, as the boy dismounted, smiling. "You walk Nightshade cool while Rob and I talk."

"You're crazy!" said Rob when they were alone. "You don't have time to give lessons. We have all we can do with…or are you thinking of Katie and her Saturday kiddies? She could teach him basic jumping, but I can't see her—"

"I hear you, and no, I don't want to push him onto Katie. But this boy's a natural in the saddle. Good seat, good hands, no wasted motion. And he probably can't rub two nickels together. I'm thinking, work two hours for a one-hour lesson. Puts me ahead a whole hour." He grinned.

"Huh!" Rob said. "*If* he can work."

"Well, that'll be the deal, won't it? You're boss, though. I want to give him a chance, but you get final say. Plan B can be Katie, provided she's willing."

Rob sighed, shrugged, and finally nodded.

Jeth turned and walked over to Cecil. "Okay, here's what we can offer. I charge forty dollars an hour for lessons," he said, matching Katie's teaching fee.

Cecil's face fell.

"But what would you think of working two hours in the barn instead of paying cash?"

A broad smile lit the boy's face, and his shoulders lifted. "I can do that!"

"Shoveling manure and grooming horses is tough work. I know how much I get done in two hours, so we'd expect you to pull your weight."

"Yes, sir. I can handle it!"

"Good lad! Now, what day would work best? You'd have to dance around whatever our weekly schedule is, so I hope you can be flexible."

"I have a night job, so most any day, any time, would work."

Jeth grinned. "Don't want you falling asleep halfway over a jump!"

CECIL DID PULL his weight—and then some. Neither Rob nor Jeth had thought the pact would last past the third lesson, but the bigger problem was prying the manure fork out of the boy's hand and getting him into his car when it was time to go home. He soaked up instruction in the ring, and even Rob stopped to watch every so often. "Have to admit—you got as good an eye for unlikely riders as for unlikely horses!"

"WITH SHOW SEASON coming up," Rob said to Jeth on their way to the house one afternoon, "we need to get you some riding gear. My breeches might fit you, but swapping back and forth would be tricky...especially if we're both in the same class." He grinned.

"Yeah, I've been thinking about that and counting up what I've saved from not drinking, smoking, or running around with tramps. It'll be tight, but I think I can swing it."

"I should pay for a good part of your outfit. After all, you're my guy."

"Right. And if I were a bum, I wouldn't even have to pay it back." He saw Rob's face stiffen and hurried on. "I know a place just outside of Carleton City that has good used stuff, along with decent-priced new. If you'd trust me with a day on my own, I think I could get what I need for close to what I've saved. Maybe I could borrow a little just in case."

"See what's in the petty-cash drawer in the barn, and if there's not enough, come back in. I trust you, but it's a long way and a lot of gas."

"Yeah, I factored in gas. It would still be cheaper than anything online."

After checking with parole officer Rick, Jeth took off early. He was back by suppertime. "Too tired to display my wares tonight. I'll do show and tell tomorrow," he said.

"Well," said Katie, "you come here and do it. Change in our bedroom. I want to be in on this!"

Cecil arrived the next morning in time for the fashion show, and the audience lined up on the living-room couch. They were properly wowed when Jeth emerged from the bedroom, dressed in black show helmet, black jacket, and black boots, with white breeches, white shirt, choker collar, and stock tie. "Even got my own spurs," he said. "I still need a pin. The few they had were pricy, and any old tiepin will do. The shirt is new; the helmet, jacket, breeches, and boots 'pre-owned' but in good condition."

"Hey, man—you done *good!*" said Katie. "I *like* it!"

"And," said Jeth proudly, opening his wallet, "here's your hundred bucks back!"

Rob eyed the cash. "Um, is this going to leave you eating nothing but crackers the rest of the week?"

Grinning, Cecil raised his hand. "I'll save leftover French fries for him. They'll be cold and soggy, but—"

Jeth reached over and batted the boy's head.

THINGS WERE DEFINITELY good in this place. If only the inner ache for Janni would go away.

6

Rob looked up when Jeth peeked in his office, hand pressed over the mouthpiece of his cell phone.

"Rob, what would you think about my going to town for supper? A guy I've known a long time—Chuck Graff—lives in Hadley. He heard I was working here and wants to get together. I'd meet him at—I think he said Sanderson's—for supper, talk a while, and come home. But I won't do it unless you feel comfortable about it."

Rob raised his eyebrows. "You did okay in Carleton City. Do *you* feel comfortable about it?"

Jeth shrugged. "He's an ordinary guy. Haven't seen him for a while. We might have a drink, but I won't even do that if you say no."

Rob smiled. "Hey, I'm not your nanny. Rick does that. You'll clear it with him?"

"Of course. First order of business. My guess is I'll be back by ten or ten thirty."

HE WAS BACK by ten—the next morning, a gorgeous spring day with birds and blossoms blissfully unaware of the unfolding drama.

Rob came out of the barn with Capstan and stopped abruptly when he saw Jeth on the bench, hunched and utterly wretched, kneading his hands. Rob yanked the horse around and snapped a tie to the bridle, his own face mutating from anxiety to relief to anger to pity. He jogged to the bench and sat beside Jeth, putting a hand on his back. He retracted it, however, when the stench of vomit rose from a full-body coating of filth and shame. Jeth's face wore assorted cuts and bruises; one eye was discolored and swollen nearly shut. He clenched his jaw, kneaded his fingers, and stared at a patch of gravel five feet away.

"Buddy, what happened?" Rob asked gently.

Jeth shook his head. His jaw was clenched, and his eyes focused hard on three dirt-brown sparrows five feet away. As he stared, words began to dribble out. "Wrong place...wrong people... wrong everything." He grimaced and dropped his head. "I've lost everything. What you see is what I am—dirty, brown, ugly..." He untangled his fingers and grabbed a fistful of hair in each hand. "I had this feeling...early...even before I found out what was going on, but I—" He drew a shuddering breath. "I should've left, and by the time...it was too late. I knew too much. I tried, but...too many to fight off. Chuck didn't join them, but he didn't help me, either. Somebody clocked me, and when I woke up, my wallet was gone, keys, car. I walked back." He studied the pattern of pebbles beneath the bench and rubbed his head, breathing hard. "I didn't want to come back and face you, but I...had to. I'm here, so go ahead. Chew me out. I deserve every word and what you'll do with me. I'm assuming Rick called when I didn't check in with him."

"Actually, he didn't."

Jeth stared at him. "He didn't call? He never misses."

"He did this time."

Jeth looked down again. "Well, there are guys out there who might pin just about anything on me, and I couldn't prove what happened, one way or the other." He stood but quickly pressed both hands to his forehead.

"Your head hurt?"

"Yeah."

"We should take you for X-rays. A concussion, maybe."

Jeth turned on him. "I'm not *worth* an X-ray! Just throw me out, throw me in jail. Get it over with!" He spun away, gritting his teeth.

"I wouldn't throw anybody in jail as dirty as you are. Let's get you cleaned up, some food in you. Come on." He put an arm around him and steered him toward the trailer.

As they approached, Katie came out of the house. "Jeth!"

Rob waved her off and moved Jeth inside the trailer.

With no help from Jeth, but no resistance, either, Rob stripped him and pushed him into the shower, then laid out clean underpants and a tee and fixed cereal, juice, and toast.

When Jeth was done eating, Rob took his dishes to the sink. Jeth would not look at him. He sat with elbows on the table, head in hands.

"Okay," said Rob. "To bed. Sleep as long as you want, and then we'll talk."

Jeth stood, eyes black with anguish. Rob looked at him a moment, then hugged him. "I'm just glad you're back safe," he said.

Jeth spun away, ricocheted off the wall, and lurched to the bedroom, shoulders heaving.

LATE AFTERNOON, AS Rob was putting the last horse in the barn, Jeth followed him in.

Rob turned and smiled. "There you are! Looking some better. Cleaner, anyway. Your eye looks awful. How's your head?"

Jeth shrugged. "I'll be okay."

"Are you up for a Meg-and-Jake ride?"

Jeth shrugged again, then slid in beside Meg and backed her from the stall. They brushed the two pleasure horses, saddled, and bridled them, all without a word. Once mounted, Rob led the way behind the barn to the trail system that formed a three-mile loop through forest and meadow.

They rode in silence, with only bird chatter and the odd cough or snort from the horses to mark their passage.

Jeth finally said, "I've got to tell you what happened."

"You don't need to. I know it was bad. That's enough. I don't need details."

Jeth turned on him angrily. "Stop trying to make it easy! I need to say the words. I want you to know everything so it can be as bad between us as it can possibly get."

"Why ever for?"

"I don't want to hide anything. You trusted me, and I blew it."

Rob shook his head. "You're a piece of work. You had to make sure I knew your prison history and everything connected with it, right down to the abortion. You came back to face me. *But you don't have to say this to me.* Maybe to God, but that's a different matter."

"Shut up and let me tell you!"

Rob sighed. "Okay, I'll listen."

Jeth said nothing. Only Meg tossing her head broke the silence. Finally, he began.

"Some guys Chuck knew came in the restaurant and dragged us out. 'You gotta come!' they said. I knew right then—my first chance to leave—this was not good, but Chuck seemed willing, so I trusted him, went along. Some got in my car, some in Chuck's, and we drove south toward Carthage and turned onto an overgrown farm road, maybe a half mile in, to one of those old orchards in the back country. There was a bonfire with fifteen, twenty, guys, drinking hard. I was the stranger, and they jumped on Chuck about me. I was okay, he said. Been in prison, he said. Played that up. Now I knew for sure—my second chance—this wasn't good, and I should've turned right around. They might have let me go.

Then more guys came in a pickup and started unloading crates. Know what it was?" He looked at Rob. "A cockfight."

"You're kidding!"

"Do I sound like I'm kidding?" he sneered bitterly. "They dragged over the first two crates, and somebody put a bottle in my hand. Without thinking, I took a slug. I know, I know—automatic. What does that tell you about me?" He looked accusingly at Rob, but Rob said nothing. "I was going to hand it back and leave, but as soon as I swallowed, I knew I'd been had. No idea what was in it, but I retched till my toes came up. As soon as I could get on my feet, I headed for the car, but it was blocked, and they took me down and worked on me. In their minds, I was a loose cannon and had to be decommissioned. I never actually saw the birds fighting, but I could hear it going on. I fought as best I could and then either passed out or got knocked out. When I woke, everything and everybody was gone, including the car and stuff. Am I going to report this? I don't think so. I don't know what God would say, but cockfighting's illegal. If you even watch, you get slammed."

"Any women there?"

"A couple. I suppose they could pin something on me, but I don't remember touching them, or them me."

"And you *walked* from there? Which way did you come? Carthage is at least fifteen miles from here."

"I tried cross-country, but it was too hard, too many swamps. I got bogged down one place and considered just lying there and never getting up. But you prodded me, made me move."

"Me? How so?"

"I don't know. I just knew I had to face you. I blew it, Rob. I broke your trust. I had at least three outs, and I didn't take them. Even when I saw roosters in those crates, I could have tossed the bottle and run out. For just a split second, I didn't want to. I didn't want to watch two birds kill each other, but at the same time…"

He sighed. "There you have it—the guy you trusted and hired. What are you going to do with him?" His voice cracked.

Rob was silent a long time. Then, as though he were starting a brand-new subject, he told his own history—rebellions, wrong choices, rotten attitude, bad moves. "She didn't get pregnant, but that was only by the grace of God, or I might have had an abortion on my back, too."

They rode without speaking for a bit. At a smooth stretch, the horses gathered themselves for their usual canter, but Rob pulled Jake back and went on with his story.

"We had a guy that hired on now and then at my folks' farm. Harley, his name was. He was…different. My dad called him a religious nut, and I guess he was. I liked him, though. I could talk, and he'd listen. Preached a lot, but he was a guy, and I learned things about living and getting along with people."

Rob pulled in a big breath and went on. "Harley told me about Jesus, that He could fix guys like me. He told me that Jesus died on the cross—for me. That His blood was some sort of legal transaction so God could forgive me, x-ing out my sin, as though I'd never done it."

Jeth looked over at him, a sharp frown briefly displacing shame.

Rob went on. "He said this transaction was free for the taking. I couldn't pay for it; couldn't earn it. Totally free. I listened to Harley, and though I was too proud to tell him, I thought hard, tested what he said, and ended up a changed man. I wish now I could tell him…" Rob was quiet a moment. "Harley moved to Georgia, and I heard a few years ago that he died."

Rob and Jeth rode in silence a moment, faces forward, as though needing to unpack some puzzling phenomenon that lay across their path. Then Rob looked over at Jeth. "What God did for me, Jeth, He can do for you. I can forgive you because of Jesus' blood that did its work in me. I can forgive you but can't take your sin away. That's God's business. Jesus' blood can cover you, wash you clean. I can't do that. I can only forgive what you did against me, whatever that amounts to. You mostly hurt yourself, you know—not me. Gave me a bad night, but the real damage fell on you—hard. And if I read you right, you'd handle a second chance pretty carefully."

Jeth looked at him. "Huh! I'd lay down my life for you. Give my blood—every pint, if you needed it."

"Come on, Jeth! That's not what this is about."

"Rob, you trusted me; gave me a job straight out of prison. I don't think you understand what a huge gift that was. Last night I had three chances to nail that trust, and I blew them all. I let you down. I will make it up. I won't break trust again." His face bore a look of hope.

"No!" said Rob. "It doesn't work that way. And I won't let you work it off. It's over and done. We're just going to move on. And besides, you will fail me again, just as I will fail you. That's life."

Jake and Meg picked up their pace, knowing they'd made the bend toward home. Neither man spoke.

Finally, Jeth, looking straight ahead, said, "The blood thing. It doesn't make sense. I don't like it."

"Yeah, seems crazy today. But if you look back, blood sacrifices have been basic religion from year one. The old guys back then knew how important blood was. Life is wrapped in blood. They had the right idea, maybe, but nobody expected God Himself to become the sacrifice. Jesus, the Lamb of God, bled forgiveness for everyone who steps over to His side. Because of Jesus' blood, I am forgiven forever. I don't understand that. You can't, either. Only God can make it happen."

"So, God slopped blood over you to hide sin. Blood is gross, especially a lot of it!"

Rob grimaced as they pulled up in front of the barn and dismounted. "Jeth, you're twisting my words. Rationalizing. We'll talk later."

As they unsaddled the horses, Jeth said, "You could call cockfighting blood sacrifice."

Rob rolled his eyes and sighed. "No, that's not the right—"

"Don't even try, Rob. I can't handle any more right now."

"All right, no more blood. You feel strongly that you've wronged me. Can you accept that I have forgiven you? All I'd have to do is call Rick. But I won't do that. I have forgiven you. As far as I'm concerned, it's over. Covered."

Jeth said nothing.

"Jeth, look at me."

Jeth looked, but his eyes would not hold Rob's gaze.

"Jeth, I forgive you. Can you accept that?"

"No, but I can grovel."

"No groveling, Jeth. Lay it down. You're not going to jail by my hand. You're not going to pay for what you've done. *You are forgiven.*"

Jeth finally looked straight at Rob, tears running down his cheeks, and hugged him. Rob held him a long while, then pushed him to arm's length. "You look terrible. Go eat. Go to bed. Get up late."

KATIE WAS WAITING for Rob when he finally came in for supper. "Is he going to be all right?" she asked.

Rob grimaced. "I don't know. His body will heal, but I don't know about the rest of him. He's got a mind I just can't get ahold of. If he comes around, it's definitely going to be God that does it, not me."

FOR TWO DAYS, Jeth felt like he was living a bad dream. Images rose to haunt him, and he half expected Rob to turn and say, "I've changed my mind."

He knew that both Rob and Katie were watching him closely, and at the end of the second day, before they left the barn, he was stopped by Rob's hand. "You're still torn apart, aren't you?"

Jeth rubbed his face. "It's like I'm in an earthquake. The ground is shifting, and I don't know how to get my footing. I know what you said, and I think you meant it, but I also know what I did and what they did, and I can't shake that."

"Come sit down. I'm going to pray for you."

Jeth stared at him a moment, then sat obediently. He couldn't have told anyone afterward what Rob said in that prayer, but he was profoundly grateful and abruptly calm.

A BUSY WEEK followed, with sales and coaching sessions that Rob sometimes offered to buyers. Jeth enjoyed these, and they helped keep his mind focused. He worked late on other chores so as not to neglect anything Rob had lined out for him. In his mind, Rob, above all else, must be satisfied.

But reality set in. A week later, at the end of a murky, grinding day, both were tired. Rob rubbed his neck. "The farrier is coming tomorrow. I'll work with him. Dynamo and all… You work as many jumpers as you have time for."

"That's what I do all day, every day. So what else is new?"

Rob raised an eyebrow at him. "Well," he said, turning away with a crooked grin, "at least you've stopped trying to earn brownie points. Get some rest. You're working too hard."

"Working too hard! I'm doing exactly what—"

Rob spun around. "Stop. Go eat. Sleep." He turned and walked away, leaving Jeth staring at the ground.

7

At church that Sunday, Maybelle came up to Jeth, wrinkle-framed eyes full of a hidden, secret laughter that he could only sense, not see. As she had promised weeks earlier, she gave him her mother's hymnbook—a small, leather-bound volume with yellowed pages and tiny print. At first he was annoyed. He had seen others slip gifts she'd given them surreptitiously behind acrylic holders on the information table. He considered doing the same, but those fathomless eyes explained how precious that book had been to two generations, and he was moved, almost shaken, by the weight of the gift. Rob had also given him a gift—a Bible, he explained, that had notes and commentary to help him understand what the text meant. That, too, had moved him; but after leafing through both volumes and reading here and there, he left them on a shelf in his trailer.

Rob came home late one afternoon from delivering Capstan to a buyer. Jeth, having groomed Dynamo for a much-anticipated after-work session, set the saddle down and helped Rob park and unhitch the trailer.

"Havener came through all right?" Jeth asked. "You thought he might back out."

"Oh, yes. Check in hand. No haggling. Another guy—Sam Jarvis—didn't make out as well. Havener had seen one of Jarvis's horses and liked how he performed, but when they got him out of the trailer, the horse bit Havener, which cooled his enthusiasm."

"Huh." Jeth glanced at Dynamo, still tied inside. "I knooow the feeling."

"The horse was a good jumper. I rode him and liked what I saw but decided that one bull elephant in the stable was enough."

"A stallion?"

"No, gelding. I don't think he's as bad as Dynamo, but he has a mouth and heels. And a name—Lord Nelson—that, in his mind, sets him up as High Chief Mucky-Muck of the Universe. Jarvis did a hard sell, but I'm not up for intergalactic jousting."

Jarvis, though, seemed to have smelled a sale. He called Rob almost every day. After the fifth call, Jeth began to sniff the wind. "The guy really wants to unload that horse."

"Yeah, but why would we want another Dynamo?" Rob asked.

"Well…depends. What d'you say we go visit Ol' Sam with pickup and trailer, park the trailer, and drive in unannounced, so he doesn't have a chance to stick him with a tranquilizer?"

Rob raised his eyebrows. "You picked up a few tricks along the way, didn't you?"

Jeth grinned wryly. "His last price was pretty good, but we might get him down some if the horse hoists his colors."

As expected, Jarvis was displeased by their sudden arrival but passed off the horse's ill humor as a temporary malaise. Jeth had learned a few things from handling Dynamo, but he played inno-cent and clumsily dodged the horse's mouth and hind feet. When he mounted, though, both he and Lord Nelson were all business. Jeth liked what he saw and was pretty sure he could work with the prob-lems. When he dismounted, a groom walked the horse, and Jeth took over the transaction—with a quick, sideways glance at Rob.

"I don't know." Jeth shook his head. "He's a handful."

"But you saw what he can do on fences."

"Yeah, if we live through him!"

"He's not that bad—really," Jarvis insisted. "A little twitchy now and then, but—"

"What's your asking price today? The last price you gave Rob—"

"Three thousand, and that's a steal."

"Three thousand! For a horse that eats jeans for breakfast?"

Jeth knew he was in the driver's seat with Jarvis, and he kept refusing every offer. When Jarvis got down to fifteen hundred, Jeth shook his head, his face expressionless. "I don't know... We'll think about that one, but we can't commit right now. We'll get back to you...when we're able."

Jarvis talked at them all the way to the truck, but they politely took their leave and drove to where they had parked the trailer.

Fifteen minutes later, they bumped up the drive, trailer in tow, and heard Jarvis angrily shouting instructions into his radio. Jeth and Rob took off for the barn and got to the stall just as the groom was preparing to inject the horse. Jeth grappled for the syringe and swore angrily. As Jarvis came in, Jeth faced him furiously. "Why would you drug him now, after we've already ridden him? At best, this horse is worth seven hundred dollars, given his disposition, but we might have paid a thousand. The most you'll get now is five hundred. Take it or leave it. And we could report you."

"Get out of here!" Jarvis punched his words. "You're not getting this horse for any amount of money!"

"That's fine." Rob pulled out his business card. "If you change your mind the next couple of hours, here's my cell-phone number."

They parked a mile down the road, and Jeth turned off the engine. "How long before he calls, you think?"

"Ten minutes?"

"Sounds good to me." Jeth looked at his watch.

The phone rang eight minutes later. Jeth laughed and started the engine. "I sort of took over the negotiating. I shouldn't have done that."

"You were awesome. You knew just what he was thinking and what he'd do. And while we twisted him a bit, I can't think of anybody who deserves it more. Now let's hope you've read the horse right. I've got doubts about a salvage, but we're not losing much."

At home, Jeth worked hard with Lord Nelson and was pleased with the results. A steady diet of kindness and carrots mellowed him, and his native strong will got him over fences.

CECIL WAS A godsend at this time, from warming even Pixie and Campion to performing menial tasks, such as setting up jumps. He could now put a new, friendly, easygoing sorrel named Peterkin over basic jumps, as well. Rob also had him on Toogie, and the colt got on well with him. Both Jeth and Rob liked the boy—his quiet, gentle ways around the horses, and how he had blossomed as a person. When Cecil let on that he and his mother were churchgoers, they bonded even closer.

Jeth's only problem was Cecil's constant refrain of "Yes, sir" and "No, sir." "Look," said Jeth, "I grew up as a stable boy. I haven't earned the title 'sir' yet. 'Yes' and 'No' will be just fine. Okay?"

"Yes...sir."

Jeth growled and got him in a headlock, and when they came up laughing, Jeth said, "You from the south?"

"My mama was."

"Well, she taught you manners. I'd like to meet her."

Cecil brought her one Sunday afternoon, shyly, ready to back off and go home. But Rob welcomed them warmly, and Katie invited them in for tea. After two hours of laughing and singing and sharing life with the warm and round "Mama Berry," they parted like lifelong friends.

8

Jeth had questions. He wouldn't let go of the blood issue and plagued Rob every chance he got. "How are these sacrifices different from, say, cannibalism? I know it's not the same thing, but one's as awful as the other."

Rob's answers couldn't satisfy. Finally he said, "How about coming with me to Bible study tomorrow morning? Maybe the other guys can answer you."

Jeth thought a moment. He had never taken up Rob on the invitation, always choosing to do double duty so Rob would be comfortable in going. "What time does it start?"

"Seven. Leave here quarter of."

"What about the work?"

Rob shrugged. "I used to get up early on Thursdays. I can go back to that."

"Okay. Early it is."

AT BIBLE STUDY the next morning, Jeth sat quietly as the dozen men chatted about their week. He knew some of them: Tom, the leader, whose truck-repair shop lay at the far end of Rob's trail system; Bennie, who sometimes helped with barn chores. After a long litany of concerns—health issues, money problems, and a marriage under repair, Tom looked at Jeth. "How you doin', young feller? Glad you're here. Rob treatin' you good? If he starts gnawin' your leg, we'll run him up a tree."

Jeth laughed and rubbed his thigh. "Rob's not the only leg-gnawer on the place. And besides," he added ruefully, "I gnaw legs pretty good myself."

He leaned forward, elbows on his knees. "I'm stuck on something, and Rob thought you might have an answer." He was quiet a moment. "His take on Christian stuff is full of blood, and that...turns me off. Cavemen around a fire, carving up a... rooster." He grimaced. "Yes, I understand that's what they did back then, and somehow God borrowed the idea and pinned it on Jesus."

The men looked at him intently. Outside, a door slammed, and a badly whistled praise song faded down the corridor.

Rob rubbed his neck. "I told you he thinks outside the box."

A stocky, gray-haired man cleared his throat and thumbed through his Bible. "Well, the blood of Jesus cleanses us from our sin." He looked up. "'My hope is built on nothing less than Jesus' blood and righteousness.' We sang that last Sunday. Were you here?"

Jeth looked at him as though he had two heads. "You *like* that song? Made me gag."

A scholarly-looking man—his neat, creased slacks a stark contrast to Jeth's stained jeans—shifted in his chair. "Our theology teaches that those old sacrifices meant a great deal. People back then knew that blood equals life. And when Jesus came—"

Jeth waved a hand. "Yeah, Rob got that far. But that still—"

"In the Old Testament," the man went on, "priests killed rams and goats and bulls, and the blood from these sacrifices atoned for sin. But when Jesus came, He became the one perfect sacrifice, and now blood offerings are no longer needed. Through Christ's finished work, we can '*boldly approach the throne of*—'"

"Look." A third leaned forward and cut in. "Forget blood for now. Think of Jesus' death as a legal transaction. He paid the penalty that—"

"No." Jeth put up his hands. "I'm not going to forget blood. If it's as important as you say, then don't dance around it. It just occurred to me: Communion—that's blood, isn't it? And you're drinking it. This isn't just a friendly little ritual that churches do every few Sundays."

Rob leaned back and shook his head despairingly.

WHEN THEY GOT home, more questions followed. "What does 'tithe' mean?" Jeth asked Rob.

"Tithe means tenth. The Bible says we're to return to God a tenth of what He gives us. Everything we have comes from Him in the first place, so it's right and good that we give back a part of what He gives us."

"A tenth. Ten percent. You give *ten percent* of all the money that comes in?" Disbelief tightened his voice.

"Yes, I do. And God makes the rest stretch."

"Stretch. Right. God gets the hunk that could buy Katie a lot of things she does without. That could fix up the barn or give you decent fencing. That could—"

"Whoa. We've got more food than we should be eating, plenty of clothes, a warm house, all those horses... Compared with the rest of the world, we're unbelievably rich. I don't begrudge a single dime I give back to God."

"So God doesn't mind your giving that tithe to moochers like Charlie?"

"No, He wouldn't mind, but our tithe—the ten percent—goes just to the work of the church and to missions. What Charlie gets is extra—an offering over and above our tithe."

Jeth spun away in exasperation. "That's madness! Why not give ninety percent and live off ten?"

Rob laughed. "I know a guy who does just that. He's making a bundle, but he's chosen to live pretty much like we do—plain and simple. Actually, things were tight around here awhile back. Then God sent you along. Now, because of you, we're making enough money so I can actually pay you. You were our test of faith." He clapped Jeth on the shoulder.

Jeth didn't laugh. He turned away, then back quickly at Rob, and closed his eyes a moment before walking away.

KATIE HUGGED JETH one too many times that week. It felt good—and then it didn't. Had she been anyone other than Rob's wife, he would have welcomed the interplay and given back as good as he got. But she was Rob's wife, and that turned the fun on its head. Rob had hired him straight out of prison. Trusted him, for no good reason. Even when Jeth had let him down, not only had Rob not tossed him out, he'd forgiven him. And now, the bond of friendship—yes, of love—had placed an even greater obligation on him. Katie, as warm and caring as she was, was becoming a burr under his saddle.

SUMMER CAME IN all its opulence—warm scents of soil and grass, birds coupling in heavy-headed trees, wildflowers working their artistry on every untended piece of ground. Horse-show season was already in full swing, and this served up a different sort of intoxication. Their heavy hitters were Pixie, Campion, Caprice, and Belladonna, and they had delayed showing to make sure the horses and riders were in top form. They would also show Lord Nelson and maybe Woodbine, but more for experience and training—and, of course, for exposure to potential buyers. They would stick to Pennsylvania shows this season, hoping to range further afield the following year. They had worked hard. Again, Cecil was invaluable and knew what needed doing without being told. Jeth wondered how the boy got enough sleep between his two jobs.

Their first events were local B-rated shows with 4-H competition and barrel racing, but each had two jumper classes. When they got to the grounds and unloaded four horses off the big fifth wheel, Jeth inhaled the horsey atmosphere and caught his breath with sudden pleasure. "Even a down-home country frolic like this is a drug fix. I didn't realize until we drove in how much I missed—" He looked at Rob, eyes shifting to panic. "What did I just say? I didn't mean—"

Rob laughed. "I know what you meant. This is where you get your rush. The statute of limitations ran out on your drug past. Now, start hustling. We got an hour to get these horses up and ready."

"You know, sometimes I just want to get down on the ground and kiss your feet."

"Here." Rob tossed a currycomb at him. "Polish Campion instead."

IN THIS FIRST show, they had entered two horses in each class, with both Rob and Jeth riding. The jumps in the ring were basic— a couple of brush jumps, a faux stone wall, and rail fences, one of which was clumped three thick. The jump pattern, too, presented no challenges: to the right over two jumps, across the bottom and left to the cross-ring jumps, a tight turn to the opposite cross jumps, across the bottom, and up the perimeter jumps. The horses would be assessed four faults for each knockdown or refusal and one fault per second over the time limit.

Each horse entered at a trot, circled at a slow canter, and then passed the timing light to start the clock. They moved easily between jumps, then gathered, soared with a grunt, and landed with eyes and ears searching out the next obstacle. The first contestant finished with four rails knocked down, giving him sixteen faults. The second horse was disqualified after a jump refusal that left the rider on the ground. Seven horses competed, and to nobody's surprise, Jeth and Campion came in first, over Rob's second on Caprice. In the second class, though, with a slight rearrangement of the jumps, Rob and Belladonna beat Jeth and Pixie. "Hmm," said Jeth. "A little homework needed. Too many distractions, even for Pixie."

The second show was equally low-key, but Jeth did poorly. He was out of sorts from the start and quickly got into an argument with Rob about who had forgotten the grooming tools. "I always put them in the box," said Jeth, "but you toss them who knows where and expect me to know where they are."

Rob shrugged. "Okay, I'll take the blame, but it doesn't change the fact that they're not here. What now?"

"Well, that's your problem."

Rob looked at him, then walked off. He was back fifteen minutes later with a borrowed currycomb and brush. He cleaned the horses silently, all the while eyeing Jeth, who sat with his head in his hands. "You're not feeling well, are you?"

Jeth grunted.

More silence.

"You want to scratch the class?"

"No!"

"Okay, we'll do what we can."

After Jeth's humiliating loss, Rob took Nightshade from him, pushed him onto a chair, and walked the mare cool. He put her away, then came back and examined Jeth closely. "You're a wreck." He put a hand on his forehead. "Fever. We're going home."

This time, Jeth didn't argue.

NEXT MORNING, JETH went to the barn, as usual, to tend the nickering, pawing horses, but Rob came in and sent him back to the trailer. "Don't come out until your fever's gone. I'll send Katie down with some stuff."

Katie came, just as Jeth had dropped off to sleep on the couch. She set a tray on the table and, with cheery prattle, heated water for tea, measured a spoonful of noxious stuff, and shoved it into his mouth.

Jeth closed his eyes, fervently wishing she'd go away. She opened a jar of linament, but he waved her off. "Leave it on the table. If I need it, I'll put it on."

She pushed out her lips and shrugged her displeasure but then lined up her ministrations within easy reach, cleared the dirty dishes, and started dusting.

"Katie." He waited till she turned around. "I'm all right. Thanks for coming."

"No problem!" She continued dusting. "I'll check in from time to time and bring—"

"Katie, go. I'll never get better if you keep stirring up dust."

"Oh, it won't take long. I'll be through in a jiff."

He got up, took the cloth out of her hands, turned her around, and pushed her toward the door.

"Jeth—lie down!"

"Not till you leave." His cell phone rang. "Go. That's probably my girlfriend."

Her eyes widened, and she stopped, but he said "Out!" and pushed her through the doorway. He closed his eyes and leaned his head against the jamb. On the fourth ring, he pulled the phone from his pocket.

"Hello? Jeth?"

"Maybelle! Is that you?"

Katie turned around and stared, but Jeth waved her on.

"Jeth, I heard you were sick."

"Now, how did you find that out?"

"You were on the prayer chain."

"Word does get around. Hasn't been long enough for me to know I'm sick."

"Well, I'm praying for you. I pray for you a lot, you know."

"Thank you, Maybelle. I'm honored that you think I'm worth praying for."

9

The first A-rated show of the season, near Harrisburg, offered serious competition. Sponsored by a local stable, it offered comfortable stalls and a large outdoor ring. Along with the usual rail jumps, the course included a faux stone wall, an oxer with the rails tipped crossways, and a tall flower box topped by a rail. One of the classes included a combination of three jumps in a row, with only two strides between. Some of the wings on these jumps were intentionally scary—bright colors, shapes, or fluttery material—and in preparation, Jeth and Rob had worked hard with bold materials to season their horses.

The first class went well. Campion came in only a few seconds slower than the first-place Mitchell Stable entry. Jeth was rubbing him down when a voice behind him jolted him upright.

"Hello, Jeth."

"Janni!" His face lit as he took in her slender, tight-clad form, dark hair glinting fire from a shaft of sunlight. "I never guessed you'd be here. I didn't see any Wingate listings." He took her hands and ran his eyes over her low-cut tee.

"One-day shows don't appeal to Dad, but I decided to check who might be riding this season." She smiled coyly. "You did well. Just a skosh wide that last turn. Could've saved a stride. Nice horse." She stroked the black gelding's neck.

"Yeah, Campion's doing okay. Not ready for a U.S. Equestrian event, but he's coming. Are you riding this season?"

"No, and probably never. Freddie's our extreme-jerk big guy now. You remember him. He wins. I seldom did—though I might have had an...*interesting* advantage here."

"Yup. My focus shot." He grinned.

"I'll keep that in mind." She cocked a hip and ran a finger down his chin. "So what's this stable you ride for? Somebody told me you're buying and selling."

"I work with Rob Chilton, not far from Oakley. Morningstar's a mom-and-pop operation. Rob is a great guy to work for. Took me on, hardly batting an eye. He knows what I did and a lot besides. I owe him more than I can say. We're a good team. He works the horses through basics; I finish them up. He had a fair clientele to start with, but word gets around that we handle good stock. The place is a dump. Well...rustic, anyway. If he didn't give so much money away, he could spruce things up, but that's not going to happen."

She looked at him quizzically. "Give money away? Who to? Not you."

"He's done plenty for me—big stuff, little stuff. Most of it, though, goes to help other people. Ten percent to the church, and he and Katie support orphans in...Guatemala? Someplace. Last week they invited a missionary for Sunday dinner, and I thought, Hoo boy, there goes the winter hay budget, off to Micronesia or wherever. To say nothing of the sots he sometimes hires to shovel manure. They don't stay long—a couple of weeks, for drink money." He raised his hand. "I'm not putting Rob down. He's got a huge heart and puts his money where his mouth is. That's the way he is, and I couldn't ask for a better place to work."

"So you go to church, too?"

"Sometimes. The Sundays we don't show are super. Everybody rests, even the horses. We sometimes ride just for fun, but the pleasure horses don't work much, either."

"That's his religion."

"Yup. Ticked me off at first—wanted to get on with things, especially Dynamo, but with what we pack in during a day, Sunday is really—"

"Dynamo?"

"Ye-a-aah, Dynamo!" He laughed. "You should see him—and me riding him. You wouldn't believe. A nasty, five-gaited stallion. He's bitten me twice, but we're beginning to see eye to eye. Probably the most magnificent piece of horseflesh I've ever seen or sat on."

"*You?* On a five-gaited *Saddlehorse?*"

"Yep. Way different all around. I'm getting the hang of it. And when he starts to rack, you know he's got the right name. In those moments, I'm one with that horse, and someday..." He gazed across the alley to a horse being hosed down. "Someday, I'll be able to say I won with that horse."

He shifted his attention back to her neck. "Yes...um...the Westmoreland show next week. Your dad going there?"

"Oh, he'll be there. Three-day shows are worth his while."

"It'll be a challenge for our little gaggle. We'll see if they're up to snuff."

"I'll look for you!"

JANNI DID COME to the Westmoreland show on Friday, the first day, and Jeth introduced her to Rob. She didn't stay, though. "I'll be back tomorrow sometime," she told him.

"What about Daddy? What if he sees us together?"

"He won't. Daddy does clubhouses, not stables. You should know that. Did you ever see him in a pair of jeans?" She tilted a shoulder toward him.

Jeth laughed. "Still wears his satin turtleneck and red weskit?"

"*With* diamond stud." She flicked a thumb at her chest, then raised two fingers stylistically. "And cigar. Don't forget the cigar!"

Over Friday and Saturday, Rob rode Gladys and made fourth. Jeth got a blue on Caprice and a pink fifth on Peanut, which pleased them. One more class was scheduled for Sunday morning, and Jeth would ride Woodbine, the auction horse they'd gambled on. Neither man expected much. The brown gelding had vindicated Jeth's assessment of his innate ability, but this was stiff competition. They hoped his potential would show well enough to attract a buyer.

10

After Saturday's classes, Janni came again. She greeted Jeth warmly. "You're not riding tonight. How about dinner with me? We'd have a chance to talk."

"I'd love it, but I didn't think to bring my weskit, and the diamond's in for an oil change."

Janni laughed and leaned toward him conspiratorially. "Where we're going, noo-body dresses up." She cocked her head impishly. "And besides, your misbegotten face goes better with jeans."

"You've always hated my face. Not pretty like Daddy's. Or yours."

"Uh-uh. I love it. The parts are all wrong—messed-up hair not wavy like his, nose too strong, chin crooked—all wrong except for these lines." She drew her fingertips down his cheeks. "Put those in, and the finished product is…" She put her face close to his and whispered, "*Perfect.*"

Jeth sucked air to get his voice in order. "I'll check with Rob. I'd have to be back by eleven at the latest, to stay with the horses so Rob can head for the motel."

"We can make that work." She flicked her tongue roguishly.

When Jeth told him the plan, Rob looked doubtful. "I promise," Jeth said, "no heavy drinking, no cockfights, no funny bottles. I'll check in with Rick. Janni says we're eating at a small bistro near the Westmoreland Marriott, and I'll be back here by eleven."

JANNI MET HIM at five thirty and took him to her car, arm tucked in his. The evening was fine, and Jeth's heart swelled with the promise of this unexpected occasion. The riverside bistro Janni had chosen was upscale, though not dress-wise, as she'd said. It took Jeth back to similar combos of glitz and grunge from years past. Now, though, he felt oddly out of place, far removed from Rob and Katie and the church huggers. But Janni was here, and that was very good—a welcome replacement for the Katie images he'd been entertaining at night. Janni hadn't changed much, but her inherited beauty bore a more settled look: the fire in her eyes, the flash of color off her raven hair, the quick laugh and sultry, mobile mouth that wore a thousand expressions. Her talk was warm and witty, evoking memories of romps and shared foolishness, of reading to each other, of long horse treks and camping under the stars. He sat back, sipping his wine. *God, I love her!*

The food was good, the noise tolerable, except for three twenty-somethings who had surfed in on whatever high. The establishment quickly ushered them out.

"Party poopers!" Janni glared at the door. "Let 'em have fun. We used to do that."

Yes, they did. Fun at parties, fun at shows, fun in bedrooms with Janni's music in the background. Albinoni's *Adagio*—good for raising his thermostat. Did she ever listen to it anymore—with someone else, maybe? He closed his eyes and could hear the aching beauty of the ancient, sultry melody.

Janni had grown up with that kind of music. Grandpa Grundel had played cello with a respectable orchestra, and her mom had inherited his passion for music. Both of these influences had slidden out of Janni's life in her late teens, when her mom had departed the Wingate establishment, but by then, music had been tattooed on her soul. She could not go with her mom; Daddy wouldn't allow it. But, while Jeth lacked her heritage, he had soaked in enough culture along the way to utilize Albinoni for his own amorous purposes.

Not all memories were benign. They had scrapped and stabbed each other. Janni had learned early on how to get at him, how to bring him to heel. Pressure from her dad and his propelled Jeth away from Janni and toward stable work and intensive jump training. And then, she'd gotten pregnant. Jeth thought of a recent suppertime conversation about a church girl in the same predicament. Abortion was out of the question for her family, but it was no-win, either way. Jeth knew that, and he'd known it five years ago. Janni's child…his child…

When the server came with a dessert tray, Janni shook her head. "I'll take the check." She turned to Jeth. I'm paying. This is my night. And I've got plans. A nice evening. Let's walk along the river."

A BREEZE OFF the water picked up and handed them, one by one, the smells of fresh-cut grass, river mud, summer heat. "So quiet here," murmured Janni. She clung to Jeth, and they strolled in silence, listening to a nearby robin and a distant saxophone. From somewhere on the far side of the river came the insistent shrill of a cicada. She smiled up at Jeth. He bent and kissed her lightly.

They talked of old times, of her mom and grandfather, of horses they both had ridden. "So tell me, how do you train this Dynamo thing of yours?" Janni asked.

Jeth laughed. "More a question of how he's training me! I've learned tons from him, especially the art of winning arguments. We've sort of figured out who's boss, but there are times when I marvel at some deep wisdom—horse sense, maybe—that surfaces, and I'd like some of that. But he's all stallion, and a tyrant, to boot. Not a shred of cordiality. We're on speaking terms, though. He knows carrots, and he knows a firm but gentle hand. We'll never cozy up—no head-on-shoulder sort of thing—but he responds and gives two hundred percent."

"An honest horse, your dad used to say."

"He's that, and then some. It's all up-front...out there in plain view. I like that. A good trait for horses and for people. I want to be that kind of man."

Soon she quickened her step and steered him across the boulevard toward a small eatery. She bypassed that and stepped instead through an adjacent doorway, pulling out a key to unlock an inner door.

"Wait."

She turned and looked at him.

"I'm not going in there."

"What do you mean? This is our night."

"No. We've had our night. We're having our night, out here along the river."

"Come *on*, Jeth. This is what I planned. A little room upstairs. Wine, music, just the right—"

"No." He planted his feet. "I can't."

"What do you *mean*, you can't?" She was getting exasperated. "You're not talking sense."

"I can't. I can't do this. That's what I mean. I work for Rob, and I can't break trust with him."

"What does Rob have to do with it? You told him you'd be back by eleven. You will. I promise. What you do between now and then is not his business. You're a big boy now. You don't have to report in every ten minutes."

"I messed up six weeks ago. I can't do it again. I promised him."

"Jeth, stop! You're being silly. You're not messing up; you're with me. We're having a good time. Rob has nothing to do with this. And I've got a couple of CDs I know you'll like." She smiled provocatively.

Jeth gritted his teeth and closed his eyes. "Rob's got everything to do with it," he said. "He gave me the job of my dreams when I was all but unemployable. He *trusted* me. Most guys fresh out of prison could rot in the street before anyone would hire them. I'm not going up those stairs. I'm sorry, but I—"

"You're refusing to lie on a bed with me. What am I, horse crap? Time was when I couldn't keep you off me. Had to crawl behind every bush to keep you happy."

"Janni, you're not even trying to understand. Rob did something for me that—"

"Rob did something for you. So now you're, like, married to him? What if Rob weren't in the picture? What if you worked for somebody else—say, my dad? Would that make a difference?"

Jeth looked away and was silent. Yes, it probably would make a difference. He'd know the messing-up part but not forgiveness, and would he even recognize messing up? Jeth didn't know. But he had, in fact, drunk out of Rob's trough, and out of that same trough came obligation. "Yes, it would make a difference. But I'm not working for your dad or anyone else. I'm working for Rob Chilton, and he works for God. He did something for me I can never, ever pay back. The last thing I want to do is—"

"Like what?"

"Like what, what?"

"Like, what did he do, other than discover you and take you on as his best rider? Don't forget that part. What makes him Mr. Wonderful, right up there next to God?"

"Like, I can't tell you. He knows what it was, and I know. That's enough. I'm not going to break trust again. Let's go walk by the river some more."

Anger blistered Janni's eyes. Her face went rigid. Her lips trembled with rage. "I go to all the trouble of planning a night that would make up for three horrible years, and along comes this holy-roller cassock in blue jeans. Well, take your cassock and *stuff it!*" She slapped him. Hard.

Jeth reeled away, then lunged at her in a fury, grabbing her shoulders. They were suddenly ten years old again, at each other's throats. Within seconds, though, he pushed her away and shoved open the outer door.

Roaring with anger, Janni followed, "Jeth Cavanaugh, if you leave now, you'll never see me again. I hate you! Get out of my sight, and don't ever call. Go *away!*" Her voice rose to an ugly screech.

Jeth stopped midstep and spun around. He said nothing but stood, staring at her, anger drifting into puzzlement, as though he did not understand what she had said. He studied her a moment longer, then turned and walked away, slowly, solemnly, frowning slightly, as though sorting through the imponderables of the universe.

JETH GOT BACK to the show grounds on his own with three minutes to spare. Rob stood and stretched, rubbing his eyes. "How'd it go?"

Jeth sank down on a hay bale without speaking.

After a moment, Rob came over and put a hand on his shoulder. "What happened?"

Still Jeth said nothing. Then he looked up. "Rob, Janni went into a lavender fury and slapped the daylights out of me because I wouldn't go to bed with her. I wanted to—badly—but I couldn't, like there was a...a wall of fire or something. I couldn't go up those steps. I wanted to go back outside and walk by the river, where it was safe, away from...what? I didn't know, but I think, somehow, the instant she whacked me, I touched down on foreign soil. Now, tell me what it means."

Rob looked closely at him. "Foreign soil..." Then, with a look of understanding, he put his hand on Jeth's shoulder. "Foreign land! That first Sunday you went to church with us, you said you were as comfortable as a stranger could be in a foreign land. You 'touched down.' Do you mean…?"

Jeth took a big breath. "I almost hauled off and gave it back to her, but suddenly it didn't matter. Nothing mattered. In seconds, I lost the love of my life and gained something way better, and I haven't the foggiest notion what it is or what makes it better. Almost like my inner compass suddenly swung to true north. Rob, I really want this…God thing, or whatever you call it."

"Hey, man!" Rob flung his arms around Jeth, pounding him enthusiastically, his grin sea wide. "You're my brother now. Both of us, the family of God! But tell me more about that wall of fire."

They talked long and late about Jeth's unorthodox entry into the kingdom, until Jeth finally told Rob to go get some sleep.

"You're the one who needs it," said Rob. "You've got a class at eight thirty."

"Well, sleep for me. For sure I won't be sleeping. Too much to process."

"Maybe we should scratch."

"Hey, if I can haul myself onto Woodbine and not fall off, I'll give it a try. Can't do worse than come up last."

"Well, we are trying to sell that horse. We got him so cheap at the auction, we wouldn't have to get much to make a profit, but—"

"I'll do my best."

11

When morning came, the air hung in thick, sultry slabs. Rob was not heartened when he looked at Jeth. "Do you feel as bad as you look?"

Jeth rumpled his hair and closed his eyes.

"Do you want to talk or go to bed?"

"I'll ride. Just need some coffee."

"Go get some breakfast."

"Sounds awful."

"Well, at least wash up. Woodbine looks good, and you should, too. You've been polishing him, I see." He ran an appraising eye over the dappled rump that shone even in the thickening murk.

"Maybe nobody will notice what I look like."

"They'll notice."

An hour later, Jeth mounted and looked at the clouds writhing overhead. "Not raining yet." He gave Rob a weak grin.

Jeth was tenth and last in the lineup of jumpers. As he waited, the air bristled with electricity, as though lightning might leap from the ground to savage the rumbling blackness overhead. He drew big breaths.

"Nervous?" asked Rob.

"I don't know what I am. I'm a foreigner here, remember?"

Rob half smiled, then looked irritably at the sky. "Why aren't they calling this class until the storm's over?"

"Huh! With just one entry to go? It's not that bad."

The preceding rider came out, and the gatekeeper nodded to Jeth. Rob gripped his leg. "Go out there and have fun. Ride safe!"

"Sure. Right. Dodge lightning bolts."

As the first few raindrops fell, Rob watched in disbelief as Jeth made one blunder after another—and finished with no faults and the lowest time. When Jeth came out, his eyes were stricken, his face ashen. "There's some mistake!"

"No mistake, buddy. Go back out there and get your ribbon."

Jeth returned and handed the rain-spattered blue to Rob, then dismounted and leaned his head on the horse, shaking visibly. "This is not right. I did not earn that ribbon. And there's nothing that can make me believe that God did this just because I signed on with Him. I've seen you pray often enough and things still go sour. Don't make me even try to believe this was God."

Rob shrugged. "I can't explain it, either. I've never seen anything like it. Becoming a Christian is not an express elevator to the top. Sometimes it's just the opposite. You were horrible in there, but still you won."

"No, Woodbine won, not me. I told you—"

"Jeth, he's not that good a horse. He shouldn't have won. I'd've been happy with sixth."

Jeth rubbed his face. "It was like a nightmare, like I was on the horse but also just watching this klutzy rider do one stupid thing after another, and I couldn't do anything to stop it. And then—"

"Rob Chilton?"

Rob turned at the voice.

"That was some ride!"

"Huh! Some *kind* of ride," Jeth muttered.

"Hal Paxton, and I'm interested in that horse of yours. Can we go to that tent over there and talk?"

Rob turned to Jeth. "Will you be okay?"

"I'll cool this guy." Jeth dragged Woodbine through the rain to the horse barn and almost lost him when he shied at a clap of thunder only half as loud as one he had ignored in the ring at the final jump. Annoyed, Jeth yanked the reins hard. But when he got to the covered walkway along the barn, he stroked the horse apologetically and whispered, "It's not your fault."

This inexplicable, uninvited intrusion into his life was not the horse's fault, but what else—who else—could he blame? As he walked, he watched the two men under the saddlery tent, gesturing and posturing, and could practically follow the conversation. "*That man of yours—never seen such sloppy miscommunication between horse and rider, but the horse—even with the storm coming on, couldn't do anything wrong! I want that horse.*" And Rob would say, "*I need to tell you, the horse isn't all that good. This was a fluke. You don't want him. We've been working with him, but he's still not what he should be.*" "*But,*" Hal would say, "*I saw him. Not only did he perform perfectly on his own, he actually made up for your man's fluffs and the weather. I'll give you fifteen thousand for him.*" "*But,*" Rob would reply, shaking his head just like now, "*as plain as I can say it, the horse is not worth fifteen thousand. He will be, but not now. That's his price, but I don't want you to buy him.*"

Hal did buy him, signing a release saying he had been told in advance what the horse was really like. Jeth went into a corner of the stall and wept.

On the way home, he slept. When he finally sat up, Rob looked at him. "You know, I been thinking. That had to be God. It was so bizarre, it couldn't be anything else. If you'd ridden like that when you first came to me, I probably wouldn't've hired you. Of course," he added, "if a judge had come along waving a blue ribbon over you, I might've reconsidered." He grinned. "But I would've wondered about the judge!" He was quiet a moment. "I've heard tell of horses sometimes flashing back to a former greatness and performing way beyond what their riders ask of them, but Woodbine is too young to have that kind of history. I've watched him enough to know his capabilities, and he was just not capable of winning that class! But he did. And it scares me."

Jeth looked at him.

Rob stared straight ahead. "It says, 'Be warned—don't mess with God.'"

"So, what happened was bad?"

"No. It's just not what God normally does. I don't understand it, but I don't have to. I do think it was somehow connected with your experience last night. Some sort of sign, maybe, for both of us. The nightmare you were experiencing, almost like God *making* you ride poorly. Why would He do that? I don't understand, but it certainly means I need to keep my eye on you!" He smiled and leaned over to squeeze Jeth's knee.

Show followed show, with no other strange happenings. Jeth won some, lost some, even failed to place in one event—against Freddie and a Wingate horse. That hurt, but Jeth bested him the next day, with a third to Freddie's fourth.

12

Jeth gave mixed reviews on his first couple of weeks as a Christian—had a voracious appetite for God, couldn't read the Bible fast enough, soaked in Maybelle's hymns. Never mind that they dated back a couple of centuries; everything was new to him. In church Sunday mornings, he stopped sitting in back with Rob and Katie and moved to the front row, leaning forward, arms on his knees. "I want to get close to the power," he said. "Plus, I get a wash from the praise team. I want to be up there someday."

His offer to sing with the team was snapped up, and though the evening rehearsals were tough after a full day's work, singing became an unexpected interpreter for what was deep within and almost totally incomprehensible. As much as he loved competitive jumping, he begrudged show Sundays when he couldn't be in church. The urgency to worship through song was an ache, almost as strong as the Janni ache in his heart. Her love for music had been reconfigured within Jeth to an intense desire to make the "God of wonders" float above Janni's sensual Albinoni music.

He returned to the Thursday morning Bible study, not to argue but to listen and learn. Many of his earlier issues had fallen into place, but the emphasis on blood still rankled. He had endless questions for Rob. What's this business of God ordering women and children and animals to be killed? That's worse than cannibalizing Jesus at the Communion table. How can a good God allow even "normal" suffering? What's the Trinity all about? How can God hear everyone's prayers all at once? Why are some prayers answered and others not? Miracles were no problem for Jeth: he'd had one dished up right at the start with his win on Woodbine. And if you could believe miracles happen, then a resurrection or two was a no-brainer.

Rob answered what questions he could and sent Jeth to the pastor for others, but when the volume became almost overwhelming, he said, "How about giving Katie a turn at this? She'd love to sit with you and try to come up with some answers."

Yeah, sure she would, thought Jeth. *Rob, is something going on here, or am I imagining things?* Someday he'd have to talk to his boss about it, but not now. He did toss questions to Katie, but only when Rob was around.

His quick mouth didn't disappear, though. He sometimes felt bad about the things he said, especially to Rob, but more often not.

He never spoke unkindly to Maybelle. When he told her what had happened at the horse show, she hugged him and cried, then looked straight at him and said, "I knew that first day you came to church that God was after you. He's in the salvage business, you know. Let's watch and see what He'll do now." Her eyes crinkled. "I hadn't heard you sing then, but I knew—"

Jeth laughed. "You knew just from looking at me that I definitely needed a hymnal. You're something else!" He turned serious. "Will you teach me to pray, Maybelle? I don't think I've ever prayed in my life, except maybe my first night in jail."

Her eyebrows shot up.

He grinned at her. "You had my number that first day, but I'm guessing you haven't totally sorted through the bag God tossed at you. You knew what I needed but not why."

"You come right over here and sit down. Never mind all the people. Now, what would you like to call God? There's Lord, Savior, Father, Jesus, Lord Jesus—"

"Pick one for me."

"No, I can pick verses for you, but not your heart's way of call-ing out to God."

"What verse you got for me today?"

"Well, let's see…" She pulled a Bible from her tote bag and opened it. "Zechariah is full of sweetmeats. Here's one that fits you. *'Now Joshua'*—might we rename him Jeth?—*'Now Jeth was dressed in filthy clothes as he stood before the angel. The angel said to those who were standing before him, "Take off his filthy clothes." Then he said to Jeth, "See, I have taken away your sin, and I will put rich garments on you."'*"

Jeth drew a sharp breath, and his eyes widened. "Let me see that." He yanked the Bible from her hands.

"'That's chapter three, verses three and four. Here's another one," and she snatched back the Bible. "Another verse, another angel. This angel said, *'Run, tell that young man, "Jerusalem will be a city without walls because of the great number of men and livestock in it."'* Here comes the important part: *'"And I myself will be a wall of fire around it," declares the* LORD, *"and I will be its glory within."'* Jeth, my heart tells me you will need that wall of fire."

She then led him patiently through the basics of prayer—wor-shiping, confessing, asking, thanking. She made him say the words out loud, and as he did, he felt enveloped in love—and he couldn't tell if it was her love or God's wall of fire.

JETH AGONIZED OVER Janni. He relived her rage and the hard slap that had seemed so totally out of character. As children, they had dived eagerly into savagery, but the buoyancy of their love had always popped them, gasping, to the surface. Love had defined them, and never had it been in doubt. This, though, was different. Her slap that night had been a shoulder-fired missile, designed to destroy, and Jeth was under no illusions that she hadn't really meant it. The pain was almost more than he could bear.

Dreams were even worse, and not all were about Janni. He writhed over the ones with Katie in bed with him. He began to monitor his interactions with her. She hugged him often, but then, she hugged everybody, even Cecil. Jeth took care not to go into the house unless Rob was there or without Cecil in tow. And he decided against accepting more than one dinner invitation a week.

One afternoon, Jeth was standing near the grain bin, studying papers the deliveryman had left, trying to figure out why the shipment of hay and grain wasn't exactly what they had ordered. Katie tiptoed behind him and scooped a handful of oats out of the bag he had just opened. She tossed it lightly at Jeth's head but jumped at his violent turn and defensive stance.

"I'm sorry—I didn't mean to scare you."

"Well, you did scare me. Don't do it again!"

"Jeth, you're angry with me. I said I was sorry."

He turned away and leaned on the feed bin.

Katie moved to his side and put her hand on his shoulder. Jeth straightened and backed away. "Katie, I forgive you, but *don't do that again!*"

THAT NIGHT, AFTER a cold and troubled supper in the trailer, Jeth pulled Maybelle's hymnbook from the shelf and leafed through it. His eyes stopped on one that raked his heart till he almost cried out. But he read on, and the words drifted over his soul like a blanket—cloud soft, down warm.

Come, ye sinners, poor and needy,
Weak and wounded, sick and sore;
Jesus ready stands to save you,
Full of pity, love and power.

Come, ye thirsty, come, and welcome,
God's free bounty glorify;

True belief and true repentance,
Every grace that brings you nigh.

I will arise and go to Jesus,
He will embrace me in His arms;
In the arms of my dear Savior,
O there are ten thousand charms.

THE FOLLOWING SUNDAY, another hymn ambushed Jeth, one he had heard countless times in nonconventional places. At the end of the first verse, he elbowed Rob, who was sitting by him up front, waiting to do a Scripture reading. "Look at these words! Have you seen them?" The level of his voice fell just under a shout.

"Of course I've seen them. Pipe down and sing."

"I can't. They're attacking me!"

"What?"

"The words. They've got me by the throat."

"Come on! Haven't you ever heard 'Amazing Grace'?"

"Sure I have. Amazing Bagpipes. Right up there with the national anthem. But I didn't realize it had words that meant anything. I just knew you needed to look solemn."

"And now they do mean something."

"Yes! Look at this." He pointed at the page in the hymnal. "'Saved a wretch like me...was blind but now I see.' And this: 'Twas grace that taught my heart to fear / and grace my fears relieved; / how precious did that grace appear / the hour I first believed.' That was written for me. How did they know?"

"John Newton wrote it in the seventeen hundreds. He captained a slave ship before becoming a Christian, so I guess he knew grace when he saw it."

"Huh. They ought to add footnotes or flags or something whenever it's sung. Put the reader on high alert. This is potent stuff!"

JETH'S BAPTISM TOUCHED off a minor war between Maybelle and the pastor. Maybelle went to him with a Scripture she felt should be read over Jeth on the occasion, and the pastor was equally passionate about the passage he had chosen. "Maybelle," he said, "I know you love Jeth and think the whole Bible applies to him— and, of course, it does. Don't get me wrong. But your passage from Luke isn't appropriate for a baptism. But Romans five says exactly what he has experienced in becoming a Christian—he's justified by faith, has peace with God, is rejoicing in the hope of glory."

Maybelle shook her head. "That's what you read for everyone who gets baptized. One size fits all. And one size doesn't fit Jeth. For one thing, you stop too soon. The next verse talks about rejoicing in suffering, and suffering produces perseverance and character."

"And hope," the pastor countered. "It's back again to hope. So, these first two verses do cover it all. The Luke passage just won't do for a baptism. 'Christ will suffer and rise from the dead…. You are witnesses…. Stay in the city'? It doesn't make sense for Jeth or anybody else getting baptized!"

Maybelle sat stiffly, lips pursed, chin resting on an elbow-propped hand. Then she tilted her chin and sniffed. "It may not fit him yet, but it will…it will."

Maybelle lost the battle. As Jeth rose up and shook water from his head, the pastor's voice soared over him: "'Therefore, since we have been justified through faith, we have peace with God through our Lord Jesus Christ, through whom we have gained access by faith into this grace in which we now stand. And we rejoice in the hope of the glory of God.'" He looked triumphantly at Maybelle.

Maybelle then proceeded to win the war. When the pastor asked for someone to pray for Jeth, she raised her hand and stood, smiling sweetly. She put her hands together and looked toward the ceiling. "O Lord God, Elohim, God of strength and resurrection power, I thank You for Your servant Jeth. He doesn't know yet how to be Your servant, but You will teach him. He doesn't see yet that his path may be strewn with suffering, but You will show him. You will sing to him when he is afraid; You will rebuke him when he needs it. You will teach him how to hug people into Your kingdom. You will reveal to him what Your Word means in Luke twenty-four, verses forty-six through forty-nine."

The pastor opened his eyes and looked sharply at Maybelle.

She spoke the Scripture clearly, not opening her eyes. "'*This is what is written: The Christ will suffer and rise from the dead on the third day, and repentance and forgiveness of sins will be preached in his name to all nations, beginning at Jerusalem. You are witnesses of these things. I am going to send you what my Father has promised; but stay in the city until you have been clothed with power from on high.'*

"Now, El Shaddai, almighty God, clothe Jeth with power from on high—whenever and wherever it pleases You. Amen."

Jeth had felt warmed by the pastor's words, but Maybelle's last words—"whenever and wherever it pleases You"—turned his body to ice. He trembled uncontrollably, and it wasn't because he was wet.

13

Jeth took a hot cup from Katie, set it on the coffee table, and went back to flipping pages of his Bible. He turned to Rob beside him on the couch. "I don't get what the books toward the end of the Old Testament are talking about. Like this." Jeth pointed to a text. "*Hear this word, you cows of Bashan.*' I love it! But I don't think it's supposed to be funny. And did you know that horses show up everywhere in the Bible—red, white, black, dappled?"

"Yeah, they do," Rob replied. "They're metaphors, like those cows. The Bible's full of metaphors. Especially in the prophets."

"Prophets. Like Madam Guccio—I read your palm?"

"No, no. Bible prophets, like Isaiah and Jonah, weren't fortune-tellers. They—"

"Jonah I sort of dig. He deserved to get dunked and digested. And Zechariah—he's got me in his sights, with his angels and wall of fire. But the others—"

"Jeth, stick to the New Testament till you get your sea legs. The prophets are heavy stuff, and you'd do better—"

"*What?* Skip those guys? Too many fun things here, as in funscary. Wheels turning every which way, dry bones and whores… yeah, I know. Metaphor. But how did those guys survive these 'close encounters'? Some big fellow comes along—"

"Um…big fellow. An angel, maybe?"

"Whatever. The big guy tells them to chill and not be afraid, but they fall on their faces, can't stand or talk. Then, later on, this line in…uh…" He flipped through the pages. "Ezekiel—yeah, he's my guy, with his lightning and wheels and glory. But get this: *'Then the glory of the Lord departed from over the threshold of the temple.'* The glory departed. Does that mean what I think it does?"

"It means the people of Israel were so corrupt that God basically walked away. Yeah, it was bad."

"But didn't you tell me God lived in the temple?"

"Back then He did, but today we're His temple. He lives in us."

Jeth blew into his steepled hands and stared at the coffee table, with its mantle of newspapers, horse magazines, and accumulated mail. "We're His temple. So, if we turn sour, He could depart from us like He did from the temple...walk away. Does God do that?" His voice skittered toward panic.

Rob grunted wryly. "Now you're into heavy theology. Is it 'once saved, always saved,' or is it 'Watch your step, pal'? But God walking out on us? I don't think so. This was a sign to the entire nation of Israel; and, yes, they did push God to the limit, but—"

"Whatever." Jeth leaned back and waved his dismissal. "I don't get much of this, Rob, but I do understand that this is how God talks in real life. I've experienced that, and this stuff in the Bible—Ezekiel, Zechariah—somehow helps me understand His everyday language."

Rob closed his eyes and shook his head slowly. "Buddy, God doesn't talk that way to most Christians. We don't have the right wireless setup and can't even tell there's a conversation going on. Obviously, you can. Keep reading Ezekiel and tell us what it means."

"Now you're really creeping me out!"

A WEEK LATER, at the end of an exhausting three days of competition in West Virginia, Rob finished saddling Lord Nelson and looked at his watch. "Jeth, you don't have time to watch that gaited class." His voice hung thick with exasperation. "You need to warm

Nelson before you ride. His muscles need stretching, and so do yours after your dustup with Dynamo this week."

"So he dumped me."

"Yes, he did, and you've been limping ever since."

"But I learned, and he learned, too—big time. It won't happen again." Jeth's body and voice took a supplicatory stance. "Rob, if you'd warm Nelson just this once, I could catch at least part of that five-gaited class. I need to watch them ride so I'll know if I'm doing it right. And 'C' Ring is just over there." He motioned vaguely. "I'll jog both ways. Please, Rob. Lord Nelson won't mind, and I promise to get a decent ribbon on him."

"Right. Why not promise a blue while you're at it?"

Jeth didn't get a blue—he barely got a white fourth—but Rob seemed happy. "Nelson is getting noticed, and that's what matters. Had two guys talk to me."

Jeth drove home so Rob could sleep on the way. With his heart still tingling after watching only seven minutes of the gaited class, he would have no trouble staying awake. Yes, those horses were flashy, well-trained professionals, but none of them had Dynamo's power or verve in even his most perfunctory sessions. Jeth hungered to be entering "C" Ring at a brisk, high-stepping trot. He would do that someday. He had to.

THE FOLLOWING WEEKEND, blistering hot, was perhaps the most important show of the season, in Altoona, within easy driving distance. How their horses performed in this show would determine their ranking with the United States Equestrian Federation. Rob had four horses entered, Wingate three. Jeth felt good about their chances and, despite the heat, did well in their first two classes. The big one was still to come, though, and early in the morning, everything came crashing down.

Rob and Jeth had been hovering over Pixie as though high polish would improve the handsome bay's chances against the best of Wingate and other top stables. Pixie's black mane and forelock had been braided to Katie's exacting standards in a way that showed off the pear-shaped splash of white on his forehead. This class would again be Jeth against Freddie. Rob rubbed sweat from his face. "Do you think you should start warming before everyone else gets in the practice ring?"

"Yeah, probably. This is as cool as it's going to get." Jeth chewed a hangnail.

"I'll go for coffee while you saddle." Rob turned away.

"Don't breathe on me when you come back. I don't exactly need caffeine right now."

Rob flashed a smile. "Keep cool. You'll do all right."

Moments after Rob left, a voice behind Jeth said, "Good-looking horse."

Jeth turned, and his smile fell away. Freddie stood just inside the shade line of the tent, eyeing the tea-colored gelding appreciatively. He came up and ran a hand along the burnished back. "Well, Jethro, it's me against you out there. Wingate against... what is it, Stardust?"

Jeth's jaw hardened at the hated "Jethro" name, and his eyes narrowed, but he said nothing.

"Tricky course today. Separate the men from the boys, eh? Different from yesterday. They put an oxer after the hogsback triple and switched the pattern to a wicked-tight turn. Gotta really concentrate, get the strides right, especially with the water jump. And in this heat... Now, which is it—left and then center and back? Or is it—"

"Freddie, I'm busy. Go play your games with somebody else."

Freddie raised his arms in a shrug. "Just thought I'd stop by and wish you well." He turned to leave, then casually reversed. "Oh, by the way, did you hear that Janni got married last weekend?

Bryan Beale, one of the old man's buddies. Huge wedding. Spared no horses, so to speak. Honeymoon safari, funded by Papa." He grinned viciously. "She finally agreed to marry somebody respecta—"

Jeth was on him, eyes blazing. "Get out! While you're still in one piece." He shoved Freddie backward.

Color rose in Freddie's face, tempered by a glint of satisfaction. "Go ahead. Clean my clock. That'd give Papa Wingate just the chance he wants to put you away for another two years."

Jeth backed him into a hay bale, then jerked him to within inches of his face. "*I will win this class!* You've only made that a certainty."

Rob returned as Jeth was ready to mount Pixie. Jeth's face and stiff-angled body showed clearly that something was wrong. "What happened?" He took Pixie from Jeth and fastened him to the grooming tie.

Jeth stared hard at the steamy mélange of flags and horses and booted riders, residual sparks arcing from his eyes. "Freddie happened." He closed his eyes and clenched his jaw. "I wanted to take him out, but that's what he was hoping for."

"What did he say?"

"He told me—deliberately, intentionally—that Janni got married last week. He wants me to crash and burn in this class, but I won't. I'll win if it's the last thing I do!" He removed his helmet and messed his hair. "I know this guy Bryan. A toad, a brownnoser. I wouldn't trust him to walk my dog. Always played up to the old man. Janni and I used to make jokes about him. This has to be Wingate's stroke. He's using Bryan for his own vicious purposes— and one of those was to put Janni out of my reach."

Rob took a big breath. "Jeth—"

"Don't give me a lecture. I know I have to calm down and think straight. I know I have to be at the top of my game and get my mind together. I know it. Now I have to make it happen. And my first job is to get Pixie warmed. In the meantime, see if the order of jumping has been posted." He turned away. "And don't even think about preaching to me about forgiveness!"

Jeth made his way to the practice ring on Pixie. He was already late, and several horses, including Freddie's, were hogging the jumps. Jeth eased into the flow around the perimeter of the ring, first at a trot and then an easy canter. He tried to keep his eyes off Freddie and concentrate instead on getting tuned to his own horse, but his heart was racing, nerves leaping. *Lord... Lord...* He couldn't even pray. He slowed to a walk and looked for an available jump.

He didn't actually see what precipitated it, but he saw Freddie's horse twist on its hind legs, throwing the rider hard onto the jump. The horse ran to the side, wild-eyed, as Freddie screamed in agony, blood spurting from his neck, his thighbone crumpled sideways. Jeth vaulted off Pixie and was beside him in an instant. As he knelt, aghast, he saw Freddie's left eye, partway out of its socket. He gritted his teeth, but tending the bleeding came first. He worked his tiepin, whipped off his white tie, and held it firmly to the wound. Ties weren't good blood absorbers, though, and he looked around. The man next to him retched at the gruesome combination. Jeth growled irritably. "Go puke somewhere else. Anyone got a T-shirt—something better than this?" he called out.

At the sound of Jeth's voice, Freddie shrank from him. "Get away!" he cried. "You'll kill me!" He screamed again from pain.

Jeth grabbed the shirt someone held out, and pressed it in place. "Freddie, killing you is way down my list right now. Lie still. You're bleeding. The show EMTs are coming. They'll get you to the hospital. You'll be all right." He looked up as the circle parted. "They're here now."

Three paramedics bent over and quickly substituted sterile compresses for the blood-soaked shirt. Jeth shifted out of their way but stayed by Freddie. "Hold my hand—hold it tight." At first,

Freddie tried to pull away, but pain tightened his grip. "It hurts. I know it hurts, Freddie. Holler like hell. It's okay. Nobody cares. Hold on. Hold on."

Rob slipped in and put a hand on Jeth's shoulder. Jeth looked up at him and said, "This sort of blows the class, but—"

"Don't worry about that. The class doesn't matter, and they'll delay for an accident like this."

"Pixie's around somewhere." As two of the paramedics moved to the broken leg, Jeth cleared sweat and blood from Freddie's face, then wiped his hand on his riding jacket.

"I see him," said Rob. "Somebody's got him."

"Hold on, Freddie; hold tight! This is gonna hurt!" Jeth said as the men straightened the leg.

Freddie's scream rose to a gargled shriek. Jeth gripped tight and bent his head over him. "God, help him, help him, help him! You're okay, Freddie, you're okay."

An EMT pushed Rob away but allowed Jeth to keep his place. For Jeth, it was only him and Freddie in this small, searing bubble of unendurable pain. Shards of conversation bounced off the bubble. "...that eye...more than one bone?...delay the class... Wingate...best horse...other rider...What must he feel like?... Chilton...why can't they...morphine..."

Once the paramedics got Freddie stabilized, they shifted him to a stretcher, pulled it to wheel position, and moved carefully over the rough ground to the waiting ambulance, Jeth walking alongside. He wanted to keep holding Freddie's hand until they got him inside the vehicle, but the men said, "We'll take it from here. Thanks." Jeth had to pry Freddie's fingers loose.

As the vehicle pulled away, Rob came beside Jeth, who was leaning over, bloodied hands on no-longer-white breeches, dripping sweat and drawing ragged breaths. A uniformed show official came up to Rob. "The judges delayed the class, but we have to start now. Do you still want to ride? If you decide not to, we'll refund the entry fee."

Rob looked at Jeth. He didn't respond.

Rob turned back to the official. "Could we have a little time, maybe let us ride last? We'll let you know as soon as we can."

"Absolutely. A terrible thing. Fine horse, excellent rider. Pretty tough on your man to watch his friend go down like that."

Rob grunted grimly and waved his dismissal. "Come on," he said to Jeth. "Let's go to the tent."

"Rob, why does God do this?"

"Well, you could say Freddie got what he deserved, that he brought it on himself, but—"

"No, I mean, why does God do this to *me*? It was Freddie who rubbed my nose in Janni's marriage, but I'm the one God knocked on his knees, pleading for the jerk's life!" He picked up a horse rag to dry his face and was silent a moment. "Maybe just...asking the question answers it."

Rob put his hand on Jeth's back. "Shall we pack up and go home?"

Jeth looked at Rob, as though he was only now hearing his voice. "The class...?"

"They started a few minutes ago. I think we should scratch and go. You're in no shape to ride."

"Is Pixie okay?"

"He's fine."

Jeth looked out over the fairgrounds. "How long do we have?"

"Fifteen minutes. They said you could ride last, but we have to let them know soon, and I don't think—"

"I need to warm him."

"Jeth..."

"I've got to ride."

"Why? There's nothing hanging on this. Freddie's out of the picture, so—"

"I've got to ride. I just do." He stood up.

"Jeth, look at you. You're covered in blood!"

"Do they give ribbons for what you look like? We're wasting time. Is Pixie—" He stopped and stared at Rob, eyes wide, then looked down at his hands and his once-white breeches.

"What?" said Rob.

"I'm covered in blood!" His voice was tight with awe. "I'm *washed in blood*. I finally get it!" He took a huge, shaky breath.

Jeth took time to watch one horse go through the jump pattern and then turned Pixie to the practice ring. Tension was high as he sat waiting to ride. Even Pixie pawed and tossed his head restlessly. "Where's Cecil when we need him?" Jeth muttered. "He'd breathe peace into both of us." As he entered the ring, only vaguely hearing Rob's "Ride safe," he had no idea what or who he was jumping against. He only knew he had to jump clean within the time frame.

He did. But so had three others. The jump-off whittled it down to two—Jeth against Freddie's horse with substitute rider—but both were again clean jumps, even with three jumps raised. The third jump-off was tightly time factored, and incredibly, they both came out exactly the same. Stewards approached both riders and asked if they wanted to jump or default.

Jeth wiped his face. "Pixie's tired," he said to Rob. "I don't want to risk him. Is that okay with you?"

Rob turned to the steward and said, "We decline to jump."

The officials huddled for a moment, and then the announcement came over the PA system: "Both riders have declined to ride again. The prize money will be split."

Jeth slid off drunkenly and buried his face in Pixie's lathered neck.

14

Jeth surprised Rob by actually taking time off the following week.
He didn't go anywhere. He slept a lot and wandered the acreage or
rode the trails, trying to unpack it all. That Janni was married was
a knife in his belly that could disembowel, if not kill him outright.
He had known that the slap was more than just temper, but a tiny
grain of hope that time might change things had lain dormant
within him. Now, though, hope withered, never to spring to life.
A couple of years ago, he would have worked around the situation
somehow, set up new motel trysts. But not now...not now. Walls
of a different sort had been erected in his heart and mind.

He talked long with Rob. "It's hard to put into words.
Freddie—a dirty, rotten sinner. His blood—the force of life—
somehow became Jesus' blood for me. I know, I know. Sounds
dippy." He stopped and chewed his lip. "I'm sort of thinking out
loud, trying to put the pieces together. I knelt there beside him,
but why would I want to do that after what he'd just done to me?"
He stopped and chewed again. "Maybelle said God would teach
me how to hug..." His voice trailed off in perplexity. "I didn't actually hug Freddie, but I did something. I had to. I *wanted* to. Was
that...Jesus there?"

Rob looked at him intently, then said softly, "This is some sort
of holy ground. I'm thinking I should take my shoes off."

Jeth was glad to get back to church. Now when he sang "His
blood has covered my sins," he didn't have to grit his teeth. Praise
singing was his tiny island of safety, of joy, of intense worship. He

poured his heart into it and often shook uncontrollably when he finished and sat down. He hugged Maybelle long, sensing that she understood his unrest better than any of the others. "Maybelle," he said, "Rob told me that most Christians don't feel God's presence in their lives or understand His language. But you understand what God is saying, don't you?" He held her at arm's length to search the woman's gossamer body and soul of steel.

To Jeth's surprise, Maybelle's face clouded. She closed her eyes a moment, steepled her hands over her mouth, then regarded him through deep pain. "Jeth, dear, I wish I could say you're wrong—that most Christians do have a lively conversation with our Lord. Instead, I see starving people seated at a full-spread banquet table, nibbling only crumbs. The food is there, but they will not eat. They're not hungry, you see. You are hungry, my dear, and that's why God has singled you out for extraordinary things."

Now it was Jeth's turn to close eyes and steeple hands. But after scratching vainly for an adequate response, he simply hugged his banquet server.

THOUGH CHURCH WAS a solace, the ride there was seldom comfortable. Katie always seemed peeved over the rush to do barn chores, clean up, and dress in time. She mostly took it out on Rob, but even Jeth had to watch what he said. This troubled him. She hadn't been that way when he'd first come, but maybe she and Rob had hidden their differences back then. He'd been around enough married couples to know that bedrooms often went into deep-freeze mode.

Katie badgered Jeth to eat with them, often using Cecil and Mama Berry to lure him there. This contrivance exasperated Jeth, but the Berrys always brought laughter and peace and pure joy, and he needed that—badly. Fortunately for him, they spaced their visits prudently.

LATE FALL SAW hay and bedding material laid in for the winter. Their number of trained horses had shrunk. They had sold Gladys, Caprice, and even grouchy Lord Nelson over the summer, but money went out fast with vet bills, much-needed equipment upgrades, and barn repairs.

Now that Cecil was through school, they figured out a way to take him on full-time, though not full salary. They calculated what he had been earning at the restaurant, plus what Rob was paying him for extra work. "That's not near enough," said Rob, but Cecil, overjoyed at the prospect, would have worked for less. "If I'm here all day, I can do stuff nobody else has time for," he said. "Do I have to do overtime to keep getting lessons?"

Jeth rubbed the boy's short-cropped head. "We should pay *you* for lessons."

They all needed a break from the intensity of the summer season, and Jeth, in particular, welcomed the time to work Dynamo. He had developed a special relationship with the horse, a passion that demanded frequent feeding. The stallion had prospered under his attention and was building endurance. Additional workouts had also improved his disposition, but he still could not be trusted.

They also worked on new jumps, including a modest water jump—a shallow, oblong pool with a simple rail gate over it. "Pixie and Campion don't mind water," said Rob, "but Peanut flips out just looking at it. We need to lunge Toogie over it, too—get him thinking it's no big deal. He's our future, y'know."

THANKSGIVING BROUGHT GREAT joy to Jeth's heart. Everyone was in a good frame of mind and behavior, and the Chiltons' table expanded to take in not only the Berrys but also three lonely church people. Katie put on her warm and loving face. She seemed made to entertain—to decorate, to cook, to open wide the door, flushed and full of welcome. The real Katie. Jeth wished this deep-down core of her constitution would last forever.

It did—almost. Once Thanksgiving was over, the Christmas season settled in, complete with the first snowfall, and Katie again had focus and purpose. If Jeth had not usurped her role with Rob and the horses, he wondered, would she be a different person without him around? She still seemed genuinely glad, though, not to have to do outdoor drudgework along with running the house. She often went for rides on either Jake or Meg and continued giving lessons to her Saturday riding students, as weather permitted, so she was not deprived in that area. Still, Jeth felt that somehow he was key to the situation.

Christmas broke over Jeth as never before in his life. Familiar carols, now sparkling with meaning, rang bells in his heart. "Joy to the world! The Lord is come." "O holy Child of Bethlehem, descend to us, we pray; cast out our sin, and enter in; be born in us today." *Yes, Lord. Come in! Let flesh keep silent. Let Ezekiel's weird creatures move in, rank on rank of them—a vanguard of Light to vanquish the powers of hell and darkness.* He tried to take it in, to understand this strange, mysterious world of archangels, virgins, God dressed in flesh. His heart enlarged almost to bursting. How many Christmas concerts had Janni taken him to? He wished he could revisit them and soak in the splendor, the glory, of that exalted music. He thought often of Janni's mother, whose vibrant beauty and passion for music had been used by Wingate just enough to enhance his status in life. How had she put up with him so long? She had finally been allowed to leave, but only when she could no longer benefit her husband and he had Janni firmly in thrall. She had left everything behind and gone to live with her father in relative penury, even taking back the Grundel name. Jeth wished he could see her now, to thank her for building Christmas into his heart in a way he was only beginning to understand.

Had Janni cared about losing her mother? She had never shown it, but her mother's passion for life and for music remained imbedded in her soul. What, though, had become of her passion for Jeth?

Christmas passed, and the grungy gloom of winter settled on hills and hearth and hearts. Jeth kept busy, riding when he could, fussing over Dynamo, searching the Internet for horses, and keeping his mind off Janni—and Katie—as much as possible. He and Rob made some sales and some purchases.

On a shopping expedition in New York, an unusual jumper caught Jeth's eye. Bicolored paints were commonplace in Western horses but rare in hunters, jumpers, and Saddlebreds. Jo Jo, though, could jump. Very well. Even Rob could see that. But the gelding was not particularly ambitious, and when neither Rob nor Jeth could push him beyond an easy canter, Rob shook his head. "The price is okay, but what good is a horse that can do only half the course before the buzzer?"

Jeth sighed. "You're right, and he's ugly. If jumpers were judged on conformation, he'd bomb right up front. But he's a born jumper. There's a slot for him somewhere that will pay off big—for somebody. I say we become that somebody. It worked before, if you recall."

Rob made a face. "Yeah—Woodbine." He studied the activity in front of this well-appointed stable complex with its copper-roofed cupola and white board fencing, then shrugged. "Okay, but he's your baby!"

Jeth grinned. "Great! I relate to ugly. Janni kept a running catalog of my facial deficiencies, but when you put them all together, she said, it comes out right. Maybe that's the way with Jo Jo."

But Jo Jo didn't work up well, though both Jeth and Rob were amazed at his ability to clear high fences. He simply wouldn't move fast enough—on principle—to be competitive. Reluctantly, Jeth turned his attention to the old standbys and their two new horses—Salsa, a red roan mare, and Indigo, a black mare with sunstruck-blue overtones.

ON A CRISP, glittering April day, a small but important ceremony took place. Rick came to Jeth with an official-looking envelope. The formal document inside stated that Jeth had fulfilled his parole obligation to the state and was thereby free to resume his place in society as a law-abiding citizen. Jeth's hand shook as he read the words. He looked as though he wanted to say something but instead gave Rick a powerful hug that the man wasn't expecting. "Thank you," Jeth managed to rasp. "I can't tell you what you did for me."

Rick looked at him, puzzled. "Hey, man—you were easy! Kept your nose clean. Can't get in too much trouble jumpin' them gates in there." He gestured toward the ring.

The parole officer, uneasy over Jeth trying to keep his face in order, felt even more awkward when words finally came: "One call you didn't make…"

Rick shuffled uncomfortably. He was used to being cussed out, offered a beer, or brushed off, but never this sort of reaction. "Well, uh, you take care now, hear?" And he walked out of Jeth's life.

JETH SEARCHED THE Internet for a low-key show for Cecil to ride in when the season started. Jumping classes in small, B-rated shows were scarce, and a couple of possibilities conflicted with other events. But the boy needed ring experience to boost his confidence, and Jeth was determined to see that he got it. Cecil didn't exactly want ring experience, and the days leading up to the show saw him in a state of ambivalent agony.

When they walked the course ahead of time, Rob pointed out that the jumps were easy verticals: a brush jump, a cross rail, and a low oxer with two sets of uprights. "No sweat," he said. "You could do this in your sleep." Maybe so, but Cecil seemed ready to melt down.

His fears were realized. He rode Peterkin, a kindly, seasoned jumper who never balked, but this time, the horse planted his feet in front of the brush jump, and Cecil found himself draped over the shrubbery. He climbed down gamely, remounted, and then, though automatically disqualified, put the horse over the fence before leaving the ring.

When he came out, close to tears, Jeth hugged him. "Hey, man, you could've crawled out in disgrace, but you got up on your hind legs and made Petie get up on his. Well done!"

Rob pushed him for a second show with a novice class, and this one went better, but Cecil's nerves still put him near the bottom. When he came out and dismounted, Rob was ready with a cool, wet towel. "If they awarded ribbons to riders who sweat the most, you'd've won for sure!" He scrubbed the boy affectionately. "That's two under your belt!"

15

Once the major events started, Cecil's show riding had to be put on hold—to his relief. He was happy to go with Jeth so that Rob could stay home now and then. At a large county fair east of Harrisburg, Jeth pulled a hard-won second with Belladonna. The chestnut mare had been dependable but never dazzling, and this red ribbon was a triumph. He left Cecil on horse duty and went to get food for them both. He was tired but felt good. The day was refreshingly cool, and he liked fairs—the warm, country ambiance provided a welcome respite from the cutthroat competition of show jumping. Large tents sheltered cows, chickens, emus, crafts, flowers, and seasonal vegetables. Beekeepers and outdoor furnaces hugged the periphery, away from the mishmash of food vendors that featured such exotica as barbequed rabbit and deep-fried Twinkies. A whimsical blend of midway music stitched everything together.

Jeth wandered past the sheep tent, pausing to watch a couple of Amish youngsters feed lambs and wishing he could be kneeling there with them. He moved on, nearing the food concessions, then froze. As though she had been expecting him, Janni stepped from the shadows and came toward him. Her smile was forced, but clearly she had abandoned her vow never to speak to him again. Jeth's face hardened, and he was about to growl, *"What do you want?"* when his mind's eye suddenly put them in a long, sterile, white hallway that blocked out even the midway music. He saw only her wan, stricken face; her dark, desperate eyes.

She chatted: How had his winter gone in buying and selling, and what were his prospects for the show season? Her movements were quick and nervous on a covert level of trying to play up to him while pretending she wasn't. They talked of Freddie. "I heard they salvaged his eye but don't know much more," said Jeth.

"Yes, they got it back in, but his leg took longer to heal."

"Can he ride? Will he be able to show eventually?"

She shook her head uncertainly. "Who knows?" She hugged her chest, then laid out a new, safe topic of conversation: "Dynamo. How's he doing? Are you still winning arguments?"

Jeth shrugged. "Most, but not all. Haven't shown him yet, but with his stellar bloodlines, we're getting stud fees. Someday..." He studied her a moment, then said, "And you—how are things going?"

She looked away, then back at Jeth. "Somebody told me—and it wasn't Freddie—that you saved his life. I asked Freddie about it, but he got mad. Didn't want to talk about it." She tried a laugh but couldn't make it work.

Jeth studied the Amish sheep handlers, then spoke carefully, eyes still on the sheep. "Just before the accident, Freddie came over to mess with my head. Told me you got married, hoping it would rattle me enough to lose the class."

Her eyes narrowed, the old, fiery rancor stiffening her face. "And you *saved his life*?"

Jeth shrugged. "I had to."

"What do you mean, you *had* to? EMTs are always on the grounds. I would've stood there and happily watched him bleed to death."

"Well, I was right beside him, and I couldn't just stand there. And I don't think you could've, either. But it was more than just my civic duty. I *had* to, as in, God made me. Like when you slapped me and I had to walk away. I was in a different dimension, and God did something, both times—something I can't explain, something…profound." He looked back at her. "You didn't answer me. How are you doing?"

She frowned. "But after what Freddie did to—"

"Never mind Freddie. He made his choices. I want to know about yours."

She looked away and pushed up the sleeve of her sweater. "Oh, fine," she said brightly, running fingers through her hair. "Finefinefine." But pretend was not in her nature. Neither were tears. She had never been one to cry easily, and Jeth caught his breath as she hid her face from him. She whirled back, however, eyes fiercely dry. "You want to know? It's hell. And go ahead—say it: 'Serves you right. You deserve double whatever you're getting.'"

"No, I won't say that. Tell me."

A rooster crowed in the distant poultry tent, and Janni's voice turned coarse and brittle. "Bryan is…an ogre…and his son a beast—a troglodyte."

"His son! Where'd a son come from? Had Bryan been married? Or maybe he wasn't."

"Oh, yes—somewhere between pop-up appearances at our place—but I didn't know about it. His wife evidently washed her hands of them both, so he needed a cook and housekeeper. The boy needs a jailer, but he didn't package it that way, and I didn't find out till too late."

"How old is he?"

"Eleven, and not hard to imagine what the teenaged version will be. Bryan can't control him, and he seems almost proud of the rotten kid he spawned. He hates the noise and nastiness when it's aimed at him but loves it when I'm the target. There's no way I can control the kid, and sooner or later…" She stopped and set her mouth, punching her next words: "And Daddy set it up." Her face turned tight and bitter. "I was still furious with you when Bryan showed up again. He was kind and laid out the bucks. Even fun, at times. But I should've known something was up when he and

Daddy starting talking alone so often. Bryan proposed, and when I considered the fringe benefits—house, honeymoon off the coast of Africa, bottomless purse, and, yes, getting back at you... It's what I didn't know that stuck fangs in me." She turned to Jeth with raised eyebrows and a fake smile. "That's what I married! You can be happy for me." She looked away again. "Bryan won't spell out the collusion between him and Daddy, but he hints at it—all the time."

Jeth grunted but said nothing.

She looked straight at him, lips trembling. "I'd give anything to go back to that night, do it over again. I didn't know..."

"There's no going back," he replied gently. "The question is what's next."

Her eyes picked up a glimmer of hope, but he quickly dashed it. "You are married, so I'm out of the picture. If he's beating you, then you need to get out. If not, then stick it out. Statistically, marriages in trouble do eventually get better."

Her eyes flashed. "Don't preach at me! I'm not a statistic."

"No, you're not, but you are married, and there's nothing I can or will do about that. I can't even be available for talking. Somebody else could be your sounding board, but for me, it's too close to cheating. Unless you're in danger. But I won't buy into games."

A bevy of giggling girls mobbed the cotton candy machine across the grass. Janni stared at them—unseeing, hard-faced, dry-eyed. Jeth hardly recognized this woman—strangely small and desolate, her soul sucked dry by this new, inchoate pain. She, whose life had been largely untouched by angst of any sort, was now chained to it. Jeth wanted badly to hold her. *Is Maybelle's upper-level course, Hugging 401, the lesson on when not to hug?* But he only reached out and squeezed her arm, then turned and walked back to the horse tent—without food.

JETH WAS NERVOUS the next couple of shows, but Janni did not reappear. He told Rob about the encounter and asked Maybelle to pray for a "friend" who was in trouble. Her eyes took in more than he had wanted to confide, but she said nothing and simply asked later how his friend was doing.

Jeth sighed. "I don't know and have no way of finding out. We're praying in the dark, but I'm sure there's trouble that's not likely to go away soon."

Maybelle cocked her sparrow eye at him. "Has she been in this trouble before?"

Jeth gave her a crooked grin. "Maybelle, you're a sly cookie. I don't even have to tell you when or what to pray for. You figure it out just by looking at me!"

He didn't dare ask her to pray for Katie, not even under an assumed name. She'd know. Katie was a more immediate need—at least, more in his face—than Janni. She was becoming two-faced—a sweet, charming hostess to the outside world but a flirty shrew the rest of the time. Fortunately, Jeth was able to keep out of her way much of the summer, spending a fair amount of time on Dynamo—the more benign of the two hellions.

Their fall and spring training efforts had not been in vain. The horses were performing well, if not spectacularly, and sales continued to be good. Jeth rode in every show, and Rob rode the horses he had worked up. Both came away with an impressive array of ribbons and trophies and prize money.

Jeth rejoiced when Rob stayed home and only Cecil came with him to shows. In the midst of the tension he and Rob were living under, the boy was a calming presence. He even breathed peace on the horses. He talked to each one, nose-to-nose, and fussed over them. Jeth watched. *I used to do that. What happened?* He locked his arm around Cecil's neck. "Hey, lug—you're good for me."

"Ow! Lug yourself! Lemme go!" Cecil laughed and clawed at Jeth's arm.

"I won't let you go till you bless me. No, that won't work. You bless me every day. What else can I get out of you?"

"I'll sic my mama on you!"

"Oh, no!" Jeth tossed Cecil onto a pile of sawdust and rubbed a handful over the boy's head. After a brief dust war, they both lay back and laughed joy into the core of their being.

16

In September, no one laughed much. Jeth hated the minefield he was in with both Rob and Katie. Katie seemed to be laying traps for him, bumping into him—literally—in unexpected places. Rob became noticeably testy, with Jeth quick to snap back. They were all tired from the show circuit, having traveled farther afield than the previous year, with two expos still to go. Cecil was often hard to find on those days.

One afternoon, Rob came into the barn with fire in his eye. "I thought I told you to unload the tack box and check the bridles to see which ones need work."

"You didn't say that. You just said to put everything in the tack room."

"We'd just been *talking* about checking them. Any dolt could figure out from the context what I was asking."

"I can't read your mind."

"Then why don't you ask questions?"

"I did what I thought you wanted."

"Well, you missed by a mile."

"What I did needed to be done."

"So did the sorting—first."

"This is stupid! What do you want me to do?"

"I want you to finish."

Jeth turned away, yanked open the tack room door, pulled down all the bridles, and put them in two piles.

Again, Cecil remained absent.

Two days later, Jeth had worked hard with Salsa, plus two new horses that needed assessing, and when he was done, he saddled Dynamo and worked him for a half hour. He was putting him away when Rob came out, having just eaten supper. "What are you doing, riding this late?"

"I didn't ride Dynamo all week."

"He doesn't need to be ridden. The others do."

"I rode them. First."

"You drag yourself in here in the morning, kill yourself all day, and then do a totally unnecessary thing like—"

"Tell me how I've cheated you," Jeth snapped back, color blotching his face. "Tell me exactly what I haven't—" He stopped and looked at Rob, almost curiously. Then he spun around and strode into the barn. Three minutes later, he dragged Meg out, bellied up bareback, and threw his leg over. Without a word he pressed the startled mare into a canter and headed for the trail.

He soon pulled the mare to a walk. He stopped at the first overlook and stared at the strong, rock-muscled hills that stood guard over the broad valley with its crazy-quilt cornfields, isolated barns, and scattered clusters of homes, churches, and fierce independence. Lights winked on, in lockstep with Jeth's tally of his mounting problems. Meg tentatively reached for a mouthful of tall, ripened grass and, meeting no resistance, explored the menu further down. Finally, Jeth pulled her head up and pushed her to a jog but then pulled to a stop and gazed through the trees. *Katie's all wrong. Everything's wrong. But whose fault? Mine? Uh-uh. Not entirely. Unless…unless just my being here touched it off. Did my coming corrupt Rob and Kate so bad that God's glory is leaving their house?*

Instead of continuing around the loop, he abruptly swung the mare around and cantered back to the barn. Rob had gone home. Jeth put Meg away, then jogged toward the house. He pulled open the screen door, and Rob raised his head. Without a word, Jeth nodded toward the door, and Rob rose and followed him out. Jeth strode through the dusk to the trailer, flipped on the light, and gestured toward the chair. Rob sat stiffly, hackles up.

Jeth perched on the couch. He looked down a moment, then at Rob. "First off, I'm sorry. For a lot of things. I've been way out of line for a long time. Almost every day I come out spoiling for a fight, and now I've got you doing it. I've been a scrapper all my life, but that's no excuse. I know better, but it hasn't made any difference. I'm going to try to stop it, but I ask forgiveness now for the times I'll mess up."

Rob just looked at him.

"But that's not what I really want to say. Something's wrong, and maybe this has brought it out in the open." He looked down again. "Something's going on with you and Katie, and somehow I'm in the middle, and I don't know how or why or what to do about it." He looked up, his face pale. Rob had his face in his hands. "If it would fix it like that"—he snapped his fingers—"I'd leave in a heartbeat, get out of the way. I love you guys too much to break up your marriage."

Rob looked up in stark horror.

Jeth rubbed his forehead. "I know—the thought scares me to death, but the last thing I want is for God to walk out on you because of me and whatever 'disease' I'm carrying. I'm trying to say I'll do whatever must be done to make things right again. But let's at least talk so I can figure out what's wrong."

Rob again covered his face, elbows on knees. He shook his head slowly, not speaking.

"Tell me straight-out: Am I the problem?"

"No. I'm the problem. Katie's the problem. You're the target; I know that. I've seen her go after you. I've seen you dodge. And I'm sure there's a lot I haven't seen…"

"Rob—"

"Jeth, this is my problem. It's not your fault."

"If I weren't here…"

"If you weren't here, it would be something else. I'm to blame. I'm not the husband I should be. She doesn't get to do anything fun. We've never had money to throw around. It's all gone to the horses, the business." He rubbed his head.

"Rob, it's not money. That can't be it. She's not a gal who has to buy clothes like other women have to breathe."

Rob shook his head. "No…it's not money. It's me. Before you came, I needed her. I was with her all the time. But when you came, she was glad not to have to muck stalls and do the donkeywork. She felt free to go do woman stuff, with Saturday morning kids and playing with Toogie her only work obligations. But it changed our whole relationship. It's a different dynamic now. Maybe her hitting on you was her way of getting my attention. I don't know. Maybe if I told her you were threatening to leave if she didn't lay off…"

"Well, she needs to quit what she's doing, but threats aren't the way to go." Jeth looked down. "A dangerous question, but here goes: Does she get enough sex?"

Rob sank back in the chair and closed his eyes.

"Okay," said Jeth. "I get the picture. You're tired enough to fall asleep at the supper table, and morning comes way too early. And Sundays—"

"Sundays—huh!"

"Well, we won't talk about Sundays."

"Before we were married, we both wanted children—a bunch. She loves kids. You've seen that—at church, in the ring. But the realities of a horse farm with just the two of us doing most of the work… She didn't want to do pills, and there was hardly ever time or energy. Then it got to be a pattern."

"You're working too hard," said Jeth. "Even with Cecil and all he does, there's too much. I can do the early work, and you sleep till—"

"Right. And you die on me from overwork. That'll help."

"Well, we need to work out a plan. But first things first. Here's what I think." He hitched to the edge of the couch and leaned forward. "You need to take Katie away for a week. Doesn't have to be glitzy; just somewhere away from horses and work. Sleep for twenty-four hours, then walk and hold hands and eat and play—and make love, man!"

"But—"

"Uh-uh. No buts." He was warming to the subject. "Cecil and I can take care of things here. This is the perfect time. No show this coming week. Did God plan that? We'll be caretakers and just keep things cranking along—no heroics. And if you're thinking you can't afford it, we'll find something, and I'll pay for it. I still owe you—and don't you dare say I'm trying to earn my salvation!" Jeth swung from the couch to the desk beside it and jiggled the mouse to wake up his computer. "Let's see what we can find."

"Now, wait! I don't—"

"Chill. I'm just looking. What radius do you want—a hundred miles? Closer? Farther is sometimes better when you need a change. Romantic resorts? As in, posh? Exotic? Uh, maybe not," he said when he saw Rob stiffen. "Let's try SuperDeals." He clicked through several sites. "September isn't a bad month for this, as in, cheaper. Here's a place. Not fancy, but it looks like they'd treat you right. And places to go, things close by, even dinner on a train."

"How much?"

"Ne' mind how much."

"Jeth—"

"What'd I say? Read my lips: I want to pay for this. It's doable. It was my idea, and I want you to take this woman off and get her pregnant!"

17

Getting Rob and Katie off brought on a bit of a dustup. Katie had been thrilled at the prospect of a whole week at a resort—an experience so far off her radar screen that it wasn't anything she even wanted to do. But the actual preparation for such an occasion brought out the worst in both of them. What would they be doing? *We'll decide when we get there.* What would they need for these activities and others they couldn't foresee? What dress clothing? *Wear grain sacks, for all I care.* Would they do anything but fight the whole week? *That's up to you.* Would they eat out every meal, or would they need some food? Finally, though, Jeth and Cecil waved them down the driveway and then knocked fists and did a little dance, no words needing to be said.

Even before Rob and Katie left, a notice for a backwater horse show popped up on Jeth's computer. He moved the mouse to close it out, but a "Hodgepodge Gaited Class" caught his eye, open to three-gaited, five-gaited, or Tennessee Walker. He'd never heard of such a thing. He guessed that somebody close by—or a couple of somebodies—had one of each, and you can't have a class with only one horse. He didn't say anything to Rob, but he did talk to Cecil. "What do you think, buddy? Could we pull off showing Dynamo?" The correct attire for saddle-horse showing might be a challenge, but he had contacts through people who had used Dynamo for breeding.

Bennie from church would keep an eye on things while they were gone. "We should be back by ten," Jeth told him. "Just keep the troops happy and pray that Dynamo doesn't kill one or both of us." Jeth clapped Bennie's shoulder and then set about loading the stallion into the small trailer.

That turned out to be less of a hassle than he'd expected. The horse was tired from his intensive three-day training and put up only token resistance. Once they got to the show grounds, however, head and tail came up, and he sniffed the breeze expectantly. "Stick to business, pal," Jeth said. "Never mind the ladies."

This particular show came as a welcome change from the high-powered events they normally entered. Big stuff for locals; but, while adrenaline ran high, edginess was nonexistent, with competitors and spectators alike milking the fun of it all. The classes ran to equitation and pleasure horses—English and Western—plus the catchall, show-horse anomaly Jeth had entered. Churches and civic organizations had food spilling out of booths, and Jeth would have loved to wander among them just to chat. Dynamo, though, could not be left alone with Cecil.

Jeth easily located the man from whom he was borrowing the saddle-seat attire that was so different from jumping breeches and high boots, and after he changed, Cecil whistled.

"Not a word, pal. Not a word! It may look funny, but it feels worse. Everything's a size too small—tight little boots, long-leg jodhpurs sort of spray-painted on. But it's only one class. I'll make do."

Jeth didn't expect much from this first attempt to show Dynamo. If nothing else, he could assess the horse's behavior for corrective work. But he was nervous just the same. As he entered the ring at a brisk trot, Cecil called out, "Ride safe!" Jeth grinned back at him.

The class consisted of two three-gaited show horses, one other five-gaited, and a three-gaited pleasure horse. These all seemed at home in a show ring with its noisy surround sound, but Dynamo found it alarming and shied repeatedly. When the judging started, he settled down but remained on high alert. Jeth wondered how the gaits would be called with such a mixed bag, but after the first walk/trot/canter routine, the steward cried, "Slow-gait or trot, please." The call to rack followed, and Dynamo steamed past all the other horses, head and ears up, flaxen mane and tail streaming. The crowd applauded, and Jeth expected to have to do battle again, but the horse stuck to business, getting the hang of the whole affair. *Born to rack*, Jeth marveled.

To no one's surprise—except perhaps Jeth's—he got the blue ribbon, along with enthusiastic applause. Back at the trailer, Jeth dismounted, and he and Cecil slapped backs. "Hey, man—you were super!" said Cecil.

"He shied and broke gait twice. What did the others do that was worse than that?"

"Like they were standing still when you went by—that's what."

"But speed doesn't count all that much. More like style, class."

"You were class, man. The others looked like yellow dogs next to Dynamo. He blew them away. Très quiche!"

Jeth laughed. "Where'd you come up with that crazy phrase?" He reached for Cecil's head, but Dynamo took matters in hand and grabbed a mouthful of jodhpur.

Rob and Katie returned, both all smiles, and Rob greeted Jeth with a surreptitious thumbs-up. Jeth and Cecil had a supper of grilled chicken and baked potatoes ready for them, and for the first time in months, everyone at the table was totally relaxed and happy.

The next morning, Jeth handed Rob Dynamo's blue ribbon. "Not the prettiest ribbon I've won or the most dramatic, but I was happy with it. We still have a long way to go with ring behavior. I was surprised that didn't put me at the bottom of the pack, but the judges were…um, *casual*, to say the least."

"A blue ribbon, eh?" said Rob. "With that on the wall, we can up our stud fee!"

THE END OF October, Katie tested pregnant. Both she and Rob were jubilant. Now that the question of having a child was off the shelf, they both had a new outlook. Katie's hormonal adjustment to the new life within her spawned a few microbursts, but the men were patient and supportive, and within a couple of months, she could not stop smiling.

This, for Jeth, felt very good. "Best money I ever spent," he said softly to Rob.

JETH FOUND A substantive, late-season show for Cecil in West Virginia—a good distance away, but the setup was perfect. "Looks good," said Rob. "But can he pull it off? I don't want him getting down on himself."

"Oh, he's got the jam for it, I'm pretty sure," Jeth said.

Cecil wasn't sure at all, but when he and Peterkin came out of the ring with a pink ribbon on the bridle—fifth out of nine competitors—he was a happy guy. His confidence soared, and even the horses began to sense that he was in charge and not to be trifled with. Toogie, especially, quit fooling around, and the two of them made great gains over the winter as they grew up together.

18

By early May, Katie had grown cumbersome and uncomfortable, and she groaned hourly about the three weeks still to go. *Nothing* was going right. Men couldn't *possibly* understand what pregnancy was *really* like. She just *couldn't* do *everything* they wanted. The men were patient, and Rob spent as much time with her as he could. Jeth and Cecil agreed to handle the early season shows and were excited about the prospects. They hoped to sell Peanut and Salsa this year, as both had worked up well. They would keep Toogie, as he showed promise of becoming as athletic and energized as Pixie. Rob had delayed gelding him. "He's a sweet guy—so far. But two stallions on the ranch? I dunno."

One morning, Rob came to the barn dressed in street clothes. Katie waddled beside him, her face puffy and blotched. "Hey, guys," Rob said to Jeth and Cecil. "What's on your plates for the day? I have to go to Simonville this morning, so you're on your own. Jeth, which horses do you have in mind?"

"Salsa, of course. And Indigo. She needs work—badly. And Nightshade could use some follow-up after yesterday. A three-mare morning." He grinned.

"Make that four mares." Rob gave Katie a squeeze. "Keep an eye on this one. She had a tough start today. And Cecil." Rob turned to the boy. "You keep on with Toogie. Maybe more this week than last? He's doing basic jumps pretty good. You could start him on double jumps today and maybe a triple next week—low, of course."

"Yeah, Cecil," said Jeth, "and try to remember to put them back up when you're done."

Cecil wriggled uncomfortably and turned to Rob with a worried look. "Maybe tomorrow? Mama has her procedure this morning. Remember I told you last—"

"Oh, yeah. I forgot. Anything serious?"

Cecil shrugged and looked away.

Rob scratched his elbow. "So, what are you doing here?"

"Barn chores. Got time for that."

Rob shook his head. "Unbelievable. Go take care of Mama and tell her the barn gang is pulling for her. And Jeth, like I said, I gotta meet Sam Johnson's lawyer in Simonville, or we stand to lose a chunk of change. With Cecil gone, Katie can keep an eye on you, dust you off if you get tossed." He grinned at his wife, who was less than amused. "So…everybody take care. I should be back by noon." He turned to Katie with a reassuring hug. "My cell phone's on, so call, even just to talk, but not at nine thirty during the appointment. And Cecil." He turned the boy around. "No more work. Get going. And if Mama needs you tomorrow…"

"I'll be here extra early." Cecil grinned and waved, then danced to his car.

Rob chuckled. "Funny he won't say what it is."

"Maybe she wouldn't tell him." Jeth shrugged. "But he's worried. He needs to be with her."

As Jeth walked to the barn, he reflected on Rob becoming a father in a matter of weeks—a proper father. *By the grace of God,* Rob had said when telling about his girlfriend not getting pregnant. Grace, indeed. Janni had gotten pregnant. Their love was undeniable back then, rolling in tall grass or in the abandoned cabin high on the hill. So simple, so elemental. No thought of consequences or of having an abortion. His child, their child…torn to pieces…

Fiercely, Jeth grabbed the full barrow of manure and wheeled it to the pile out back. He forced his mind to a different track and hummed through the days of Elijah, Ezekiel, and David. He put out to pasture the horses he wouldn't be working, then saddled Salsa, all the while "riding clouds, blasting trumpets" full-volume. He stopped suddenly, head at full alert. He heard it again—Katie screaming. He yanked the horse to the nearest stall, then headed for the house on a dead run. Katie stood in the bathroom, doubled over, dampness creeping down her pants. "My water broke! Oh, it hurts!" She screamed again. "Rob! Get Rob! The baby's coming!"

Jeth froze, frantically trying to think what to do. He took a big breath. "Katie, come sit on the bed, and let's figure out how much time we have."

"I can't! I'm wet!" Her cries rose to a scream. "It's coming! It's coming!"

Jeth half carried her to the bed and put pillows under her head and shoulders. "It's okay. Never mind wet. We'll do what we need to." But Katie squeezed her eyes tight and began to push, and Jeth saw in an instant what he was up against. This was not good. More than not good—all wrong. If anyone other than a doctor had to deliver this baby, it should be Rob. And with not even Cecil here… though that was probably good. If "procedures" upset the boy, this would blow him to the next county. Jeth grabbed the phone by the bed and punched 9-1-1. Stretching the cord as far as it would go, he laid the receiver on the floor so he could work on Katie. Why didn't they have a wireless phone in the bedroom? Why had he left his cell phone in the trailer? He shouted Rob's cell phone number and the house address but couldn't hear much in return. He was on his own. He'd helped deliver a couple of foals, but this was way, way different. Katie was going to have a baby on his watch, and from all the signs, soon.

He ran to the bathroom, grabbed every towel in sight, and slid one under her hips, moving her to where he could best work. Between pushes, she was screaming and clutching at him. Finally, he stopped and put his hands on either side of her head. "Katie, look at me. You're going to be okay. I'm here, and we're going to get this baby delivered. Take short breaths, like they told you. That's it. You're doing fine. I've got to take your slacks off. Babies don't come through clothing, at least that I know of." He draped a towel over her prodigious belly—more for her sake than his—and worked her pants off.

She seemed to calm a bit and was no longer crying, though her pushes ended with a shriek. "You're doing great," said Jeth. "I can see the head. That's right—push!"

No, don't push. Got to clean off horse dirt. "Short breaths. I'm going to wash my hands, but I'm right here."

Sweat poured off Jeth. *Rob—please come! Where's the rescue squad?*

Katie screamed. "Jeth!"

With no towels left in the bathroom, he ran out, wet-handed. "It's okay—I'm here. You're doing great. Push! Push! It's coming. Hang in here with me, Katie! You're going to have a baby! Push! Push!"

The baby came just as two paramedics called from outside, then found their way into the house. They took in the situation, one moving to Jeth, the other to Katie, checking her vitals. Jeth took a huge breath, closed his eyes, and dropped to his knees as the infant gave a lusty cry.

"Hey, you the man!" said one of the paramedics. "If your day job falls through, consider midwifery." He looked the baby over quickly. "Good job!"

Jeth smiled weakly. The paramedic left the child in Jeth's hands and set about delivering the afterbirth. Jeth looked long at the little one, then laid it gently on Katie's breast. "You got a little girl, honey. Just wait till Rob gets home!"

Katie sobbed as she stroked the damp fuzz on her child's head. "Is she all right?"

The EMT looked up. "Push one more time, sweetie. Atta girl! We'll check her over, but she looks good. And you're some kinda pro at having babies. How many times you been through this?"

Katie smiled and looked wryly at Jeth. "My first."

"You gotta be kidding! First babies don't come that easy. The name's Clarence, by the way, and no jokes on that—hear? My buddy here is Mel. We'll check out Missy once you get through playing with her." He grinned. "We don't often get to do this. Most calls are heart attacks or folks down and can't get up. This is fun, though—especially when somebody else does all the work. We'll have Daddy cut the cord."

Jeth shook his head and backed off. "Daddy, uh-uh. Stable boy. I think that's Daddy in the driveway now."

But it wasn't. A policeman sauntered in, looked things over, and phoned the station. Then he turned to Jeth. "Everything under control, I see. You're kind of a mess!" He surveyed the smear of blood on Jeth's cheek, then turned to Katie. "What've we got— boy or girl?"

"A little girl," said Katie. "Her name is Jessie."

"Congratulations, Dad!" The officer held out his hand to Jeth, then withdrew it upon seeing the gore still covering his. "Bet you didn't expect to be doing this when you got up this morning."

Clarence looked up and winked at Jeth. "Yeah, I'd lay money on that one!" He looked back at Katie. "We'll get you bundled up, honey, and take you and Jessie to the hospital. Not ripped too bad for a first-timer, and the bleeding's normal, but—"

"Oh, please, can't I stay here till Rob gets home? Jeth will be with me."

Jeth froze. He opened his mouth to protest but couldn't find the right words. Clarence, however, turned authoritative. "Sweetie, I can't make you do nothing you don't want, but you need a profes- sional from here on out, and that's not us. Breathing, blood, heart- beat—our big issues. And with a new baby, blood's a big player.

We wanna make sure you keep most of yours. Isn't that right, Mr. Midwife?" He turned to Jeth.

Jeth, his face drawn and disordered, nodded emphatically at Katie. "You need to be taken care of. You did a super job, but..." His voice trailed off as Katie cried into the black head moving about on her breast. Almost in despair, he said, "Katie, you need to go."

"All right," she said at last, "but call Rob and tell him to hurry!"

Jeth reached for the phone, which had been kicked out of the way but not replaced on the cradle. He punched in Rob's cell number and was surprised to hear his frantic voice after only one ring.

"Jeth! Is that you? What's happening? I've been trying to call but couldn't get through."

"She's okay, Rob. The baby's okay. The EMTs are packing them up, taking them to the hospital. They're asking Katie the doctor's name right now. They think she's fine but want them both looked over. Where are you? How far away?"

"I'll go straight to the hospital. Be there when they arrive."

"Yeah, you need to be there." His voice held an edge.

As though across a vast desert, Jeth watched the paramedics load mother and baby onto the gurney, wrapping and strapping them carefully. Outdoors, the action turned to slow motion as they opened the back door of the ambulance, lifted the gurney head, folded the undercarriage, and pushed the load into the vehicle. After an eternity, Mel jumped from the back, closed the door, waved at Jeth from across the desert, and climbed in the driver's seat. Jeth saw the policeman, then the ambulance, disappear into a hazy, endless stretch of sand.

He stood there, unable to sort through the perfect storm of emotion within. He looked at his hands. *Need to get back to work. Salsa's saddled, but...hay in the stall? Can she work on an empty*

*stomach? Can I? Maybe unsaddle her, give hay, ride Meg on the trail.
She won't care about blood.*

After staring through his ambivalence a full minute, he wandered toward the barn, marveling at how uneven the ground had become. After taking care of Salsa, he again stopped and stared. He had delivered a baby. Katie's baby. *Wrong—all wrong.* But, wrong or not, it had happened, and he thought of the mess she and Rob would come home to. He took a breath. That was work he could do. A clean bed, for starters. Food? He shook his head. One thing at a time. Bed first.

He returned to the house and stared at the bloody towels on the bed, wondering how deep the stain had penetrated—through the bedspread and maybe the entire mattress. Down to bedrock, perhaps. He dragged the mess to the bathroom tub and turned on the cold-water faucet. As the tub filled, he watched as red swirls released their hold on the terrycloth and pirouetted through the water in a ghoulish ballet. He closed his eyes, then went to the bedroom to inspect the bedspread and bedding beneath. Not bad. Spot soaking, maybe. He tore the bed apart and returned to the tub.

Blood again. Washed in blood. But this was Katie's blood, not Freddie's. Was Katie's different? Freddie had made one blatant, frontal attack; Katie had come at him subtly—how many times? But this was different. New life from this blood. A baby, yes, but this blood also marked a change in Katie, in her focus, her actions. He had panicked when she had wanted him to stay till Rob got home, but what new mother wouldn't be afraid and in shock? She needed room to change, to make mistakes in the process, to deal with her own covering of blood.

He wrung the rinsed towels and dumped them in the washing machine, starting it before tackling the bedding. Two loads ought to do it, as the sheets looked okay.

He had just finished remaking the bed when Rob drove up. Jeth opened the door and waited as father, grimacing mother, and sleeping baby shimmered across the expanse that still held desert qualities. He tried to smile a welcome.

"Hey, man—there you are!" said Rob. "Can you wait a few minutes till I get the troops bedded down? Then we'll talk."

Jeth nodded, then retreated to the living room sofa to examine the remnants of blood on his arms. Too late to put the towels back in the bathroom. He had folded them—sort of—but hadn't put them away. As he grappled with this weighty issue, Rob came out, all smiles, but stopped when he saw Jeth. "Hey, buddy, you don't look so good."

Jeth stood and drew a shaky breath. "I'm okay. How's Katie?"

"She's fine. Needed minor repair, so she's sore, but everything's fine. And little Jessie couldn't be sweeter. They cleaned her up and looked her over real good. You did a terrific job, man!"

Jeth grunted. "The towels..."

"Yeah, where are they? I found one small towel hiding on the top shelf, and I think I'm only beginning to see what you did here today."

"They're on the dryer. Not folded as good as—"

"Jeth." Rob looked at him closely. "You're a disaster. Go home and sleep. I'll check on the horses while—"

"Salsa's okay. I took care of her. If you don't need help in here, maybe I could take Meg out?"

"Do it. I'll put my radio on. Make sure yours is, too. I'll call if I need you."

19

Jeth finished saddling Meg and had her bridle in hand when an SUV pulling a two-horse trailer bumped up the driveway. A man, short and lumpy, with close-set eyes and a horseshoe of graying hair, got out and looked toward the pastured animals. "Hallo there," he called as Jeth came from the barn. "Jake Hawkins. They tell me you got fine jumpers here." His attention shifted to the blood on Jeth's arms.

Jeth closed his eyes, hoping the man wouldn't bother to ask, then said, "Yes, we do. Interested in young stock or ready to go?"

Jeth needn't have worried; Hawkins went on as though programmed. "I'm trying to build my stable with horses that are promising but not there yet. Show me what you got." He again inspected the grazing horses.

Jeth ticked off the for-sale horses, and Mr. Hawkins wanted to see them ridden.

"I can show you three. The fourth isn't available." He didn't say that the far pasture was too much for him right now, but his heart sank when he saw Hawkins peering in that direction, hand shielding his eyes from the sun. Jeth pulled Salsa from her stall and grimly resaddled her, trying to hide his own bones and sinews that were melting relentlessly. He then exchanged Salsa for Indigo, but when he finished and opened the gate to get Nightshade, Hawkins stopped him. "Never mind another horse." He pulled a briefcase from his car and opened it on the bench under the pine tree. Jeth could see packets of hundred-dollar bills in neat, shimmering layers, and he looked away in an attempt to keep his stomach in place.

"I'll give you thirty thousand for both of those horses," said Hawkins. "Cash. I like 'em. Just the stage of training I'm looking for. No point seeing anything else." He began to count packets, but when he reached twenty-one, he straightened. "You fellows... seems I heard you're religious. What church you go to?" He set the money back on the case.

Desert was again encroaching on Jeth, but he responded haltingly, aware that fully half of Hawkins' attention remained on the far pasture. He closed his eyes and reached in his pocket for the radio call button and pushed one long and two short. Within a minute, Rob jogged into the yard.

"Rob, this is Jake Hawkins. Wants to buy Salsa and Indigo, the two for thirty thou. Cash." The hair on his neck rose even higher than the miasma that was engulfing him. He looked as straight as he was able at Hawkins, then picked up the case and handed it to Rob. "Check this—*carefully.*"

"Never mind," said Hawkins, and he snatched the case and ran for his car. Jeth was on him within seconds and pulled him down, money packets flying. "Call nine-one-one, police." He closed his eyes and fought dizziness and nausea while kneeling on the writhing, bellowing Hawkins.

After making the call, Rob picked up a packet. "This funny money, you think?" he asked Jeth.

"Everything's funny." He looked up, taking sharp breaths. "Rob, call back. Tell them to look for a truck and trailer on the road with horses in it—ours."

"What horses?" asked Rob. "Not Salsa and Indigo. They're— What are you talking about?"

"Just call!" Jeth shifted to sit on Hawkins, unmindful of his squirming and swearing. He rubbed his head and eyes.

"Jeth, are you all right? You look awful. Why don't you get up, and I'll—"

"No. Easier just sitting here."

After a short search, the police did find a trailer holding Pixie and Campion. And though the officers had to inspect the worn money closely, it was indeed "funny."

"You fellows been busy here today, haven't you," said the policeman who had appeared earlier. "If you drive anywhere, try not to get caught speeding. That'd wrap your day up g-double-o-d."

AFTER THE HORSES had been put away and everyone had left, Rob came to the barn and found Jeth nearly catatonic, seemingly unable to unsaddle Meg. "Here. Let me do that. This has been a day." After putting the saddle in the tack room and tossing hay into the mare's stall, he gripped Jeth's arm and moved him outdoors. "Come in the house while I check on Katie." He guided Jeth up the walkway and settled him in the living room, but when he came back, he couldn't rouse him. "Jeth! What's happening? Jeth, answer me!"

Jeth's eyes remained open and staring, but he didn't respond.

Katie came gingerly from the bedroom, alarm in her voice. "What's wrong? What's the matter with Jeth?"

Rob ran his hand through his hair. "I don't *know*! What else can happen today?" He pulled out his phone and dialed 9-1-1—again—and talked to the dispatcher. Katie, crying, knelt beside the chair and stroked Jeth's head. "Jeth—please say something." Rob stuffed the phone in his pocket and paced from chair to door till he saw flashing lights.

"What you fellows doin' out here?" Clarence bent over Jeth. "Midwifing get to this guy?"

"I guess. Don't know what else could be wrong. He's almost never sick."

The men checked his pulse and blood pressure and listened to his heart. "Did he fall? Hit his head? Any heart problems? Diabetic? Chronic troubles?"

"I don't think he ate much today. Maybe just breakfast."

Clarence shook his head in perplexion. "His vitals are in the park, but somethin's wrong somewhere." He rubbed Jeth's breastbone. "C'mon, guy. How about it?" Finally, the medic stood. "We'll take him in, get him looked at. And please, both of you—just go to bed and stay tight till tomorrow, will you?"

Rob looked at the men, then at Katie. "I want to go with him, but—"

"You stay here. Take care of the wife and kid. Trust us. We'll drive real easy."

AFTER MULTIPLE TESTS and X-rays, hospital personnel still couldn't discover a reason for Jeth remaining unconscious. They put him on an IV, called Rob, and kept Jeth overnight.

Rob called early the next morning and was relieved to hear that Jeth was awake and alert but couldn't explain what had happened. As soon as Cecil came in the drive, Rob pulled him to the house to stay with Katie and then drove to the hospital. He found Jeth in a chair, staring out the window.

"Hey, man—you look better than you did last night."

Jeth grunted and studied the wastebasket across the room. He looked up. "Katie and the baby all right?"

"They're fine. This new little person makes a pretty insistent alarm clock. Going to take some getting used to. You okay, buddy?"

Jeth smiled wanly. "Define 'okay.'"

Rob pulled a chair over and sat down. "Hm. Not okay. Do you hurt?"

Jeth tented his hands in front of his mouth. "*Hurt* isn't the right word, but do I feel good? No. I don't know what's going on. Something...deep, but I don't know what."

"Deep, where?"

"Deep inside. In my spirit. Does God zap people?"

Rob looked at him, reaching for something to say. Then he leaned forward. "Having to deliver the baby made you feel bad, didn't it?"

Jeth again looked out the window. "You should've been the one—not me." His voice was husky. "I had no business—"

Rob put his hand on Jeth's knee. "My friend, I wasn't there. Maybe a bad call on my part, but I can't think of anyone else I'd rather have had take my place. Everything you did was right and good, and Katie can't say enough about how strong and calming and capable you were."

Jeth snorted. "She's easy to fool!"

"Maybe you didn't feel calm, but that's how you came across, and I'm everlastingly grateful for what you did. Could've been a disaster. This was a God thing, Jeth. Her water broke; she went right into hard labor, gave birth with only a small tear, nothing else wrong; and I was back in time to help deal with Hawkins. How many more evidences do you need that God was pleased—that you did a great thing?"

"Evidence, yeah. Baby evidence, Woodbine evidence... When God does that sort of stuff, even you ask questions, and don't tell me you don't!"

They sat silent for a minute. Rob leaned back. "When did you wake up?"

"I don't know. I didn't know where I was."

"Were you afraid?"

He thought a moment. "Not afraid of a strange place. Maybe afraid of how I got here."

"Tell me about the Hawkins thing. How did you know he was phony? What tipped you off?"

"There's another 'evidence.'" He looked up plaintively. "I just knew. The money...eye signals, maybe. He kept looking at the far pasture. The religion talk seemed forced."

"Religion talk?"

"Yeah, he'd heard we were, quote, 'religious,' and started asking questions. I was feeling bad, but when somebody asks... Somehow along the way, in spite of how I felt—or I'm thinking maybe *because* of it—I knew what I needed to do. Rob..." He looked at him with wide, frightened eyes. "This scares me to death, and I have a feeling it's not the end of it."

20

Jessie appeared as a Fourth-of-July starburst in their firmament. Cecil especially, after his first shy peek at the newborn, found every possible excuse to offer flowers or a toy to mother and child. Though Katie dearly loved this long-awaited baby, the sudden hormonal shift in her body and the unreasonable demands of this new person triggered a fair amount of seismic activity. Rob took big breaths and shifted his shoulders, getting the feel of this new daddy cloak so strange and awkward upon him. And Jeth, once he recovered, asked for a crash course in diaper changing so he could babysit while Rob took Katie out for the occasional, much-needed lunch date or ice cream break. None of them, though, could get enough of this little peacemonger who had so deeply impacted their lives. And, discounting the earthquake aftershocks, never had Jeth seen Katie so happy.

But horse shows were also on their doorstep, and the rest of May was taken up with preparation. Most of the horses they would be showing had worked up well, but Jo Jo, the bicolored paint purchased over a year ago, became a bone of contention. Despite Jeth's best efforts, Jo Jo refused to be rushed, and neither Jeth nor Rob thought him worth much more time. They had even tried to sell him but couldn't get potential buyers past his lumbering gait. "We've got to show him this year—somewhere," said Jeth, "and I think Clarksville's the place."

"Clarksville! He's totally untried," said Rob. "We can't take him to a Grand Prix event. This isn't a comedy show where buyers laugh as he fizzles. And they would laugh: you can't build a big enough fire to get him even halfway around the course in the allotted time."

"That's exactly why I want to take him to Clarksville. They have an open jumper class with minimal time restraints—the only show I can think of where a horse can practically walk around. It's perfect for him. He's not fast, but he can jump anything—*if* he can take his time. The only alternative is a puissance class where jump height is everything. None of those around here."

"We don't even know how he'd behave in the show ring. And he's too slow to test out anywhere."

"Hey, he's so laid-back, nothing short of a nuclear bomb would rattle him. He'd be great for teaching kids to jump, but that's not our game." Jeth rubbed his neck. "Rob, there's only two things I ask for this summer: that I can ride Jo Jo at Clarksville, and that Cecil can ride in two good shows."

Rob hissed his annoyance but went out of the barn to watch Cecil a moment. He turned to Jeth. "All right, but you better get that horse ready to jump the moon. Cecil—yeah, he deserves a worthwhile ribbon." And he walked away.

DESPITE CECIL'S BUDDING confidence, Jeth knew the boy was both scared and ecstatic at the prospect of riding in a major show. He was spending even more time on the job. "Turn that boy loose," said Rob, "and he'd clean cobwebs out of the pine tree." Sometimes Cecil brought Mama Berry along to help Katie, which pleased both of them. Life had turned sweet on all sides.

Jeth found himself under Maybelle's surveillance at church. When she learned he had been in the hospital, she questioned him closely, and Jeth could not hide his misgivings concerning what it had been about. With a finger across her chin and mouth, she said, "My dear, I can see that you don't believe any more than I do that your body simply went *kaflooey*. Remember when we talked about the prophet Daniel going senseless after the angel appeared to him in chapter ten? Do you think Daniel was just having heart palpitations?"

Jeth laughed, then closed his eyes with a grimace. "It was God, wasn't it, Maybelle?"

She cocked her head. "Perhaps, or maybe a signal from God—a signal you could run with or run from."

"Maybelle…"

"Jeth, dear, running with God, no matter how dangerous it appears, is always safer than heading toward what you think is safe. You need Zechariah's wall of fire around you, and I'm going to pray it up."

He hugged her warmly. "Maybelle, I feel like I'm in the arms of God. Are you my angel?"

WITH THE IGNOMINY of his first show in mind, Cecil showed serious stage fright when they got to one he'd chosen to ride in. "Forget trying to win," said Jeth. "Just go out there and get over the fences—preferably in the right order. Judges notice things like that. And buck up! You and Salsa are a tight team. You've worked her hard, and she's right up there." But when Cecil put on his new riding outfit and fastened his helmet with shaking hands, Jeth thought he was going to cry. "Come on, buddy. You've done this before. Leg up. You the man! Ride safe!" He slapped him on the knee and sent him into the ring.

He rode respectably well, getting only eight faults; and, as it turned out, his time pushed him into a sixth ribbon. He came out all smiles, swung his leg over Salsa's neck, and fell onto Jeth, who pounded him gleefully. "Good job!" Jeth said. "A green in this show trumps your pink hands down. Wait'll we tell Rob. He'll be proud! Let's take care of the little lady here and then go get something to eat."

THE CLARKSVILLE SHOW was something else. Everybody was uptight just driving onto the white-railed grounds and feeling their way between turreted buildings and multiple rings. Jo Jo was assigned to stall number 223, a twelve-foot enclosure with a small-mesh sliding door. Horses were everywhere—being ridden, being walked cool, being hosed down. The warmup rings, even those under cover, were busy. Once Jo Jo was settled, Rob, Jeth, and Cecil took a look around and sized up the entry list. Wingate Stables had several horses, and Rob looked glum. "I hope you know what you're doing," he said to Jeth.

"Yeah, I think I do. I'm going to ride Jo Jo everywhere they'll let me—get him used to the noise and bustle. He's a trooper. He'll stick to business."

The open jumper class, held at night, was a big draw, closest to a puissance class, where jump height is everything. With this crowd, high was good; time meant nothing.

Freddie was still out of the picture, and his replacement took no notice of Jeth. Jeth, in turn, kept his distance.

When he mounted, the horse felt good under him—alert, energized, yet fully in control. Jeth knew what was at stake in this class, but he felt confident. As the horse ahead of him came out, Jeth looked at Rob and was pleased to see a convincing smile. Rob slapped the painted rump and said, "Ride safe!"

He did ride safe—and well. No faults. Four jumps went higher; two other entries were eliminated. Again, no faults. Now it was Jo Jo against a Wingate horse, with the four remaining jumps higher still. The crowd was tense, cheering each jump. Incredibly, they both came through clean. Rob was a wreck, and Cecil stroked him the way he would quiet a horse. Jeth alone seemed calm and patted Jo Jo's neck. "You can do it, old boy," he murmured. "Let's go out and show 'em!"

Jeth trotted through the gate and, with a big breath, eyed the four looming jumps. "Okay, guy—let's go!" He put the horse into a slow canter and eased up to the first jump. Clean. The second. Clean. The third was also clean, but Jo Jo stumbled coming down, and Jeth lost both a stirrup and a rein. The crowd groaned. Cecil cried out. Rob put his face in his hands. Jeth, though, didn't miss a beat. He gripped his knees tight, grabbed mane with his left hand, and willed the animal toward the final, highest jump. In that instant, they were one, and with ground-shaking strides, they surged at the seven-foot jump and soared over. Clean. Jeth powered his left arm triumphantly.

The crowd roared in a moment no one would forget. The Wingate horse still had its turn, though. The rider did not dilly-dally, as Jeth had, and took the first two jumps nicely. But the top rail of the third jump teetered for an instant before tipping over. The crowd went wild. Cecil leaped up to hug Jeth and nearly pulled him off the horse, while Rob pounded Jo Jo's neck. "I'm a *believer*! *Never* was a win so sweet!"

AFTER RECEIVING THE trophy and the purse, Jeth handed both to Rob and dismounted. He started to lead the horse back to the stall to rub him down, but Rob took the reins. "You're gonna be mobbed, buddy. Cecil and I will take care of Jo Jo. You go soak it up. You deserve every minute!"

Jeth talked with people, including a couple of reporters, for nearly an hour. One young boy looked up at him and said, "How did you stay on the horse with no stirrups?"

Jeth smiled. "Hey, I had one stirrup. I prayed, and God helped us over the jump."

Wide eyes were the boy's only response.

Jeth winked and roughed the lad's hair.

When he talked to Rob the next day, he said, "One bit of lace got the idea of having me sign her program, which started a run on that—everything from old, crumpled receipts to the inside of a birthday card. I got 'em good, though. I wrote:

Glory goes to God, not—

Jeth

That night, however, when the congratulatory line had ended, Jeth turned to look for Rob and Cecil. One more person, glowing cigar at his side, stepped from the shadows, eyes steely, unfriendly. The last person Jeth expected to see.

"Mr. Wingate!"

"Congratulations are in order. Fine horse. Is he for sale?"

Jeth chuckled to himself. "Probably not. Not right now, anyway."

"Fair enough. But—"

"Jo Jo's an old-style jumper. Doesn't know the word 'fast.' Takes his time to get the job done."

Wingate raised his eyebrows. "Then are you for sale?"

Jeth was taken aback. "Me?"

"I'm offering you a position—a hundred thousand a year to start. You would have a say in purchasing, oversee all training, and, of course, be our top rider in shows. I'll set you up with a house, car—what else would you like thrown in?"

He spoke with an unsettling economy, and Jeth was dumb-founded. This man, who had loomed so large in his life, for good and for ill, was now exhibiting a condescension Jeth had never seen. He studied the diamond-studded turtleneck, the paunchy eyes, the coarsely corrugated black hair, and thought of Lord Nelson, the surly but businesslike horse they had bought from Jarvis. Jeth spoke carefully. "I appreciate the honor and trust, especially against our past. This means more than you can ever know.

But—" He stopped and examined his boots. "I'm totally committed to Rob. He gave me my life back. I came to him fresh out of prison—no track record, no reason to trust me. He not only gave me a job; he became my friend. No amount of money can match that. I love him and his wife. I love the way he does business, the way he cares for little people. I love the horses."

Wingate inspected the glowing end of his cigar, and even in the dim light, Jeth could see his jaw muscles tighten. "Of course," the older man said, "Janni wouldn't be far away. A house of your own, time on her hands…"

Now it was Jeth's turn to clench his jaw. "Janni's married. That changes everything. And I want that marriage to stick. Being thrown together wouldn't help either of us. Again, thanks, but—"

Wingate flicked his cigar, turned on his heel, and left.

ROB FOUND JETH hunched at the far end of the horse barn, alone and staring. He put a hand on his shoulder. "The day catching up with you?"

Jeth looked down and shook his head almost imperceptibly.

Rob frowned. "What's up? What's going on?"

Jeth leaned back and looked at him. "Wingate came and offered me a job. A hundred K, house, car. I'd be top trainer, buy and sell as I wanted."

"What did you say?" Rob's voice was tight.

"Huh! Goes without saying—flat-out no. Respectful but straight. Then he tried to throw Janni into the deal. I nearly lost the respect part at that point."

Rob sagged against a barn timber in relief.

Jeth looked at him curiously. "Did you really think I'd jump ship on you?"

"It's an offer you deserve, one I couldn't match in ten lifetimes." Rob leaned down. "Jeth, you could be a Grand Prix rider. You know it. I know it. None of our horses is there, but you are, and staying with me...you're stuck with what we can afford. Wingate has at least two Grand-Prix-grade horses. Why wouldn't you take the offer and go where it takes you?"

"Let me count the reasons: Wingate's got money; he'd like to own me. Have me under his thumb, once and for all. I lived there, remember? I know him and what it's like to work there. Toxic climate. I'd never know where I stood, with Wingate or anyone else. He'd expect me to be a Freddie clone—cheat, maneuver. Winning is everything, no matter what it takes. No Sundays off—none. The cocktail circuit. You think I want that?"

Rob shook his head in disbelief. "But with—"

"Do you *want* me to leave and go with Wingate? Did you hear what I said?"

"Of course I don't! And yes, I heard, but—"

"Rob, look at me. No amount of money or perks or the Grand Prix circuit could make up for you and Cecil and Katie and Jessie and Maybelle. You're stuck with me, pal, till death or God do us part."

Rob closed his eyes against tears that threatened to break through. "You're going to the motel tonight," he said roughly. "Cecil and I will do guard duty. You need a good night's sleep."

Jeth didn't move and continued to stare. Rob looked at him with even more alarm. "You are having second thoughts."

Jeth looked up sharply. "Read my lips: Wingate could offer me the moon, and I wouldn't work there. You said I did a good job tonight. He'd never say that, no matter how many rabbits I pulled out of his hat. I'd never trade my life here, no matter how many houses, cars, or women he threw in."

Rob straightened, his entire frame relaxing. "Okay, then what's the problem? I see a pattern here: The greater the victory, the deeper the gully afterward. You delivered the baby—tailspin. You caught on to Hawkins—fell off the planet. Tonight—the class of your life. Who could have done what you did? Now look at you."

Jeth lifted his head, the old frightened look in his eyes. "Rob, why does God do this to me? It's not right. I get the feeling He's setting me up for something."

Rob looked away and sighed. "I don't know. Since you came on the scene, I've felt I don't know much at all about God. It's not that you never make mistakes or act brain-dead stupid—I've seen enough of that—but, at certain times…"

Jeth was silent. Then he said softly, almost to himself, "I feel like Moses by the burning bush, that I should take my shoes off, on holy ground." Rob looked at him curiously and watched him bow low and fall prostrate, with his arms stretched forward, as though reaching for something. Rob rubbed the prickling hair on his neck, not knowing what else to do, and then he felt it—a warming, palpable presence as from fire, and in the shadows, a horse nickered a welcome.

ON THE WAY home, Jeth said, "I think we should sell Jo Jo."

Rob looked at him. "*What?*"

"I got several offers last night—one was eighty thou, and I think we can parlay that to at least eighty five. The guy gave me his card. He's a great jumper, no question about that, but he's not going to win consistently, at least within normal time constraints. Push him, and his ears go back. Yeah, we'll tell buyers up front, but I doubt it'll make any difference. He's a hot item right now, and he can only cool. We didn't pay much for him, and we could use the money. Your house is way due for an indoor facelift. The barn needs maintenance, to say nothing of fencing. I'm just being realistic, thinking in ways you never would."

"Top of the list is the trailer. It—"

"No. The trailer's off-limits. We got it insulated last fall, and it's too big a job to do again. I'm fine there."

Rob whistled tunelessly through his teeth and stared straight ahead. "I don't think I'll ever understand the way your brain works."

THEY DID GET a handsome price for Jo Jo, despite having made multiple disclaimers. When they loaded him into the trailer, Jeth stroked him regretfully. "You gave me the ride of my life, buddy. I won't forget."

Jeth pushed Rob to have a new kitchen installed, and Katie was ecstatic. They also had enough to add a sprinkler system in the barn, and Jeth was ecstatic.

Cecil rode well in his second show, getting a red and a white ribbon. He kept saying it was a small show, but clearly he was pleased.

21

In mid-July, Jeth was working his second horse when he began feeling strange. He took a drink, went to the bathroom, and stretched out in the shade for a bit, but nothing helped. Rob saw him lying down and came over. "You okay?"

"I don't know." He rubbed his head. "I think I've been here before."

"What do you mean?"

Jeth took several big breaths. "Something's going on that I need to pay attention to."

"As in Hawkins?" Rob's voice went thin and tight.

"Yeah, but no Hawkins today—just you and Cecil. Rob, I don't like this."

"Do you want me to take you to the doctor?"

"No, I need to think. Is it okay if Meg and I go for a ride?"

"You want someone with you, nine-one-one in hand?"

Jeth laughed ruefully. "You don't deserve being stuck with me. I think I'll be all right. I just need to figure it out."

"Take your radio and call if you need help. I'll buzz every half hour, and if I don't get a response, I'm coming after you."

"Due diligence. I hear the threat."

He was back in less than an hour, face white and hands shaking. Rob said, "You look terrible! I'm taking you—"

"No. That's not it. Rob, I've got to do something I don't want to but can't get out of."

"Like what?"

"Like going to Janni and Bryan's, and the sooner, the better. Maybelle, where are you? Rob, tell me I need a shrink. Tell me to go to the doctor, take two dark chocolates, and I'll be better in the morning."

Rob didn't laugh. He stood back and studied Jeth. "I can't figure out you and God; I just know not to get in the way. But good idea—call Maybelle. Or wait till you feel better. Uh, no—I can see that. How about I drive you?"

Jeth shook his head. "If God wants me to go, He'll get me there. Maybelle would only tell me I can't run from these things. Just *pray*, my friend. Please pray." He looked up plaintively. "Rob, is there anyone else in the whole world that God works with this way?"

Rob laughed grimly. "Talk to your friend Ezekiel on that one! I've known people who speak in tongues, have weird dreams, hear God's voice, but this isn't like that." He shook his head. "Yeah, go to Ezekiel. He might be your guy."

JETH MADE THE hundred fifty miles in good time and got to Billingsford just after three thirty. Before hunting for Bryan and Janni's house, he stopped at the police station and explained what he was doing, what his record was, and why he wanted to get involved. Sgt. Reye dutifully entered everything into the computer, as though this were commonplace. Jeth shook his head on the way out but felt good about the detour.

He parked in front of the house and was surprised by its stodginess. The entire neighborhood could have come straight out of the "Gracious Living" section of a mid-century Sears, Roebuck & Company catalog. Set in the bedroom district of Billingsford, with stately trees lining the broad avenue appropriately named Maple, the house was moderate-sized—two stories, with a sunroom on the left, a two-car garage on the right. Jeth knew that

Janni never would have chosen such a plebian dwelling. Was this Bryan's notion of gracious living?

Jeth was going to sit a moment before going in, but the compulsion to act came on strongly. With a shaky breath, he strode up the walkway and rang the doorbell. After the third ring, he heard footsteps, and Janni opened the door, looked at him, and fainted dead away. Jeth leaped to her and saw something fall from her hand. He picked it up—a prescription bottle—and didn't have to guess what it was.

Within seconds, she opened her eyes, then squeezed them against tears he knew she wouldn't allow. He wanted to hold her but instead helped her up and led her to a chair. "Are you alone?" he asked.

She nodded, breathing heavily.

"Tell me what's going on."

Her mouth convulsed. "I can't...do this any longer. It's...stinking hell in this house. Bryan is bad enough, but Brandon..." Welding sparks flew from her eyes.

"He's eleven, you said?"

"Twelve now. A fat lunk. Almost big enough to knock me flat, and Bryan doesn't even try to stop him. He hates him as much as I do, but I think he's hoping Brandon will take me out, and the kid will be trundled off his hands without his having to lift a finger."

"You need to get out of here. If you're not safe—"

She laughed ghoulishly. "Not safe! You got that right, and there's not a thing I can do about it. I can't leave. I can't lift an eyebrow without Bryan's permission. He's got some legal hold over me that I can't begin to understand. With Dad's collusion, of course. Yes," she said at Jeth's frown, "the 'legal' part may not be legal. It's probably not, knowing the way they operate. But if I make a move to counter it, I'm toast. I know for a fact there's nothing I can do. Except die. *That* I can do."

Jeth heard the garage door open.

"They're here," she said grimly. "Please, Jeth—just go out the back door and let me do it my way."

"No. I'm not leaving. And I've got the pills. Where can I get out of sight? I want to hear the show before I step in."

"Over there, through that door under the stairs." She pointed. "The sunroom. Neither of them goes there."

Jeth slid out of sight just as a door slammed beyond what he took to be the kitchen. Father and son spilled into the living room, fighting as they came. Seeing Janni, however, they coalesced and turned on a common enemy, spewing harassment every bit as noxious as she had described. Whose car was out front? Who had she been making out with? Janni screamed and spit and tried to get away.

Jeth stepped out, and both Bryan and Brandon stared in amazement. "You!" said Bryan. "I should have known! What are you doing here?"

"God told me to come, and I came. And just in time, I'd say."

Bryan snorted, then threw his head back and laughed. Brandon joined in, braying with coarse embellishments. "Get out," said Bryan, all laughter gone from his voice.

"I'm not getting out."

"You will. I won't have my wife's tomcat in my house."

Jeth's eyes narrowed. "I'm not your wife's tomcat, and I'm not leaving till I know she's safe. We will sit down and talk sensibly." He stepped forward, overshadowing Bryan by about two sizes in all directions.

Bryan stepped back. "I'll call the police. I think they'd be interested in an ex-con trespassing."

Jeth raised his eyebrows and fished his cell phone from a pocket. "Here. Sgt. Reye will probably answer. He knows all about me. And about you. I'm sure he'll send somebody right over."

Bryan's face went blotchy. "What do you want?"

"I want this situation to change. For starters, I'm proposing to take Brandon with me, get him out of here. When does school start? End of August? Six weeks of peace and quiet for you to get your house in order and take better care of your wife.

"Brandon's my son!" Bryan bellowed. "You can't come in here and steal him out of my house!"

"No, I can't, but I believe we can come up with a mutually agreed-on arrangement that would make it legal. If you don't go along on this, then I'll be the one to call the police. It's either me or the Department of Social Services. I don't think it would be too hard to show that the boy is a menace to Janni, and from the look of him, he'll soon be able to take you down, as well." Jeth bit back a smile. Brandon looked incredibly like a colt version of Dynamo; and, like the stallion, his future might possibly improve. "You pick," he said to Bryan. "Me or D.S.S. If I take him, I guarantee he'll come back a different boy. I'll treat him well but with behavior change as a goal. That's my job with horses; it'll be my job with Brandon."

Brandon looked from one man to the other as though trying to grasp what Jeth was proposing. Then he exploded—all over the house. He swore; he raged from room to room; he ran upstairs, hurled books and clothing down the steps, and then continued his wave of destruction on the lower level.

Jeth looked inquiringly at Bryan, who, though shouting and swearing at the boy's behavior, did nothing to stop him. Jeth shrugged. "Okay—duty starts now." He grabbed the boy on his manic sweep through the living room, put enough pressure on his shoulder to stop his thrashing, and sat him in a chair. "You sit there until I say you can get up."

Brandon tried to slide away, but Jeth stood in front of him until he sat still. "That's better. Thank you. Now—" He turned to Janni. "If you'll get a piece of paper for me, I'll draw up a release form. Both of you can look at it and make whatever adjustments we can all agree on. Then we'll each sign multiple copies, and Brandon and I will be on our way."

Bryan glowered. "You'll take him off and make a pervert out of him!"

Jeth shook his head in disgust. "You know I'm no pervert. You don't like me—that's clear—but my goal will be to make Brandon easier for you to live with."

Bryan continued to argue halfheartedly, but Jeth could tell that the prospect of Brandon being out of the house for six weeks sounded good. Bryan finally went to a room on the right, Jeth's paper in hand.

Jeth turned to Brandon. "And while we do the paperwork, you go upstairs and pack whatever clothing you want to take. No iPhones, no radios, game things. Just clothing, a toothbrush, and a comb. Do it, or live with whatever Janni packs for you."

"Don't I get any say about going? I'm not signing papers."

"No, you won't, and no, you don't have a say. You lost that privilege, at least till things change. Now go upstairs and get your stuff."

Bryan came out of the room with four copies of the agreed-upon release document. Jeth laid them out. "One for Bryan, one for Janni, one for me, one for Sgt. Reye at the police station. Now, sign each sheet, and we'll be all set."

Brandon, his future being signed away, stomped up the stairway and came down a few minutes later with a plastic bag. Jeth took it from him, dumped the contents on the floor, removed contraband, and repacked the few items of clothing. "Not much here, buddy. Want to add anything? Maybe from the stuff you tossed down the stairs?"

Brandon swore. Jeth shrugged.

Parting was tense. Though Bryan was clearly benefiting from the arrangement, his face displayed major defeat. Janni said nothing, but her glistening eyes spoke volumes. Jeth spoke to her softly. "You'll be all right now. I'll talk to Sgt. Reye again and have him check on you from time to time. And both of you"—his eyes took in Bryan—"try to work things out. If this 'arrangement' you have with Papa Wingate is a long-haul affair, then you might as well make the best of it. I'll be in touch."

22

After the stop to show Sgt. Reye the goods in hand, the first real test was supper at McDonald's. They both ordered, but when Brandon unwrapped his burger, he lifted the bun and swore at the thin layer of mustard. Jeth looked at him. "That's what you ordered. I heard you say 'mustard.'"

"Mustard's for hotdogs. What lunkhead puts it on burgers? They gotta make me a new one."

Jeth stood, gathered up his own burger, and hauled the boy out to the car.

"I haven't eaten!" Brandon protested.

"Too bad. You could've, but you chose not to eat what you ordered. We'll bed down early at a motel and stop somewhere for breakfast. Maybe that'll taste better to you."

At the motel, Jeth slept on the floor, his body blocking the door.

On the road in the morning, Jeth put up with the boy's mouth for a half hour, then hauled him out of the car and ran him till he was ready to drop—which didn't take long. They got back in, and at the first smut out of Brandon's mouth, Jeth stopped again.

"Okay, okay," said Brandon. "I won't say anything!" He huffed a fair amount but kept his word and said nothing the rest of the trip.

They got home by noon, and after Jeth had handled introductions all around, Brandon made the mistake of muttering an epithet after meeting Cecil. Without a word, Jeth took him outdoors to the roundpen and ran him around the perimeter until he cried and fell down. Jeth yanked him up and put his face to the boy's nose. "Don't ever let me hear that word again," he said softly but with fire in his eyes.

Again, Jeth slept on the floor, at the door of the trailer. He fixed all their meals except on Sundays, when they were invited to join the family. Brandon expressed displeasure with the dietary change—heavy on fruits, vegetables, and "pig bread," as he called anything whole-grain. Jeth felt satisfied, though, that the boy had learned not to complain and was generally hungry enough to shovel down anything put in front of him.

Brandon's first work assignment was manure, his first tool a close-tined fork. Jeth worked beside him, showing, directing. Brandon did make bold to object—tentatively—but Jeth just raised his eyebrows and motioned for him to get on with it. And he did. When he did a job well, Jeth lavished praise and took time to joke and fool around. He thought playing catch would go over well. It did, but Brandon hardly knew what a ball and glove were.

The first week was up and down, with a fair amount of time spent running in circles. One time, Brandon crawled under the bars of the roundpen, but Jeth was quickly behind him and, after a tackle that produced scrapes, got him up and running again. "I don't much care where you want to run, but run we will."

Brandon loved to ride, and Jeth put him on Jake and set Cecil to teaching him. He began to lose weight and look better. They sometimes went on the trail together, which Brandon enjoyed. He chattered continuously, to Jeth's surprise. "What's the matter with that tree over there? Got a big lump on it."

"That's a burl—a growth that some trees get. People sometimes make bowls out of them."

"Cecil told me to post up when the horse's inside foot is on the ground. What about when you're trotting a straight line like this?"

Jeth smiled. "Post any way you want."

"I don't know anybody at school who can post. Geez, if they got on a horse, they'd be like, I mean, totally flum-dummed. Why does that big horse you rode last night kick all the time? He got a mad on?"

"Yeah, I guess you could say that. He's a stallion that, for some reason, always gets up on the wrong side of the bed. He's also dangerous. That's why I told you to stay way back."

"You don't make him jump. How come?"

"He's not a jumper. He's an American Saddlebred, a horse bred especially for showing off his gaits."

"What's a gait?"

Jeth explained. He also told the boy of his desire to show Dynamo at a major horse show. "He's a horse that's made to rack, and I want people to see him at his best."

Brandon liked horse shows and quickly entered into the satisfaction of blue ribbons. He went to church, unwillingly, and put up with devotional times at home, but he began to listen when Jeth made use of teachable moments.

And Jeth hadn't needed to sleep in front of the door since week one.

AS THE WEEKS went by, Brandon improved his throwing skills and could even hit a few gently tossed balls. Sometimes Rob and Cecil would join the mock ball games of just throwing and catching, with Jeth providing running commentary. "Stee-*rike*—right over the plate. A grounder to center field, and Brandovski scoops it up. A high ball to left field, and Robbins is there for an easy catch. Oh, no! Jetson fumbles the ball, and Cecilsan advances to third, in scoring position." At the end of the "game," they all would pass Brandon with shouts of "Gimme five!"

Brandon ate it up. He continued to have explosions, but his time in the roundpen dwindled to almost nothing.

Early one morning, in the middle of the fourth week, Jeth had to renege on his promise to take the boy to the water park in Appleton. "We'll still do it, but not today. An important buyer is coming to look at Belladonna. I've got to get her ready and be here. I'm sorry. Maybe we can squeeze out an hour for fishing or something equally awesome, but—"

"I *hate* fishing! Nothing's awesome like a water park." Brandon stormed to the barn and kicked the feed bin, timing his blows to mimic Dynamo's in the far stall. Then he stopped and looked toward the noise. His eyes narrowed. He walked softly to the stall, slid back both latches, and opened the door wide. Dynamo came out, snorting fire, but instead of running out of the barn, the stallion turned on the boy and set about systematically destroying this young nuisance, now in easy reach. Brandon screamed and fell beneath the horse's front feet. With nothing restraining his rage, the stallion bit the boy viciously, struck fiercely with his foreleg, and turned to kick whatever remained. Meg, two stalls down and in heat, neighed. Dynamo stopped, raised his head, and responded to a more primal urge.

Jeth, hearing the ruckus and Brandon's screams, came running and with difficulty got Dynamo back into his stall. For an instant he closed his eyes and leaned against the door, catching his breath. Then he turned to where Brandon lay huddled and crying. He did a quick assessment for broken bones or spinal injury, then carried him outside and laid him on the lawn. "Your head looks okay. Nasty scrapes, dirt, but at least he didn't come down on it hard. Tell me where you hurt." He moved the boy's arms and legs.

Brandon winced and drew shallow, shaky breaths. "He bit me. Ow!" he cried as Jeth felt around his shoulder and again along his thigh.

Cecil, just arriving, saw the checkup in progress and came over. "What happened?"

"He tangled with Dynamo."

"Shall I get Rob?"

"You might alert him, but I think he's all right. Nothing seems broken. He'll be sore, but if Meg hadn't been there…"

Brandon looked at him with wide, frightened eyes. "I'm sorry, Jeth, I'm sorry. I didn't mean it." His breath came in short bursts. "I'll run the circle a hundred times. I'll clean stalls all by myself. I'm sorry. I didn't mean it!"

"Can you sit up? Your head doesn't hurt bad?"

He shook his head, and Jeth helped him stand. "Let's go sit on the bench."

Brandon was shaking, his face chalky. "Jeth, I didn't mean it."

"Yeah, buddy, you did mean it, and that's what we need to talk about. Years ago, I did something I knew was wrong, but I was only sorry about getting caught and what came of that. Another time, I went back on Rob. At first I thought I just needed to clean the barn, work my tail off to make up for it, but Rob showed me that's not God's way. First comes saying we did wrong, then comes forgiveness. And Rob forgave my bad, just like that."

Jeth put his arm around the boy. "Buddy, you did a big bad. You did it because you were mad at me for scratching the water park. You wanted to get back at me. Isn't that it?"

Brandon looked up with stricken eyes. His rapid breaths became sobs, and he buried his face on Jeth's chest. Jeth held him tight and let him cry loose the toxins that had corroded his soul. Rob came over, saw from Jeth's face what was going on, and walked softly away.

When the crying subsided, Brandon began haltingly to line out his inner anguish—how he hated everything and everybody, including himself. Kids at school hated him, but, being bigger, he could level them. His teachers hated him. He got kicked out of school regularly, but his dad would make them take him back. Brandon swore fervently, his voice raspy and hard. "I hate him." He began sobbing again. "*I hate him!*" He gripped Jeth tightly and, after a few minutes, said with equal fervency, "I wish you were my dad."

From that moment on, Jeth could do no wrong.

23

The calendar was now their mutual enemy. Four weeks behind them, only two weeks to go. The mourning began. Jeth used every available moment to instill survival skills in the boy—how to be a man, how to make right choices. His parents would be the tough nut, and Jeth could only hope that the positive changes in Brandon would put Janni, at least, on his side, and that Bryan might alter his behavior for the sake of a little peace in the house.

When the dread moment came, Brandon hugged Rob and Katie and Cecil and baby Jessie. "I don't want to go," he sobbed.

Rob put his arm around him. "You're welcome here anytime. If things get too tough at home, this is your place. We love you!"

The ride home was quiet. Jeth suggested that Brandon might want to consider getting rid of junk in his room that would only do him harm. The boy stared hard out the window but then nodded. "I guess." Jeth reached over and squeezed his knee.

When they got to the house, Jeth led the way through the door. He looked at Janni and Bryan, who were clearly tense over Brandon's return, and said, "I'd like to introduce this swell kid Brandon. You may not recognize him. A bit changed from when you last saw him."

Changed, indeed. The boy had lost weight and gained muscle; he was not screaming and swearing. He even mustered a small smile. Janni had the presence to pick up on Jeth's cue and held out her hand. "How do you do, Brandon? I'm very glad to meet you!" She smiled warmly, and anxiety fell from Brandon's shoulders.

Bryan nodded stiffly behind a thin smile but said nothing.

Jeth turned to Brandon. "Buddy, why don't you go upstairs and sort stuff in your bedroom, like we talked about? Maybe 'toss' or 'keep' piles. I'll come up in a bit and see what you got."

Once Brandon was gone, Jeth motioned for Bryan and Janni to sit down. Janni looked at him. "What did you *do*?"

"I did what I said I'd do. I loved him, got him moving, set boundaries. And it worked." He rubbed his neck. "Almost too well. He didn't want to come home. You guys have your work cut out for you. You can conserve these changes, or you can blow them in a single night." He went on to make suggestions about practical ways they could help Brandon stay in control. "He doesn't want to revert. He likes the new Brandon, but without help, he's a goner. I'll keep in touch often enough to see how it's going, and I'll also ask Sgt. Reye at the police station to monitor things. I know that's not how you'd like it," he said, noting the sudden hardening of Bryan's veins, "but that's the way it has to be—for Brandon's sake. The last thing any of us wants is for him to morph from Jekyll to Hyde again."

He went upstairs and looked approvingly at Brandon's selections. "How about a third pile?" he suggested, looking at some prized possessions in the discard pile. "You might store a few things in a box to decide on later."

Brandon grinned at this small reprieve.

Leave-taking was tough. Jeth knew the chances of lasting success were low. He and Brandon clung to each other. Janni's eyes glistened, but Bryan stood back, stiff and silent. Jeth finally pried off the boy's arms and ran to the car.

JETH WAS MOODY when he got home, but the pressure of catching up on work kept him going. He and Rob would be riding at three major fairs and expositions, along with an important sales event.

Then an idea perked him up. "I'd like to show Dynamo again. Not a two-bit show like last time, but a big one. Like maybe Candlewood Expo in October. They have an open class Wednesday night. That way, we could be back in time for the Allendale show on Saturday."

"Candlewood! You don't want much, do you?"

"Dynamo's a piece of work. It's time we saw what we have on our hands."

"Do you know how far Candlewood is? Practically the middle of Kentucky! Two days there, two days back."

"Nah. One long day each way. Go Tuesday, book it back Thursday. Think about it. Won't take much time for me to work him up."

In Jeth's mind—though not in Rob's—it was a done deal. He became absorbed with Dynamo, and while he wouldn't neglect his other work, the toll told. "We need help," he said to Rob. "We've got more work than three of us can handle."

Rob's mouth became a hard, straight line. "Maybe a little less time on Dynamo?"

Jeth grimaced. His anger flared, but all he said was, "I do Dynamo on my own time. But, even leaving him out, it's still too much. I think even you know that."

Cecil was tired, too, by day's end, but Jeth wanted his help in training the horse with crowd noise, flashing lights, even gunshots. "I'll pay you extra. A half hour every once in a while is all it'll take."

Cecil kicked the ground uncomfortably. "I don't think Rob would like me doing that. We're all doing more than we can..." But eventually, Jeth got his way.

ONE EVENING, A car came up the drive, thumping at 7.5 Richter-scale volume. Jeth felt it even while riding Dynamo. A young man, defined by long, stringy hair and tattoos, unfolded from the car and walked to the ring, then stepped back as the stallion's golden, deep-driving pistons sent up shoulder-high spumes of sand. He watched with interest, as though he hadn't expected to see such a horse at this stable. Jeth called out as he cantered past. "Can you give me five minutes? And please knock down the decibels."

The man waved and bent to moderate the thumping, then peered around at the modest operation. Jeth dismounted to walk Dynamo and frowned at the pulsating car but said only, "Hi. I'm Jeth."

"Todd Jenkins. Some horse. Big sucker." His pallid face wore extensive ornamentation—nose and ear studs, lip ring, and an inch-wide strip of unremarkable beard down his chin. Though nearly as tall as Jeth, he seemed unable to fill his faded T-shirt, and slouched with a defining hopelessness. His eyes shifted to the stallion. "I'm…uh…lookin' for a job. Wondered if you might…uh… need some help. Maybe not with that one." He laughed nervously and looked everywhere except at Jeth.

Jeth studied the bony face. "Tell me about yourself."

Todd lined out considerable riding experience that included show jumping.

"Any ribbons?"

"Yeah, some."

"And you've worked only at…where'd you say? Collins Ranch and where else?"

Todd rubbed his nose and looked across the ring. "Place in Petersboro."

"And that's all?"

"Some small stables when I was growin' up."

"I'd need names and phone numbers. Are you married?"

"No." He shifted his weight.

"Have a girlfriend? Maybe a live-in?"

Todd nodded and bit at his chin thatch.

"How about her phone number?"

"Uh…the number's in my cell phone. Don't have it with me."

Jeth looked at him but said only, "Let me put Dynamo away, and we'll talk more."

When he got back, dusk shadowed Todd's face. Jeth drew him to the barn and into the glare of light. He faced him head-on, eyes narrowed. "Lying seems to be a problem with you," he said.

Todd flinched, and his face bleached even whiter. "I haven't lied." He straightened indignantly. "I'm religious, you know."

Jeth laughed out loud. "Is that so?"

"Yeah. I go to church, an' I—"

"Great. Tell me the name of your pastor and his phone number. But maybe that's in your cell phone, too." He stepped around Todd, amusement dropping away, eyes boring laparoscopically through the young man. "I was going to ask how long you worked for Wingate, but I think a better question—"

"I don't—didn't work for Wingate! I didn't give his name!"

Jeth cocked his head and touched Todd's chest. "Then you really shouldn't be wearing a shirt with his old logo on it."

Todd clapped his hand over the faded, scarcely legible imprint. "That don't say Wingate! It's just—"

"I wore shirts like that for years. Papa Wingate didn't tell you that, did he?"

Todd went rigid and turned to leave. "Well, uh, I guess you don't—"

Jeth grabbed his arm and pulled him back. "Um, we need to talk more, if you don't mind." He studied the unrest that was creeping over Todd's spare frame. "You're a Wingate plant, aren't you? He put you up to this to sabotage us in some way."

"No! That's not true!"

"He picked a good enough rider, maybe, but a lousy liar. I have your name, place of employment, license plate, and I can put the police on you if anything unexpected happens here." He put his face up close to Todd's. "And I will hold you personally responsible."

Again Todd tried to get away. This time, Jeth's face softened. "A minute more. A bit of friendly advice. I know Mr. Wingate very well. I spent two years in prison because he doesn't like people who cross him. He will not be pleased with your performance here. If I were you, I'd steer clear of King Herod and go back to your girlfriend by another route."

Todd looked at him. "King Herod...?"

Jeth raised his eyebrows impishly. "Oh, since you're religious, I thought you might know about the wise men and the birth of Jesus."

THEY ENDED UP hiring Todd, after all, but it was at Rob's insistence, not Jeth's. They both saw immediately that Todd had been thoroughly shaken by hearing of Jeth's prison experience, and that Jeth's dealings with Wingate had rung true. Todd's manner changed abruptly, and with ashen face he pleaded with the two men to give him a chance. "I got the chops for this job. I know I can win classes for you. You got good horses. You train good. I wanna be here. I don't wanna be there."

Jeth looked at him closely. "There's something going on that you're not telling us. Rob hasn't given his speech yet, but one very important item in it is that we don't lie here, and we don't tolerate lying. Mistakes and accidents we can handle, but liars can't be trusted. Your truth record hasn't been good so far."

Todd's face went from paste to chalk. He looked down and scuffed the dirt. When he looked up, fear had rearranged his drawn features into something almost unrecognizable. He stuffed his shaking hands into the pockets of his jeans and licked his lip ornament. Jeth put a hand on his arm. "Steady on, old man. If you didn't kill anyone, it can't be all that bad."

"Wingate'll think it's bad. I done somethin' he don't know about, an' if I go back, he'll find out."

"And you think he won't find out anyway?"

"It wasn't that bad, an' if I'm gone, nobody won't think to talk about it."

"Suppose you tell us the bad thing."

Todd turned assorted shades of red, green, and then gray before finally relating that he and some friends had gotten drunk at an after-show party, and Todd had dressed in multiple costumes representing the Wingate family: Papa, with his cigar and signature white turtleneck and red weskit—which Todd had purloined out of the old man's car. Mama, loaded down with jewels and wobbling on stiletto heels. Daughter, wearing only enough to make it interesting.

Jeth's eyes narrowed, but he said nothing.

"He'd be God-awful mad if he got wind of it," said Todd, "and the reason I said I'd come here and try to hire on was so I could blank out that stupid, dumb-a—uh, um, wrong word. Anyhow, this seemed a way to get on his side."

Jeth shook his head. "I hope you're a better rider than you are a thinker. Hiring on with us puts you in far greater jeopardy with Papa Wingate than your little dress pageant. You need to know that. He's got a long arm."

Jeth and Rob went to the office and talked long and hard about hiring Todd. Jeth stipulated that loud music would have to be tacked on to the "no smoking/drinking/drugs" list. "It's hazardous to *my* health, let alone the horses'."

Rob looked out the window at the gathering darkness and laughed wryly. "A few years back, a guy came to church so addicted to noise that he set his GPS for the wrong direction, just to add a nagging voice to the din in his car. For him, anything seemed better than the terrifying silence threatening his life. We began to love him and fed him CDs to play during his commute. That started to make a difference, but he moved away, and I haven't heard anything about him since."

Jeth almost laughed. "GPS. Wrong direction. I'll have to remember that." But his back stayed up over taking on Todd.

Rob finally shrugged, raised his eyebrows, and took a big breath, then opened the office door and found Todd outside on the bench—smoking. He explained his usual requirements, at which Todd immediately extinguished his cigarette. Rob added not only the noise factor but also going to church with them at least twice a month. "Church won't make you a Christian, but it's a better place to be than some I can think of."

"And church is not a place Papa W. would think to look for you," added Jeth wryly. "Look for you he will, though. He knows you're here. And by the way," he said, as an afterthought, "Mama Wingate was a real lady. She bailed out long before you came on and before Papa had a chance to trash her. Has he got another woman you thought was her? And believe me, I'd better not hear anything nasty about Janni."

Jeth remained testy. He acknowledged Todd's riding skill—a couple notches higher than Cecil's—and that he arrived on time each morning and worked hard. Jeth was carefully gentle when correcting him but never got close to hugging terms. Rob said nothing, but Jeth knew he was watching—and praying fervently that he had been right in taking Todd on and that Jeth, for once, had been wrong.

To everyone's surprise and joy, Rob hired another full-time worker—a young Mexican—to take over the barn chores. They all greeted Alejo warmly and wildly, and wished him well in whatever odd Spanish phrases they could muster. He grinned nonstop, even while moving mountains of manure.

JETH GAVE THE Beale family time to settle in together, but when he called, Brandon reported that his dad was acting bad and claiming illness as an excuse. Jeth decided to follow up. Janni offered to meet him halfway—leaving Bryan home alone to be sick and grumpy at will.

At their rendezvous in St. Marys, Brandon fell out of the car and leaped into Jeth's arms. Janni stood by, watching wistfully as the two laughed and cried and rolled on the ground.

Jeth saw changes in Brandon. "Hey, look at you! What's it been, a month? How could you grow so much? Some pimples, even! A man in the making!"

They had ten hours. How would they use them? "I've got an idea," Jeth said. "You guys up for an adventure?"

They drove to the city outskirts, where Jeth cruised a poor neighborhood, finally stopping in front of an unkempt yard surrounded by a metal fence and an imposing gate that spoke elegance in past tense. "Just what we want," he said. "Come on." They went to the door, and Jeth knocked. An old lady peered through a crack measured in chain links. "Good morning, ma'am. Would you mind if we painted your gate? We'd like to make it look nice again. Won't cost you anything, and we don't need to go into your house. Would you like it to be white? Or maybe another color?"

She eyed them suspiciously. "Don't give me no line about paint. What you want?"

"We don't want anything. We'd just like to do this for you."

She shook her head, unconvinced. Jeth took it as a positive. "We'll choose some paint and be back shortly."

At a nearby Wal-Mart, Jeth and Brandon found paint, while Janni bought a bag of groceries and some flowers. The lady became even more skeptical. "Why you doin' this?"

"It's a God thing," said Jeth. "We're celebrating ten hours of just being together. It makes us happy, and we hope it does you, too."

As they painted, the lady came out and watched from the tiny porch, then came closer and lined out a story of hardship, loss, and deprivation that spanned two lifetimes. She went back indoors and came out with lemonade and cheap store-bought cookies and seemed pleased when they all ate and drank. "Don't know when food ever tasted so good!" said Jeth. "Can you tell us your first name? I'm Jeth, by the way, and this is Janni and her son, Brandon." Janni arched an eyebrow.

"My name's Stacia—Stacia Walker." She seemed proud to have been asked.

"It's an honor to meet you, Stacia," said Jeth.

When the job was done, Stacia was clearly pleased and invited them inside. Jeth shook his head. "I don't want to give you even a moment of worry that we might rob you. I would like to pray for you, though." They took her plump, brown hands, and as Jeth prayed, she sniffled. When he finished, she hugged them. "Are you angels?"

"No, but we're not here by mistake. God pointed you out for us to stop."

AT LUNCH, THEY talked about safe, outside things—Bryan, school, friends. Finally Jeth asked Brandon, "How do you feel inside?"

The boy looked down. "Not good."

Jeth leaned back. "It's hard, isn't it, to do and say the right things? Anything that tears people down makes you feel bad. Good choices are hard, but the payoff is extreme."

After lunch they played miniature golf, then found a lakeside park where they walked and crunched pinecones and skipped stones and laughed a lot.

Supper was quiet, subdued, each dreading the leave-taking. Jeth hugged Brandon long and hard, then pushed him to arm's length. "I can't hug Janni, but would you hug her for me? She's your best ally at home. Talk together. Listen to each other. Tell about inside stuff. Will you do that?"

As Jeth drove home, he didn't feel good inside, either.

24

The approaching Candlewood Expo drove everyone to the edge. For one thing, Dynamo kicked Jeth's thigh—hard. Rob watched Jeth limping around the barn, and he spewed fury. "How many times has he nailed you, and still you can't keep out of his way? I can't afford fractures here, and ask Freddie about the pain of a broken femur. But maybe a good dose of pain would teach you something."

"Yeah, as though I need more lessons, especially from you. He won't do it again—you can bank on that!"

Jeth also blew an easy win in a small, local show and again brought down Rob's wrath for staying up late visiting Web sites and Saddlebred chat rooms. "I'm sorry," Jeth said in a tone far removed from contrition. "I keep apologizing to everyone. Why doesn't anyone apologize to me?"

Anger—and a splash of vanity. He needed proper clothing for the show. No, he wouldn't borrow again. He wanted his own. Once he had it in hand, he wouldn't say how much he had paid.

Everyone gave him a wide margin—except Katie and Alejo. The little Mexican was indomitable. He worked and sang at the top of his lungs. "Alejo!" Jeth bellowed. "*Shut up*! My head is splitting."

"Okay, señor," Alejo replied. "From now on I spleet your head better."

Jeth headed toward him but turned aside as Rob came at him with fire in his eye. "He knows perfectly well what he's saying," Jeth snapped. "Don't give me bull about his 'language deficit.'"

As Rob walked away from that confrontation, Todd came out of the ring, clearly uncomfortable. "Uh…is it okay to rearrange the jumps, like, uh, make the layout harder? Pixie's gettin' lazy, and I thought…"

Rob shrugged. "Sounds okay to me. Did you check with Jeth?"

"Um…." The ground held his attention, and his arm needed rubbing.

Rob looked at him. "Does that mean you didn't ask him, or you did and he said no?"

"Uh…well, I sorta asked, but he didn't seem… Well, he didn't actually say, but—"

"You thought it might be safer to ask me."

"Jeth—I don't think he likes this dude. Didn't at the start. Doesn't want me around."

With a sardonic laugh, Rob chucked Todd's shoulder. "Man, right now, Jeth doesn't like anybody. Don't let it get to you. In a couple of weeks he'll be a different man. If he should happen to win, he'll be insufferable, but I don't see that happening. His sights are up there in horse stratosphere. He's trained himself as best he knows, but Saddlebreds are a whole different world, and Dynamo has almost no experience. Jeth will be disappointed, but he'll settle down, at least till next year. And God help us then! Come on, show me what you want to do, and I'll give you a hand."

Todd looked nervously at Jeth, just entering the ring on Indigo. Rob put a hand on Todd's shoulder. "Buck up, man. Last time I checked, I was still Alpha Male around here."

THE FINAL WEEK was bad. Bad weather, bad mood, and everything breakable broke. Rob teetered on the edge of the cliff. He couldn't sleep Saturday night, trying to decide whether to castrate Jeth's dream or not. Katie came out of the bedroom and sat on the couch beside him. "This is madness!" he said. "None of us will live through it."

"Let it go, Rob. Maybe you're part of his problem. You go ballistic over the least little thing. I've heard you get on his—"

"You think I'm ballistic! You're not out there listening to his mouth and his even nastier body language."

Katie's back went even straighter than the line of her mouth. "Well, I'm in here, having to listen to yours." She flounced away from the couch and pulled a tissue out of her pocket.

"Great! Two noxious people on the acreage, one of them pulling the ultimate weapon! At least Jeth hasn't inhaled tear gas."

Katie turned on him, eyes flashing scimitars, and stormed into the kitchen, where she found two open cupboard doors just begging to be slammed—which woke Jessie.

A half hour later, after everything had settled, Katie again sat by Rob on the couch. "I'm sorry," she said in a small voice. "I know it's been bad. He doesn't snarl at me...and he's got every reason to." Her tone was heavy with sorrow and regret.

Rob put his arm around her. She laid her head on his shoulder. "Cheer up, hon!" she said. "By this time next Saturday, it'll be over, and he'll settle back to earth."

Rob snorted. "Saturday is the Allendale show. It'll be another God miracle if he's able to even get over the jumps. He's killing himself. Do I just stand by and watch him do it?"

"Rob, you've got to let him do this. From the day he came here, he's wanted it. He's trained that horse, you might say, like God is training *him*. I know, I know..." She sat up and smoothed her hair. "Training is a nasty business sometimes, but Dynamo was made for him to ride, or maybe he was made to ride Dynamo."

THE NEXT MORNING, Jeth didn't want to go to church. Rob said, "You *will* go to church." And Jeth knew exactly the consequences of not going.

He went, but more out of fear of what Maybelle might say than to avoid Rob's displeasure. Following the service, Maybelle looked him up and down and said plenty. Jeth immediately regretted coming, but in the end, he clung to her and didn't want to let go. "You're my lifeline, you know that?" he whispered.

She drew him to her seat and opened her Bible, which she rooted through, pulling out a wrinkled piece of paper covered in tilting lines of her scraggy handwriting. "This is from Psalm one thirty-eight, I believe from *The Message.*" She turned it over, as though to verify the source, and then handed it to Jeth. "I couldn't see at the time why it struck me, but now I think I know."

Jeth read silently. "*When I walk into the thick of trouble, keep me alive in the angry turmoil. With one hand strike my foes, with your other hand save me. Finish what you started in me, God. Your love is eternal—don't quit on me now.*"

He looked up with stricken eyes, then bent to hold her once again.

THE FOLLOWING DAY in the barn office, Rob tried one last time to persuade Jeth to give up the trip or at least modify it. "It's less than three hundred miles—eight hours, maybe. The class is at night. If we left at five, or even six, on Wednesday morning, we'd get there in plenty of time, and then come back Thursday."

"Can't do that. I need to be there the day before to get him used to the surroundings. What's the problem with Tuesday? Cecil and Todd can take care of things here."

Rob turned away, shoulders slumped in defeat. "At least we can take the small trailer—if he doesn't kick it to pieces."

THEY LEFT EARLY enough Tuesday, but everything went against them. The dawn sky, thick and spectral, soon spewed forth a traffic-stalling downpour. Fog dogged them, the truck transmission turned ugly, and they got lost trying to find a service station. With the delays, they had to unload and reload Dynamo twice to keep him from destroying the trailer. They ended up sleeping in the truck—Rob in the cab, and Jeth on bales of hay in the truck bed—and arrived late Wednesday morning. Jeth was snappy. Rob said, "Is this worth it?"

"Is childbirth worth it, especially when the daddy's not there?"

Rob clenched his jaw.

Candlewood was a sprawling multiplex thick with horses, riders, trainers, grooms, and transportation rigs that varied in size from trailers like the Chiltons' to glitzy, stainless-steel eighteen-wheelers. The place reeked of money, of measuring horse against horse, of "go for the gold." Yes, there was laughter, joking, and horseplay; but underneath lay a brittle, calculating substratum that Jeth had known well during his Wingate days.

He had little time to acclimatize the horse, but the noise practice with Cecil seemed to have paid off, and the stallion remained steady in the unfamiliar surroundings. Though the show would be indoors, an outdoor practice ring allowed for adequate warm-up. At least the weather had cleared.

Jeth changed into his riding outfit with its jaunty hat and red tie. He couldn't cast off his angst, though, and Rob could only mutter, "I can't help you, Jeth. You're totally out of reach."

When the class was called, Rob offered to pray, but Jeth said, "No time. Get the chains off his feet. I've got to get in there." When Rob stood after unfastening the chains, Jeth headed Dynamo through the wide tunnel carpeted with wood shavings to the class holding area. Just beyond was the well-lit stadium, which could have held four rings the size of Rob's at home. The crowd acknowledged the ringmaster and other officials dressed in formal attire and began clapping as the horses came through the gate.

From the moment they entered the ring at a smart trot, Dynamo was perfection—head up, knees rising almost to his chin, with the weight of the chains suddenly gone. His coppery coat glowed, his mane and tail flaxen and swirling in the wind of his own making. Jeth could feel the ground-shaking dynamo beneath him, and never had he felt more one with a horse—except for that night on Jo Jo. The stallion was a well-oiled machine—totally honest, all business, with a way-out-front heart.

The high-stepping competition was stiff indeed, a world apart from the locals who had cobbled together a class for themselves. But now that he was actually in the ring on Dynamo, Jeth didn't care how it came out. Six ribbons, seven horses. He could be out of the running, but this moment—right now—was all that mattered. This was their common destiny, what they were made to do, and they did it with gusto—all flags flying. *Born to rack.*

Trot. Walk. Slow gait. Rack on! Walk. Canter. Reverse. Trot. Walk. Slow gait. *Rack on!* Jeth passed three horses as though they were standing still. Four…five. The call came to walk, but still he pushed on—and passed the sixth horse. Walk. Canter. Walk.

They lined up in the center, the sides of the horses heaving. Dynamo stretched like a bronze statue as the judges walked behind the contestants. Decisions made, they handed in their cards, and with the horses walking stiffly around the upper part of the ring, the call-out began. "Sixth: Martin's Maiden, owned by Laramie Humboldt, ridden by Robert Caldwell. Fifth: Bellefonte, owned by Charles Hasker." The countdown continued, and Jeth's heart picked up its pace. *Third…. Second….*

Two horses left. Jeth eyed the other and took a deep breath. Finally, "First: Dynamo, owned by Rob Chilton of Morningstar Stables, ridden by Jeth Cavanaugh."

Face flushed, Jeth trotted Dynamo to the ring steward, who hooked the blue ribbon on the stallion's bridle—with only token retaliation from Dynamo. The donor of the trophy, a Mrs. Haverstone, moved uncertainly toward the unfriendly stallion and signaled the steward to be the go-between. Jeth accepted the trophy and posed for the official photo. Then, holding the plate precariously, he chose to make the victory lap. Dynamo was tired; he knew that. But this was their moment to savor, and they would do it with banners streaming. He put the horse to a rack—down the first side, around the bottom, and full speed up the far side. He was about to slow for the gate when it happened—a crack, a stop-motion moment of horse down, rider underneath, a cloud of anguish billowing from the heap to engulf the entire crowd.

25

Rob was over the gate in an instant and sprinting toward the wreckage. Dynamo had rolled off of Jeth's inert form, and Rob stared, aghast, expecting the scene to vanish like a bad dream. When it remained terribly real, he fell to his knees and stroked Jeth's head, loudly demanding God's help, until a medic moved him aside. He could hear a rising vortex of voices centering on the horse's broken leg, but nothing was making sense. He bent and scooped up the dress hat from mid-track as though dusting it off might somehow rescue Jeth.

The veterinarian came to him, reaching for what to say. "I'm sorry...your horse...the right cannon is badly fractured...shattered, actually. A catastrophic compound break. Even without X-rays, it's obvious to me...I think you would agree...there's no way he can be saved. Such a fine animal. Some horses do recover, but with gross contamination of the wound—"

Rob waved him silent. "Do what you have to. Give me a paper to sign...whatever. Right now, Jeth..." He turned back, watching the medics stabilize bones, back, and neck, then pump oxygen into his lungs.

Rob spent a long night outside the local emergency room before being told they would airlift Jeth to Lexington. "He needs surgery," an intern told him, "and for now, we're treating him as critical, though they won't know exactly what's going on till they get in there. He's got multiple fractures—clavicle, arm, ribs, pelvis; collapsed lung; assorted internal injuries."

Rob closed his eyes, wishing the nightmare would wake him up.

"He's reasonably stable. He looks to be strong and healthy, but I can't give any assurance at this point."

Rob nodded, pressed a hand to the intern's arm, and walked away.

Jeth didn't regain consciousness for twenty-four hours after the surgery. Rob was with him when he began to come around. He drifted in and out, acknowledging Rob's presence with a squeeze of his good hand, but could not talk around intubation. Pain was a major issue, but questions in his eyes rose above it and demanded answers.

Rob started simply. "You had an accident. But you're alive, and you're not paralyzed." That worked for a while, thanks to medicational oblivion, but soon Jeth's hand became insistent. Finally, the savage words could no longer be put off. Rob took a big breath, closed his eyes, and dragged them out of the depths of his stomach: "Dynamo is dead. His foreleg shattered. He had to be put down."

Horror took over Jeth's face. He could only stare disbelievingly at Rob.

Rob considered diverting Jeth's thoughts to his big win. He had a handful of news clippings he could show him, but he knew Jeth too well to even try. Such devastation could never be remedied.

Janni and Brandon came, but even they got only token acknowledgment. They grieved with Jeth but didn't stay long. When Jeth stopped staring at the window and would not open his eyes, Rob suspected that he had switched from mourning Dynamo to flaying himself over an unfathomable catalogue of personal sin. But when the tube finally came out and he could speak, his first hoarse words were, "You didn't say 'Ride safe!' That's why it happened."

Rob didn't respond. Was this stupid accusation the first of an endless blame-Rob litany to fend off the deadly malignancy attacking his soul? But as Jeth went on, Rob began to wish that was all it was. Bit by bit, the unbearable weight of guilt, laced with physical pain, came pouring out, and nothing Rob could say made any difference. Jeth, he knew, saw far too clearly just what he had done and the steps along the way.

Rob had to get back home but didn't want to leave Jeth alone in such a state. He searched the phone book and made multiple calls, looking for a pastor who not only would be willing to visit Jeth but might be able to connect with him in his grief. He met with several and settled on one who seemed to grasp the layers of Jeth's anguish.

WITHIN A DAY, Pastor Rick Kelsey came in and said who he was and why he was there. Jeth looked hard at him and said, "Are you my parole officer? Tell me if God's glory left the temple—this temple right here," pointing to himself. Rick blinked and could produce nothing but platitudes. Jeth fell asleep.

His next visit, Rick said, "Can we spend at least thirty seconds, maybe even forty-five, on trivialities? I can do a pretty mean weather report."

He won a small smile, but at least Jeth stayed awake. "Read me Psalm one thirty-eight something," Jeth said.

"Something...hm."

"Not the first verses."

"There are only eight. How about if I start at the end? *The Lord will fulfill his purpose for me; your love, O Lord, endures forever—do not abandon the works of your hands.*'"

"That's it, but it's not right. Something about God not quitting on me."

"Maybe a different version. I'll see if I can find it at home. And maybe next time you could tell me why you think I might be your parole officer."

On his third visit, Rick innocently laid out grace as a topic appropriate for Jeth's obvious need. Jeth flinched as though he'd been slapped. With tears and convulsed breathing, he told his whole, lengthy history. "The long and the short of it is, I'm terrified of God."

Rick took a big breath. "Okay. I get the Rick/parole officer connection. You're thinking my job is like his—to keep you on the straight and narrow. I can see why boilerplate blather won't work with you. No wonder your friend was anxious to get the right guy in here. I'm not sure I can fill the bill, but let's try."

The next time in, Rick said, "I thought talking about Lamentations might be helpful."

Jeth frowned. "I don't like Lamentations. Too gloomy. Don't need that."

Rick looked at him a moment. "Well, I say you do, and today I'm Rick the parole guy. You need a professional lamenter like Jeremiah to help you name the pain that's eating your gut. Only then can you begin to heal. Not all of it fits, and we'll talk about that, too. How about it?"

Without waiting for an answer, Rick started to read.

"'I am the man who has seen affliction by the rod of the LORD's wrath. He has driven me away and made me walk in darkness rather than light…and has broken my bones.'…Um, 'Yet this I call to mind and therefore I have hope: because of the LORD's great love we are not consumed, for his compassions never fail. They are new every morning; great is your faithfulness.'…Let's see…'Though he brings grief, he will show compassion, so great is his unfailing love. For he does not willingly bring affliction or grief to anyone….I called on your—'"

"You're skipping verses." Jeth frowned.

"How do you know I'm skipping? You got the book memorized?"

"You're reading and stopping and reading. You're leaving out the bad verses."

"All right—let's talk about the bad verses. Here's one: '*Even when I call out or cry for help, he shuts out my prayer. He has barred my way with blocks of stone.*' Let me tell you what that doesn't mean."

They talked back and forth, Jeth fighting Rick all the way. Finally, Rick sat back and looked long at him. "I came here tonight planning to give you Communion. Now I'm not sure whether you need it badly or that you're in no shape to take it."

Jeth looked away and stared toward the window. Rick was about to pack up his things and leave when Jeth said in a small voice, "Yes. Please."

With a nod, Rick picked up his case from the floor, opened it, and poured juice from a vial into two tiny cups. He unwrapped a chunk of bread, then prayed and spoke the words of Christ: "This is My body, broken for you." He tore the bread in two and held one out to Jeth.

Jeth stared at him without taking the bread, eyes panicked. "*My* body...broken...*by* me," he whispered. "*His* body, broken *for* me." Tears coursed onto the pillow. He flung his good arm over his eyes, and his body shook with wracking, wrenching sobs, to the point of Rick's embarrassment to even be there in the presence of such appalling desolation. Rick closed his eyes, rubbed Jeth's bad arm gently, and began to sing, "Amazing grace, how sweet the sound that saved a wretch like me."

Jeth fumbled for Rick's hand and clung tight until the sobs began to ease. Rick disengaged and stood, reaching for a handful of tissues to wipe Jeth's face. He then turned and broke off a morsel of bread and put it to Jeth's lips, his other hand on his head. "Come," he said gently. "This is Christ's body, broken for you. Eat of it."

Jeth stiffened but then opened his mouth and accepted it.

Rick then put the cup to Jeth's lips and said, "This is the blood of the new covenant, Christ's blood shed for you. Drink." He set the cup down, put both hands on Jeth's head, and prayed. "Lamb of

God, slain from the foundation of the world, please come to Jeth in his brokenness. Cover his sin with the blanket of Your love. Bring peace and healing to his heart and body. God of wonders and way beyond, be Jeth's God…right now…right here. Thank You."

Jeth lay quiet, his eyes closed. Rick backed away slowly, gathered the Communion things, removed a piece of paper from his Bible, and left it on the bedside table.

AFTER RICK HAD gone, Jeth opened his eyes, saw the paper, and found on it the verses he had asked for. He read it over and over until he could say it by heart: "*When I walk into the thick of trouble, keep me alive in the angry turmoil. With one hand strike my foes, with your other hand save me. Finish what you started in me, God. Your love is eternal—don't quit on me now.*"

He put his arm over his eyes and wept once again, but not from sorrow. He had turned a corner.

26

Three weeks later, when Jeth was ready for rehab, both he and Rob wanted a hospital close to home. That didn't sit well with the medical people. "It could kill you," said his blunt, forthright surgeon. "Stay local so I can keep an eye on you. I stapled, titanized, and wired you with dazzling skill. Now you want to hike off and muck it all up. You can go that far only by plane or helicopter."

"No way. Don't have that kind of money. Rob'll get me there somehow. I'm going, permission or not. I'll sign myself out."

The surgeon threw his hands up and walked out of Jeth's life.

Rob arrived in a borrowed conversion van fitted with an air bed. Todd would drive, and Rob would sit with Jeth, but it took the two of them plus hospital help to get Jeth settled. With Jeth grimacing in pain, his face the color of oatmeal, Todd got behind the wheel as quickly as possible. Jeth had been medicated heavily, but heavy wasn't working. This was going to be a ride that could last forever.

Just before they left, Pastor Rick came to say good-bye. Jeth couldn't speak and just clung to his hand. "Brother Jeth," said Rick, "there's no doubt in my mind that God's glory still roosts in your tabernacle. It's there. I've seen it. God gave me a word this morning that I believe He meant for you. I was reading Henri Nouwen, and you need to read his stuff."

Jeth continued to stare, eyes burning.

"I'll send you a list. He was talking about poverty, that it has multiple dimensions. There's material poverty—not enough money. There's physical poverty, and I guess you know about that. But he says there's also mental poverty and, beyond that, spiritual poverty. And that's where you are, thinking God's glory has left you. None of us believes it, but it's what you're *feeling*. But take heart: beyond spiritual poverty is nothing—nothing but naked trust in God's mercy.

"Jeth, you've got a soft bed to ride home on." Rick patted the air mattress. "Rest all the way—and beyond—on the mercy of God."

Jeth scrunched his eyes against a firestorm of emotion.

"And don't forget—you've got Moses and Elijah and Ezekiel and John the Baptist and Rob and me..."

Jeth opened his eyes and worked his mouth to a wan smile. "And Maybelle. Don't forget Maybelle."

"Right. Maybelle. We're all cheering you on. Love you, brother!" He clung long to Jeth's hand.

THE TRIP TOOK longer than forever. Todd misread the gas gauge, and they ran out of fuel. He swore—loudly. Rob didn't actually swear, but he might as well have. In the midst of the recriminations, Jeth called out, "Todd!"

Todd stopped talking and rubbed the back of his head. Rob bent to see what Jeth wanted.

His eyes were closed, and with slurring words he said, "Todd... go. Gas...circles around..."

Rob put a hand on his shoulder and turned back to Todd. "He's not making sense, though the 'out of gas' part seems to have gotten through. Let's try nine-one-one."

They had help and gas within twenty minutes, but when the van moved again, Jeth cried out.

"Keep going," said Rob. "We got at least two hours more."

Rob began talking to Jeth about home and going home and getting close to home, and the very word seemed to have a sedating quality; but by the time they reached the rehab unit, Jeth was unconscious. Rob panicked. Had the trip killed him? He was too tired to do more than stand by while the hospital staff took Jeth inside and put him in bed.

THE NEXT MORNING, Jeth was awake and sitting up when Rob came in, and though his color wasn't much better, he managed a small smile. Katie followed her husband, with Jessie in her arms, and she leaned down and kissed Jeth on the mouth. Then she stood up, clutching the baby, and glared. "Don't either of you say a word! He needed that, and I gave it to him."

He did need it. His eyes filled, and he lifted his good hand to squeeze Jessie's leg.

AFTER A DAY or so, Rob gave the all clear for visitors. Church folk came by the dozens, the best medicine Jeth could have received. He tired easily but wouldn't allow the door to be closed to anyone.

One evening when Rob came alone, Jeth, sitting in a chair, asked him to close the door and to let no one in: "I have to say something I know you won't like, but I *need* to say it. Will you let me?"

Rob pulled a chair over and sat down uncomfortably, eyes searching for an escape but seeing none.

Jeth methodically lined out his grief and pain and anger over Dynamo in all its stages. He should have felt signs of a stress fracture and stopped the horse in time. He had killed a valuable, irreplaceable horse. He had cost Rob a huge amount of money just on medical expenses and transportation. Then the lead-up—his single-minded plunge into destruction. He had failed Rob, failed Brandon, disregarded all the signals—the things he had said and done from the very start, caught up in his passion for the task, all the while certain that he was doing God's will; that God would bless him as He had in the past. "Dynamo was an idol." He looked at a splotch on the wall that blinked red from an ambulance outside. "Every bit as deadly as the golden calf at Mt. Sinai."

Rob, too, stared at the splotch. "Idol, maybe. I hear what you're saying, but look at it this way: God gave you exactly what you wanted, except for the end. You couldn't have sent Dynamo out in a greater blaze of glory. It was a superb performance, an extraordinary win. My jaw was on the ground the whole time you were out there. I've never seen *anybody* ride as you did. I've got a stack of e-mails and newspaper clippings at home. I'll bring them in someday."

Jeth was silent. "Yeah, I won. But the *price*! For Dynamo, for me. It's as bitter a pill as I have ever swallowed. My life is mutilated."

"Mutilated? No, too grisly. I'd say you bumped pretty hard, but now you're back on track."

"Not yet." Jeth glanced away, then looked directly at his friend. "Rob, I'm sorry. A word you hate, but I have to say it. When Rick came to see me, we talked about grace. This is a harder, deeper grace than I ever imagined. I will always bear the mark of it. Everything up to now was just practice. Rob, I'm *sorry!*"

Rob didn't respond right away. Instead he got up and moved around the room, hands in his pockets, eyes everywhere but on Jeth. "I'm the one who should apologize, Jeth, not you."

"Rob," Jeth began, annoyance edging his words, "don't try to make me feel—"

"Just let me tell you what *I* need to say." Rob's hand plowed hair and anguish. "For a week before Candlewood, I couldn't decide between letting you ride or pulling the plug. Katie and I even fought over it. I know now that I should have stuck to my guns and said no. If I had, none of this..." He sighed. "You would be whole. Dynamo would be alive."

Jeth sat up, stark horror freezing his face.

"I know—there would have been hell to pay," said Rob, "but, as you said, the *price*..." He fell silent.

Jeth couldn't speak. He continued to stare and breathe heavily. Finally, he closed his eyes, slowly shaking his head. "Rob..." His voice quavered with dismay. "I don't think you could come close to picturing the horrible, ugly scene that would've come from that. I could not have borne you forbidding me to ride. No, change that: I *would not* have borne it. Thank *God* you didn't pull the plug!" He put shaking hands to his head as though to hold it together. "Everything I said above still applies. I killed your horse. I cost you a lot of money, a lot of heartache, a lot of trouble. But *I didn't destroy our friendship*! And if you had said no, I would have. When I look at the ugliness inside of me back then... Rob, I..."

Rob clenched his jaw against an emotional tsunami. He knelt by Jeth and held him long. When he could finally speak, his voice was rough. "I forgive you, Jeth. Can you let God heal your heart as well as your body?"

Jeth leaned back and wiped a sleeve across his eyes. "I'm groveling, Rob—before God, before you. But it's the posture this piece of dust needs to be in right now."

Jeth looked up, and Rob saw that though he was visibly drained, peace had settled over his entire body.

ALEJO CAME, FULL of language-fractured jokes and banter, and Jeth cracked up. His last belly laugh seemed years ago. "Alejo, man, you *bueno mucho* for me. *Gracias!*"

Cecil visited several times, twice with Mama Berry. They too were good for him and got him singing, but it was Todd that Jeth was looking for. "Cecil, why hasn't Todd come? And don't make up some excuse for him. He's mad at me? He hates me? He's got every reason to."

"Well…" Cecil grinned. "He's not minding you not being on his back. I'll see if I can get him to come."

"Tell him the lion has been declawed."

Todd didn't come right away, but one evening, five minutes before visiting hours were over, he sidled hard-faced into Jeth's room. Jeth was about to doze off and almost missed him, but he pulled himself up and smiled. "Todd! Good lad, stout fellow! I know what it cost you to come, and I won't drag it out. I just want to say I'm sorry for everything. My mind's been working through all the people I hurt and used and had no time for, and you rise to the top of the pile in almost all of those categories. I want to start over, but first comes being sorry, and I am that. My bad. Will you forgive me?"

Todd clearly wasn't ready for that bundle of words and looked at Jeth as though he were speaking Chinese. A voice boomed from the hallway, announcing the end of visiting hours, and Todd's face lifted.

"One of my rehab assignments," said Jeth, "is to practice shaking hands with this bad hoof of mine. Can you at least do that?"

Todd looked at the flaccid hand but shook his head, waved, and made his escape.

Jeth leaned back and whispered, "Will I ever stop paying for that victory from hell?"

27

Maybelle had not come to see Jeth, either, so when she appeared at the side of his bed on Christmas Day, his heart bounced out of the shapeless sadness that had settled on him. "Merry Christmas, my dear one!" she chirped.

"Mother Christmas herself! Rob told me you haven't been well. What have you been doing without me to keep an eye on you? Too much partying?"

She smiled coquettishly. "I have other boyfriends, you know."

It seemed to Jeth like a dream, that Maybelle had floated into his room, entering insurgent territory to disarm land mines and lead him to a place of safety. They talked long, and Jeth told her of his agony in the hospital and of Pastor Rick's attempt to give him Communion.

She sat silent, eyes closed, as though searching the far reaches of the universe for the right words to say. She leaned forward. "The tipping point," she said, then leaned back again.

Jeth looked at her, trying to fathom this far-off nebula she had plucked from the heavens. "Explain?"

Maybelle pursed her lips. "Some might try to divide your life into 'Before Dynamo' and 'After Dynamo'—B.D. and A.D. But I believe it is more like life 'B.C.'—before Communion—and life after—'A.C.' In that moment of Communion, you tasted broken-ness, and only through being broken can one truly engage life, with its joy and sorrow and hidden traps. That was your tipping point, and I feel certain that God will use that moment of brokenness to mend other lives."

Jeth laid his head against the pillow, struggling to assimilate her words. She was holding out the nectar of joy, yes, but sorrow and...*traps?* His breathing became uneven.

Maybelle put her hand on his arm. "What can I do for you, my dear?"

Jeth had to clear his throat before he could speak. "Please, Maybelle—would you read from your hymnal?" He took it from the stand beside the bed and handed it to her. "Your choice. I need your voice right now."

He closed his eyes while she searched the sibilant pages. "I think you'll like this one," she said.

> *O Love that wilt not let me go,*
> *I rest my weary soul in thee;*
> *I give thee back the life I owe,*
> *That in thine ocean depths its flow*
> *May richer, fuller be.*
>
> *O Joy that seekest me through pain,*
> *I cannot close my heart to thee;*
> *I trace the rainbow through the rain,*
> *And feel the promise is not vain,*
> *That morn shall tearless be.*
>
> *O Cross that liftest up my head,*
> *I dare not ask to fly from thee;*
> *I lay in dust life's glory dead,*
> *And from the ground there blossoms red*
> *Life that shall endless be.*

Jeth's eyes stayed closed for a long time, and when he opened them, Maybelle was gone, the hymnal beside him on the bed. Had it been a dream, after all?

THERAPY NOW BECAME the focus of Jeth's life—stretching, pushing through pain to new strength. He could see it happening bit by bit but far too slowly. So, in typical fashion, he upped the pace and tried to pretend he was improving.

"What *are* you trying to do?" Katie asked. She stood with Rob at the foot of his bed, surveying the widening puddle of pain. Then she leaned toward him. "Stop it, Jeth! I don't know what the therapy guys are telling you, but I'm telling you that slow is the quickest way to fast. You know it's true with horses. People are the same. Now, chill out!"

Jeth put his head in his hand, then looked up sheepishly. "I love you guys."

"Well then, rest. You'll get home faster."

Jeth looked past them and asked the big question: "Will I ride again?"

Rob sighed. "I don't know. Nobody's saying one way or the other. I don't think anyone knows yet."

The day he got on his feet was a big one. Even navigating the length of the parallel bars was huge, with pain still in his arm and pelvis. But when he graduated to a walker, he became unstoppable and began to visit other patients. By the third morning, he had made it down to room number five. He turned in and said, "Hi."

"Get out of here."

"I'm Jeth. What's your name?"

"None of your business."

"Shall I call you 'None' or 'Mr. B'?"

"Go to hell."

Jeth laughed. "I'm pretty sure I won't be going there. How about you?"

"Get outta here and I'll be glad to go."

Jeth looked at the small man ruefully. "Maybe not, when the time actually comes. Been here long?"

The man swore.

"I take that to mean too long. What happened?"

"A horse fell on me."

Jeth stiffened. "You're kidding!"

"Would you kid about that? You're on your pins. How about if you couldn't never walk again?"

Jeth fell silent. Yes, what if? Had God treated him—who deserved nothing—better than He had this man? "I'm sorry."

Jeth turned and left, noting the nameplate outside the door. *Stokie Handers.*

He went back the next day. "Hey, Stokie—tell me about the horse that did you in. I'm guessing you were a jockey. Where did you ride?"

The man thought a moment, then listed a number of race-tracks, including big names like Aqueduct and Saratoga.

"Huh! Sounds like you've seen plenty of good horseflesh. Way before your time, but you probably know about Secretariat, the racehorse that won the Triple Crown in nineteen seventy-three."

"I saw the movie."

"Yeah, but did you know that the jockey that rode all three races later broke his back and was in a wheelchair the rest of his life?"

"That supposed to make me feel better?"

Jeth quickly changed the subject. "What was the best horse you ever rode?"

Stokie reflected. "A three-year-old mare. Cantabulaire. Called her Candy. She could run...all heart." A long silence.

Finally, Jeth said, "The best horse I ever rode...a nasty SOB. I killed him."

"That bad?"

"No, that good. He won blue in a top-notch open five-gaited Saddlehorse class."

Stokie snorted. "Pretty-boy show horse," he said disdainfully. "No better'n a jackass, an' better off dead."

"If you'd seen him, you wouldn't say that. He was the finest piece of horseflesh God ever created."

"Leave God outta this!" Stokie said with surprising vehemence.

Jeth let it pass. "It wasn't enough that I won. I had to show off one more time. In the victory lap I pushed him to a full, storming rack. His leg had to be hurting, but he didn't let up. His leg broke, and he rolled over me. I woke up in the hospital." Jeth studied his walker. "And I caused it. Wanted to win so bad that nothing else mattered. I may never ride again. Walk, yes, but not ride or jump or know a horse like I knew Dynamo."

Two days later, Stokie handed him the perfect opening. "How d'you figure your comin' outta this walkin', with all you said you done, and I come out paralyzed? I didn't do nothin' but ride like I was paid to."

Jeth pulled in a big breath. "I can't explain it. It doesn't seem fair, but I know God well enough to understand that He's got something else in—"

Stokie's face went black, and he began hurling—with skill and accuracy—his lunch dishes, one by one, directly at Jeth. Jeth tried to duck, but the sudden twist left him in a heap on the floor. A nurse hurtled in and bellowed like a drill sergeant at both of them. She yanked the ammunition-laden tray out of Stokie's reach, then turned her wrath on Jeth after confirming that he was still in one piece. She got him on his feet and out the door, where she left him to shake in his own juices.

Jeth went back the next day, but Stokie was a brick wall. Jeth sat silent, trying to piece together the few clues he'd gathered. Had God hurt Stokie badly, or had people who represented God crushed the life out of him? Later in the evening, Jeth learned that Stokie would be released the next day. He had just one more chance with the man. He called Rob and asked him to pray and then thought through an approach he was sure would work.

Early next morning, before hardly anyone was up and about, he went down the hall to make his farewell plea. He rehearsed what he would say. *You hate God, and you think God hates you. He doesn't. He's just not through with you or with me. Test out that love side of God. Test Him. Someday you may find that not being able to walk was the best thing that ever—*

He stopped, dumbfounded. The bed was empty and Stokie gone. Even the nameplate by the door was empty. *Why, God? Why?*

28

Three months in hospital and rehab. Three long months. But going home in late January was thrice sweet. For one thing, he pulled a fast one on Rob. The afternoon before his planned release, Cecil and Mama Berry came, and through the happy conjunction of cooperative staff and the right doctors, Jeth's suggestion that they take him home was approved. He balked at using the walker and insisted on just a cane—and that only after the drill-sergeant nurse vividly lined out the horrors of falling and rebreaking his pelvis. They pulled up to the house, and Jeth was fully satisfied by the splash his entrance generated. Almost before the flutter ended, he went straight to the barn and sat with his eyes closed, wrapped in the warm fragrance of horse and hay and leather.

He was home where he belonged, with people who loved him as he had never before been loved. Alejo drew him in freely, brushing aside Jeth's Before-Dynamo vitriol. Todd kept his distance but was not hostile. The next day, Jeth limped everywhere, seeing, smelling, listening to horse talk. He tired easily and couldn't do much, but he was home.

He wanted to go to church that first Sunday, but Katie put her foot down. "It would be one thing if you'd go late, sit in the back, and leave before everyone grabbed you and talked you to the ground, but no, you'd be up on the platform doing praise songs, praying over this one or that, and first thing you know, you'd be back in rehab. No. You're not going. Not this week."

Home, but broken goods. True home would have been back in the saddle, putting a horse over a jump. But he was not in the saddle. He couldn't sit a horse—not even kind, sweet Meg. He gradually settled into a reflective gloom over being there but no longer part of it, and even that much was punctuated by exercises and therapy sessions. Being back at church was good, and he could play a bigger part, especially once he was able to drive. Rob found jobs he could do, and he was invaluable for Web-site improvement, Internet searches, and lining up appointments; but time went slowly, and watching the men jump was almost unbearable. He couldn't even shovel manure, though he tried with his left arm. Alejo sang Mexican songs to turn his mind from what he couldn't do. He could clean tack, take horses to pasture, check fencing, and deal with clients, but these chores were a major comedown for a star player. He was—in his mind—even lower than Alejo.

ROB SAW THE gloom and decided to do something about it. He tossed an ad onto Craigslist. *Looking for gentle, cushion-backed horse for rehab purposes. Looks don't matter.* He responded to five leads that looked promising and got back one reply that intrigued him. The woman, identifying herself as Cindy, asked if this was a mental or disabled rehab. And she wanted to talk. Rob called and arranged to meet her.

The day was thick and mucky, and the leaden sky quickly gave way to a sullen rain. The guys wouldn't be riding, so Rob gave Cecil the day off and sent Alejo for a load of sawdust. "Be here early in the morning, though. It's hard to surprise Jeth, so if I get this horse, it'll be worth an early rise." He hitched the small trailer to the pickup and then collected Katie and Jessie for an "impromptu" outing, leaving Todd and Jeth to look after things.

They drove four hours to the address Cindy had given them and found a small spread—cottage, tiny barn and paddock, and modest ring against a rocky, sloping pasture. The garden and yard were sewn loosely together with last year's blossom heads and vegetable stalks. Flower remains cascaded with a hint of grace from enormous pots that marked the start of a ragged flagstone walkway.

Cindy came to the car with outstretched hand and smile. "I'm so glad the rain is gone! I worried about that." Their bond was immediate. When Rob mentioned Morningstar Stables, Cindy's eyes widened. "Oh, as in '*bright Morning Star*'? That's a Jesus name. Did you know that?"

"You got it!" said Rob. "Just why we picked it."

"Oh, I'm so glad! Is your friend a Christian, too?"

Rob smiled wryly. "Very much so, but on a whole different plane from the rest of us. That's a story in itself."

Cindy led them to the tiny paddock and was welcomed by an affectionate nicker. "This is Dusty." She took a big breath. "We've loved her for fourteen years, and I can't believe I'm doing this."

Katie put an arm around the woman. The small, friendly, dirt-gray mare was immaculately groomed, and her alert ears and slightly dished face quickly won both their hearts.

Cindy was a single mom trying to hold everything together, and with the horse requiring more time and money than she could spare, she had been pushed to this heartbreaking decision. She obviously cared deeply for the animal but bravely saddled and bridled her, then invited them to try her in the ring. Rob rode first and found she had a comfortable amble quite like Dynamo's slow gait. "Perfect!" he said. "I hadn't thought of this possibility, but it seems God did. If we can get Jeth on her, it couldn't be a better match." He dismounted and raised the stirrups for Katie. "See what you think."

Cindy would take no money. "I want only to see the horse loved and cared for." She looked away and blinked hard. "Dusty is special to me."

That was fair enough, but Rob asked the name of her church and wrote a check, to be used for a missions trip or other project needing money. It was an emotional parting, and Katie and Jessie hugged Cindy while Rob led the mare into the trailer.

AFTER ALEJO LEFT with the truck to get sawdust, Jeth retreated from the unrelenting rain to a nook in the barn where he often sat to think and pray and contemplate pain. Most of the horses were inside, and the comfortable sound of chewing, snorting, and pawing comforted his soul. But with Dynamo gone, only the steady tattoo of rain on the metal roof over the alcove broke the tranquility.

He heard Todd come in and open the office door—to Jeth's relief. He wasn't up for meaningless conversation. A bone-deep tiredness had taken over him—from pain, perhaps, from the weather, or from—

A noise cut through his introspection. A desk drawer had opened—from the raspy sound, the petty-cash drawer. He stood and limped noiselessly to the office door.

Todd jerked with surprise and quickly returned what was in his hand to the drawer, then slammed it shut.

Jeth looked at him and shook his head.

Todd turned the color of claret. "I thought you—I was just—"

Jeth sat down. "Todd, you're more klutsy at thieving than lying. Don't quit your day job."

"I was just gonna borrow some...to tide me over."

"Okay." Jeth pulled out his wallet. "How much do you need?"

"No!" Todd pulled himself up fiercely. "I can't take no money from you!"

Jeth raised his eyebrows but said nothing.

"I can't, that's all." And he pushed out of the office and ran from the barn. Jeth watched him go, then folded his wallet and laid it on the desk. Within minutes, Todd was back, soaking wet from the rain, out of breath, and panicked.

"Sit down, Todd. We need to talk. Here's a towel. Dry off. We've needed to talk for a long time, and I blew it. I'm sorry. Let's start over. Can you tell me what's going on?"

Todd glowered. "I was just gonna borrow, like I said."

"Have you needed to 'borrow' some before?"

"No! I swear to God, I—"

"No swearing to anything. Just yes or no. And look at me."

"No, I never did, I sw— I didn't." His eyes did not waver.

Jeth nodded. "I believe you. Now, tell me why you're in such a bind. And eyes here."

Todd sighed nervously. " I…well, I…" His eyes drifted to the floor. Jeth touched Todd's knee and pointed to his own face. Todd took another big breath. "I…lost money…gambling."

Jeth leaned back. "Gambling. Okay. Not on cockfighting, I hope."

"*Cockfighting!*" he cried, bewildered.

"Yeah. It's illegal, even if you just watch. And if you happen to be on parole, and you told your parole officer you'd be home at a certain time and weren't, that's even worse. And if you didn't want to be there and tried to get away and got beat up, that's about as bad as gets."

Todd looked at Jeth, dumbfounded. "That happened to *you?* You gotta be kiddin'!"

Jeth steepled his hands in front of his mouth. "My parole officer forgetting to check on me is just one of the many miracles God has done in my life. Another major one was Rob forgiving me.

"Todd, don't gamble," he went on. "It's dumb, it's stupid. Not good. Even when you win, you lose in the end. Now, how much do you need to get by? If I don't have enough here"—he opened his wallet—"we'll get it somewhere for you. Todd, I won't tell Rob about this, and I won't hold it over your head. No pressure. I want to be your friend. I'm late in coming to that, but here I am now. Can you shake my hand this time?"

Jeth was gratified by Todd's surprisingly strong grip.

29

Rob and Katie took their time driving back, stopping for supper at a Kings Family Restaurant, which they both dearly loved. When they got home, Jeth was in his trailer, and Rob unloaded Dusty with little noise.

Next morning, Jeth came to the barn at his normal hour but was not first this time. The others were busy at work when he came in. "Out partying last night?" asked Rob. "You slept late."

Jeth looked at his watch and was about to mount an argument when Rob cut across his bow. "We're done this side. You start over there," and he motioned toward Dusty's stall, at the same time hollering toward the back of the barn. "Yo, Alejo. *Atención* here!" They chattered back and forth till they heard Jeth say softly, "Hey!"

They gathered around him. "Hey, what?" said Todd.

Jeth opened the door and stared at the little gray animal, who stared back curiously. "Who's this little charmer? Where and why did you come up with him? It is a him? No, a her," he said, looking down the mare's side.

Rob put a hand on Jeth's shoulder. "This is your replacement five-gaiter, except one of the gaits is missing."

"Mine? You're kidding!"

"Yours. Few problems to overcome, like how to get you on her. She's small, but not small enough for you to just sit down on her back."

"What's her name?"

"Dusty. And she's been loved to death all her life."

They saddled and bridled the little mare, but after trying several ways of getting Jeth's right leg over the horse's back, they stepped away and studied the situation. "Block and tackle, maybe?" Katie suggested.

"Hey!" said Todd. He trotted to the rear of the barn, where Alejo had been shoveling manure into the tractor bucket, started the machine, and unceremoniously dumped the bucket. "Don't know if the horse'll take to it," he hollered as he backed out of the barn, "but don't hurt to try."

With only a few anxious glances, Dusty accepted the approach of the tractor. Jeth stepped onto the flattened bucket, turned carefully, and hung on as Todd slowly raised it. Dusty stood like a rock while the men helped Jeth sit sideways. But how to get his leg over?

"I have an idea," said Katie. She ran inside the barn and came out with an armful of hay, which she put on the ground in front of the horse. Dusty's ears went forward, and she bent her head to the hay. With a little help, Jeth swung his right leg easily over her neck. He winced and drew his leg back. "Maybe without the saddle?" he said.

They got him back in the bucket and removed the saddle, and this time, after an initial wince, his face cleared. They went slowly at first, Todd leading the mare until Jeth took over the reins with a look of triumph. "Push her just a little," said Rob, and as Jeth tightened his heels gently, Dusty readily went into the smooth, fast-walk gait that did not require posting. "Oh, man!" breathed Jeth. His smile flashed bright as the rain-washed sun, and he circled the ring until fatigue and pain pulled him to a stop. "What can I say?" He looked at them all. "You guys..."

With more hay from Katie, the mare obediently ducked, and Todd pulled Jeth's leg over and helped him slide to the ground. Jeth held up his bad hand and got a robust slap and a grin.

RIDING WAS GOOD therapy for Jeth, and the pain worked out slowly. He graduated to a saddle and learned to mount by himself. "It's not pretty," he said, "but I get up there." He sometimes put Jessie in front of him, to the huge enjoyment of them both. He tried to ride Meg, but she was broader and more of a challenge.

Rob had, of course, told Jeth about Cindy's circumstances and explained why she needed a good home for her beloved pet. Jeth called to thank her, and they had a long, cordial exchange.

A month and several e-mails later, Cindy called to say she needed to drive to Cranmer. Would he consider meeting her there? It was a small town, so finding each other wouldn't be hard. Jeth was surprised at his own interest in the idea, and Rob grinned. "Don't want company, do you?" Despite himself, Jeth turned red. He had heard nothing from Janni, and her phone was no longer in service. That worried him, but with no listing for either her or Bryan, he could do nothing. Brandon was, of course, a major concern, and Jeth could only hope that the gains he'd made with the boy had brought a thread of stability to their home. He could recall Janni and Brandon coming to the hospital, but with so much grief and pain, the two had seemed far-distant specks. Clearly, his injury had affected more than just his inability to show jump. Maybe interacting with another woman would serve as a different sort of therapy. And, she was a Christian; Janni was not.

At the appointed time, Jeth saw Cindy in front of the Cranmer post office. She hadn't spotted him, and he sat in the car for a full minute, drinking in the sweet nectar of this brand-new sensation. Aside from passing lust, he had never considered a woman other than Janni, and he didn't quite know how to act. He took in her rounded figure—fuller and not as drop-dead beautiful as Janni's; her halo of coppery hair the color of Dynamo; the open, expectant look on her face as she scrutinized passing cars. He liked what he saw, and that gave him courage. He opened the door, pulled himself out, and limped toward her. Her face lit as she stepped forward and reached out both hands. Jeth carefully negotiated the curb and gave her a warm hug. It felt very good. "There," he said, putting her at arm's length. "I had to do that. I'm grateful. But now I'll back off."

He felt attracted by the soft pleasure of her face and an indefinable air that revealed to him the cardinal compass of her life. She was almost the exact opposite of Janni—muted and mellow versus resplendent and animated—and his eyes kept tracking the play of sunlight over the gold cloud of her hair. She was a comfortable alternative for him, especially right now.

"I was going to suggest a walk to a nice little pond I came across, but…" She surveyed his gimpy leg. "Maybe you're not up for that. We could—"

"Hey—walking's my prescribed therapy. No power walks yet, but getting to a pond should be doable." With the sensuous sights, sounds, and smells of May beating around them, they walked and talked and sat and talked and walked more. Jeth told his story. "I spent two years in prison, and a horse fell on me, with a lot in between."

Cindy's life had not been easy, either. Her husband had walked out on her and her son, and she felt fortunate to have a good job and her little spread. "You can't believe how awful it was that first week with Dusty gone. But I've got more time to garden and give Devon the attention he needs, and that's good. So, you see, you've helped me as much as I've helped you."

They talked of the ways of God, but Jeth had far too much pain to do more than skim the surface.

Saying good-bye was hard. They were bound by a horse, but a new thread was beginning to fasten on his heart. Cindy reached up and hugged Jeth. He reciprocated but cut it short. "I don't want to step over any lines," he said softly, "yours or mine."

She nodded and with tears in her eyes let him go.

Rob was still up when he got home. He came out, and Jeth told of his ambivalence. "It's a whole new idea. I'm not sure where my life is headed—on any front. I'm even on different footing with God, like trying to read tea leaves." He looked at Rob ruefully. "And what to do with two women in bed with me every night? Janni, and now Cindy." *At least Katie is safely in her own bed,* he thought.

JETH WENT BACK to doing this and that at church and at the farm. He got good at changing diapers, rewiring fence posts, and winnowing out dead-end clients. Watching training sessions pained him, especially with the show season starting up, and he tried to keep out of the way, giving advice only if asked. But when prospective buyers came to try out or receive training for their horse of choice, Jeth proved invaluable for coaching and helping bond horse with rider. After successful sales, Rob often turned toward Jeth with a grateful thumbs-up.

Toogie was responding well to Cecil, and both Rob and Jeth felt good about their decision not to geld him. "He'll be a stallion— that's clear," said Jeth. "He's already got a mouth, but Cecil stands his ground and won't put up with nonsense. And Toogie doesn't mean anything by it. Just trying out his hormones." Jeth grinned. "I love the way the two of them spar. Cecil bats his chin; Toogie comes at him with ears back and mouth open but then waits for Cecil to go back at him. About as sweet as they come. The absolute opposite of Dynamo. Bat his chin and he'd take your nose off."

Todd was doing far better than Jeth had ever expected. Rob had seen the promise, while Jeth had seen only Wingate. And Todd was finally accepting Jeth as a friend. The tractor-bucket mount had cracked open the book, and the day Todd paid back the gambling loan and looked him straight in the eye, Jeth could almost see a new leaf turning. "Good man!" was all he said, but he gave Todd a quick hug and was pleased to have it accepted.

JETH DID GO to a couple of big shows to help as he could, but running into people who knew him—especially those who had not heard about his accident—twisted his gut with the telling and retelling. Rob was winning some respectable ribbons but only the occasional blue, and Jeth felt his disappointment and frustration. However, Jeth's quality photos and video clips of show riding earned significantly more traffic on the Web site when added to the posted bloodlines.

He continued e-mailing Cindy and called her every week or so. Jeth mentioned shows he had gone to but not the effect they were having on him. She told of swimming with Devon and how well her peas had done this year. "I never had time for peas before. Used to be a pain tying string for them to climb, but with the new plastic netting, it's a cinch. I still have to shell them, but I'm getting to like snap peas almost as well. So now I'm wallowing in peas!"

ONE QUIET AFTERNOON, Todd came to Jeth, his face the color of bonemeal. He had a letter, and his hand shook as he showed it to Jeth. "You was right: Wingate's gonna get me. I didn't think he'd bother, but this says he's gonna press charges. But I didn't do nothin' like what this says."

Jeth read silently. "Legal gobbledygook," he said, "drawn up by whatever lawyer is currently in Wingate's pocket." He ran a finger along a line. "Says you destroyed a truck by deliberately driving it into an...'anaerobic lagoon'? Oh, must mean the barn wastewater dump. Who'd want to do that? Did you?" He looked hard at Todd.

"No! I didn't! I swear to God I didn't—and I mean that. I'm not just sayin' it. I drove that truck lots, but I never went anywheres near the lagoon!"

Jeth continued to search his face.

"Jeth, you gotta believe me! I never did—"

"I believe you," Jeth said softly. "You're too scared to lie to me again. My guess is that somebody drove it in, and you happen to be at the top of his extermination list." He turned. "This is not good. Get in my car. We're going down to the police station."

Todd stared at him in horror. Jeth pushed him toward the car and got in the driver's seat.

At the station, Jeth asked the dispatcher to call up his name, spelling it carefully. He explained his long history, both locally and in Billingsford. "I think you'll find Mr. Wingate's name mentioned in the record. He had it in for me, and it seems he also has it in for Todd, here. I will vouch for this guy. He has worked for us nearly a year, and we have nothing but good to say about him. You can check with Rob on that. He's a hard worker, competent with the horses, and generally behaves himself." He could sense Todd stiffening beside him. "I think we need to get our lawyer to write a letter in response, but I wanted to report what's going on—keep a running police diary, if you will. And say hi to—can't remember his name, but a year ago we kept him and Clarence and Mel pretty busy one day."

"Oh, yeah!" The dispatcher grinned. "We remember that day! You been staying out of trouble pretty good lately."

When Jeth and Todd got back in the car, Todd looked at him. "You didn't squeal on me."

"Of course not. I gave you my word. As far as I'm concerned, that episode is gone, erased. If you were to do something equally stupid, I'd probably tell Rob, but this one is forever off my plate. And if you've picked up anything 'religious' along the way while you've been with us, you might want to remember that God erases slates—clean—when we turn to Him."

After that day, Jeth could do nothing wrong in Todd's eyes.

30

I think I should go see Cindy again," Jeth said to Rob. "What do you say? Could be good, could be bad. I've got to tell her about Janni—sometime. I wish I could get in touch with her and Brandon to find out what's going on. But even if I could, she's still married. And even if she were totally out of the picture, I still don't know if seeing Cindy is right or wrong."

"Buddy, you're asking the wrong oracle," said Rob. "I don't do platitudes and simplistic advice anymore, remember?"

"Pastor Rick said the same thing."

"Not surprised. Anyone with sense keeps a good distance from you in thunderstorms. I can only stand here and pray. And hunker down till it's resolved."

Jeth called and made arrangements about when and where to meet. He was nervous when he left. "Do I look all right? With Janni, I never had to worry what I looked like."

"You're fine. Go for it, dude!" Rob grinned and slapped him on the back.

They met in a larger town, and this time, Cindy had Devon with her. This jolted Jeth, and he didn't know exactly why. He had accepted the existence of her son, but it had somehow passed by as not part of the equation. He was able to talk easily with the boy and guessed accurately that he was into soccer. But when he learned that he was Brandon's age, he knew immediately why it had shaken him. Somehow, Brandon was speaking through Devon, and Jeth needed to listen.

Jeth insisted that they eat lunch at a restaurant of Devon's choosing. They laughed and joked and stole French fries from each other. Afterward, they walked a couple of blocks down the street to a movie theater. "Okay, pal," said Jeth, "which movie do you want to see?"

Devon's eyes lit up, and he studied the options carefully. He looked first at Jeth, then at his mother, and said, "That one there—*Singhi Waters.*"

Jeth cocked his jaw at an angle. "Nope. Not that one. Has to be PG-thirteen or better."

Devon frowned. "But that's the one I want to see. It's, like, wicked awesome. You said I could pick." He looked at his mom.

"No," said Jeth, "over here. This is not playing me against her. I'm buying the ticket. I have the final say."

Devon kicked the mosaic floor, then muttered, "Okay...I'm sorry."

After he made his second choice—sullenly—and they had seen him into the approved theater, Cindy looked at Jeth. "I'm sorry I brought him."

"No, it was the right thing to do. I wasn't sure what to do or which direction to go till I saw him. Then it clicked."

"You're really good with kids."

"Yeah, maybe. At least short-term." Pain crossed his face. "He's the same age as Brandon."

"Brandon? A...son? You didn't tell me." Her tone was accusatory.

"Yes...no...sort of." As they walked, he told her the whole story, choking on Brandon's "I wish you were my dad." "So," he went on, "your baggage, my baggage...and I have no idea how God will sort it out. Technically I'm free, but not emotionally, and that's why I've been drawing lines. Maybe the lines will be taken away, or maybe they'll be cleaned and polished. I know that doesn't help you, but it helps straighten my thinking a little. I know now that I can't forget Brandon. When I first saw Devon this morning, I felt like I'd been slapped, like Brandon had been calling and calling my name and I hadn't been listening. I am, after all, the closest thing to a real dad the boy's ever had. I'm sorry I can't be more hopeful. I care for you very much. Under different circumstances, and with time, I could probably say I love you, but for now..."

"The lines."

"Yes, lines."

They picked up Devon and then, at Jeth's choice of a restaurant, listened to a rehash of the movie, recounted enthusiastically.

The three of them took the parting hard. Jeth suggested a group hug, and it was a long one.

31

Jeth found Rob asleep on the couch in the trailer. The latter sat up groggily. "Are you okay?"

"Yeah. It came clear almost right away. I still don't know which way to jump, but I do know I need to do something about Brandon. That hit me in the face. But how or what is the question—especially if I can't get hold of him or Janni."

"Have they moved, you think?" asked Rob.

"I doubt it. They pulled their number offline, obviously. Janni may have a new cell-phone number, or Daddy...I don't want to think about that. I'll just go. Can't do it tomorrow. Maybe Thursday, unless something urgent turns up here."

Jeth slept late in the morning. When he finally dragged himself out, he said, "I feel like I've been run over."

"Why don't you go back to bed?"

"No, the Askerly boys are coming today, and we need to have Indigo and Duchess looking pretty."

"Have you eaten?"

"Some coffee. Not hungry."

He tried to bulldog through, but within an hour, Rob said, "Is it nine-one-one time?"

Jeth went white and wide-eyed. He said nothing and got Dusty out of her stall, but he was back in ten minutes. He slid off and cried, "Help me, Rob!"

"Come over here and lie down."

"No. I don't know what it is. I can't see!"

"You mean that figuratively, I hope."

"No. I can hardly see you. Pray! What am I supposed to do?"

"I'll pray, but you have to lie down. You're too big to catch and lay out, and that's what's next. We've been there."

Jeth crumbled to the ground. Rob knelt beside him, his hands on Jeth's head and eyes. Jeth grabbed Rob's arm, his breathing just short of sobs, then struggled to get up. "Help me to the trailer. I've got to go."

Rob took the obvious meaning and hustled him along.

"Brandon. I've got to get to Brandon."

"Tomorrow, when you feel better."

"No, today. Right now."

"Jeth, you can't drive."

"I have to."

"I'll take you."

"No! I'll get there. I'll be all right."

"Take the truck. The GPS'll tell you when to turn. Not good, but better than not seeing anything, and it might get you there in one piece. Watch the step."

"Right. Like you don't need the truck. God only knows how long I'll be there."

Rob sighed. "This is crazy." His eyes followed Jeth as he stuffed things into a trash bag. "At least you can see well enough to pack."

"Think. What do I need?"

"Toothbrush? Shaver, underwear, shirts, pants…"

"My Bible." He grabbed it, along with other books, seemingly at random. He pulled a twist tie from a drawer to fasten the bag but dropped it to rummage through the closet for a baseball and glove. "Make me a sandwich. Enough food to get me there. And water."

"You need money?"

"Look in my wallet."

"You've got a fair amount. Plus a credit card. I'll give you some ones for tolls. Too bad you don't have E-ZPass in your— Wait! I'll get mine out of the truck."

"No! Just give me ones. That'll be good."

The two of them hauled his stuff to the car. Jeth turned and hugged Rob.

Rob stepped back. "You look awful. You sure you don't want me to go along?"

"I feel awful, but I can see pretty well. I can do it—I know that much. I'll call when I can."

Rob watched him leave, then went to the barn to unsaddle Dusty and turn her out, muttering grimly to himself.

At suppertime, Jeth called Rob and got a relieved, *"You made it! I've been kicking myself for letting you go."*

"I'm in town but haven't gone to the house yet," Jeth told him. "I called now because I don't know when I'll have another chance. I felt awful, Rob. Like driving through thick fog, but God was better than a GPS. Got me through traffic, made the right turns when I could hardly read the signs. I can't explain. But Rob..." He paused long, then went on. "The sense that I was to do this thing was so heavy on me that I just...kept driving, *feeling* but not *knowing*... I'm not—" He sighed. "I don't know how to say it. God was pushing me, and there was no turning back. All the way, Maybelle's verse about being clothed with power from on high kept pounding at me. God...Maybelle...Ezekiel..." His voice trailed off. "Yeah, I'm here, all right. Standing at the base of some unclimbable mountain, or maybe a bottomless pit or unbridgeable chasm. I've never been so afraid in my life. Everything up to now—all just practice. This is what I was made to do, Rob. I'm sure of it. Not ride Dynamo, but...*this*...and I don't know what *this* is! A book has been handed to me, and I'm scared to death to look at the first page."

"Maybe that's the way Jesus felt on that donkey ride into Jerusalem. Hell lay ahead, but the size and the shape..."

"Yeah. The size and shape. I'm heading for the police station right now, like last time. If Sgt. Reye isn't there, they'll be able to pull the record. At least I got those guys on my side."

A half hour later, at the house, Jeth took a big breath and opened the first page of his unknowable book by ringing the doorbell.

32

Brandon jerked the door open, his fractional look of surprise turning to volcanic rage. Jeth managed to shoulder in before the boy could slam the door. He was shaken by Brandon's fury but stayed quiet. After discharging his entire toxic vocabulary, Brandon spun around and pounded up the stairs. Jeth followed but fell on the third step, just as Janni came screaming from another room downstairs.

"Shoot!" Jeth picked himself up. "Can't do two steps at a time."

"Jeth!" Her hands flew to her face. "Is that you? Are you all right?"

"Yes. Stay there. I'll be down in a bit."

Brandon slammed his door repeatedly until Jeth neared the top of the stairs. He banged it once more and turned the privacy lock. Jeth examined the doorknob closely and inserted a fingernail to unlock it. He listened a moment to the mayhem inside the room, then opened the door. Brandon saw him over his shoulder and tried to run out. Jeth grabbed him, knowing full well that the boy was now tall enough and strong enough to get away easily, but memory and the tight grip of Jeth's left hand turned him back. He threw himself on the bed, shaking off Jeth's grasp. Jeth knelt beside him but didn't touch him.

"You called me, buddy, but I didn't hear you till yesterday, and then I came as fast as I could. I'm here and not leaving till you say it's okay. I was sick this morning and couldn't see much, but I came anyway, and I'm not leaving."

"You won't stay."

"I will."

"You can't."

"Who says?"

"If you don't know, you'll find out. Go away now. You'll only make it worse. I hate you!"

"Yeah, I can tell. I can tell you hurt bad. I didn't come soon enough. I'm sorry."

Brandon lifted his head to look at Jeth. "You think sorry makes it okay?" he roared. "That you can fix it? And fix Janni?"

"I'll get to Janni. Right now I'm here with you. We're nowhere near the fix stage yet. You can't fix what you can't see."

"You can't ever fix it. Get out!"

"Roar at me all you want. I'm here for the duration. Stay here while I see to Janni."

He found her sobbing on the couch. This was not good. Janni's emotional control had always been proverbial. On principle, she willed away tears. He ached to hold her but knew he'd lose any traction he might have in this household. "I'm here to help, but it has to be without touching you. That's the rule we have to play under. Now, stop crying so we can talk. I want you to start at the top and tell me what's happening. Where's Bryan?"

"He's dying."

"Well, I hardly think that's what set Brandon to spitting and clawing. What from?"

"Cancer. Prostate, liver—don't know what all. Even he doesn't know. Just gave up." She wiped her eyes and blew her nose. "Doesn't matter. He's got us chained and penned, right where he wants us. If we escape the chain, there's still the pen. No matter what happens, we're dead. If he dies before August eight, I'm up on a murder charge. If he dies later, he's rigged it so I'm ruined and Brandon entailed by the state. He knows he's dying, and his death wish is to take us both down with him. Jeth, it's a tangle of razor wire. I can't begin to understand the legal part, but I know clearly—he spells it plainly, again and again—that he and Daddy have full control over my life, now and forever."

Jeth whistled through his teeth. "Brandon wasn't kidding. What's your father got to do with it? I thought he pushed you into marrying Bryan so I'd be out of the picture once and for all."

She looked away. "Oh, he did. But when he heard you took Brandon, he didn't say anything, but I could tell I was cooked. He doesn't forget grudges—ever.

"And it gets worse every day," she hurried on. "Bryan can't take care of himself, can't even get out of bed. I desperately want to walk out on him, but Daddy would find me, no matter where I went. I know he would. But staying here…" She stared at the blackness outside the window, her eyes dull and lifeless. "I have to do loathsome things…and I can't."

"Would it make any difference if I were the one who was helpless?"

"Of course it would. I hate Bryan. I want him to die, except if he does, I'm dead, too."

"How about Brandon? Is he on your side or in limbo somewhere?"

"Huh! The good you did is long gone. It was one thing when he was in school, but now that it's summer, he just holes up in his room and marinates in the mess."

Jeth rubbed his chin. "Seems I got a jungle to whack through. I'll need a—"

"You *can't* stay here, Jeth. That will only make it worse."

"That's what Brandon said. Janni, you don't know what God put me through to get me here. I'm not leaving."

"Don't forget: My father—dear Daddy—is the silent partner in this business. I don't know how, but he is. And he'd put you back in prison in a nanosecond. You know that."

"I'm here to stay. We'll take each day and whatever it brings. I will not leave either you or Brandon alone in this. Now, where can I sleep? It's been a long, hard day. I don't need much. The floor in Brandon's room will do. Had experience with that. We'll tackle Bryan in the morning."

Janni looked at him, mouth trembling. "I don't know how your coming can possibly help, but in this nanosecond...I'm glad you're here."

33

Jeth was awakened in the morning by shouting downstairs, but before he went down, he woke Brandon. "I'm still here. I want you to know that. I'll be back after I've bearded the lion in his den."

After a stop in the bathroom and a splash of water on his face, Jeth followed the sound of heated conversation and found Janni and Bryan in the small room off the far end of the living room. Bryan's office had evidently been retrofitted as a bedroom. Bookshelves straddled the front window, and assorted photos and certificates on the garage wall framed a hospital bed. Two mismatched nightstands were on either side: to the right, a small black one with a lockable drawer and an open shelf; to the left, a larger, two-drawer stand holding a medium-sized lamp, assorted bottles and glasses, tissues, and a small basin of water. Another door to the left led to the kitchen. A cheap plastic wastebasket and folding chair between that door and the bed finished the décor.

Bryan looked up when Jeth darkened the doorway. He was a gaunt, disheveled skeleton, his face further marred by sharp-graven lines of pain. The wrath native to his eyes turned steel-hard on seeing Jeth. "So. You're the hornet that sneaked in last night to sting my wife and son!"

Jeth scratched through his uncombed hair. "Yeah, it did cause a stir, didn't it? We'll have to work on that, but right now you're next in line."

"Get out!" Bryan shouted, then immediately grimaced.

"What's happening here?" Jeth turned to Janni.

"He's not passing water, and he wants me to put a catheter in. I can't do it! We have to call someone."

"No! You *can* do it. You *will* do it!" shouted Bryan, his voice rising in pitch.

Janni turned away, fighting tears.

"Yes!" Bryan hissed. "Your lover comes on the scene, and along with him the waterworks. Cheap act. Get out!" he roared at Jeth. "Get out, or I'll call the police!"

Jeth picked up the kit that lay on the bed and turned the box over. "Go ahead. They know me. Tell 'em Jeth sent you. Now, this can't be all that complicated. The idea is to break through the stoppage and get the liquid out of your bladder. They did that on me in the hospital."

"Don't you dare touch me!"

"Well, I'm the alternative to the rock—in this case, your full bladder—and the hard place, which is Janni not wanting to do anything about it."

"I'll have you arrested!"

"You said that. Well, not 'arrested,' but same thing. That's what it would take to get me out of here. I told Brandon I wouldn't go unless I was dragged out. In the meantime, let's get your bladder emptied, and then you can roar more comfortably."

Jeth laid out the equipment on the bed and looked at the directions. "This is what goes in, prelubricated, it says. Okay. Simple enough. Install the piping and let the water flow. Says to clean you up first. Gloves? I suppose that would be smart—for both of us." He grinned.

Janni reached inside a drawer and wordlessly pulled out two gloves, a bag of cotton balls, and a bottle of antiseptic.

"Okay, we're in business." Jeth leaned over Bryan and began to pull down his pajama bottoms.

Bryan grabbed his arm. "*Don't touch me!*" he snarled.

Jeth's eyes went steely. "If I were to put my hand in the wrong place and lean a little, you definitely wouldn't like it. Now, put your hands where they belong, and let's get on with it."

Bryan, sweating and gasping, released his hand. Jeth worked slowly, gently, talking softly the whole time. "Janni, get something to catch it in. There's no bag here. Didn't think of that." When she returned with a bedpan, he worked the tube in until urine began to flow. "A lot there. No wonder you were bellowing. Let's roll you on your side so it'll drain—that's it. Feel better?"

Bryan lay pale with his eyes closed. Jeth finished up, gave the tube to Janni, and took off his gloves. He wrung out the washcloth in the basin of water and wiped Bryan's face.

"Go to hell!" Bryan snapped without opening his eyes.

"Um…not today, thanks. Been there, though. Now I'm here, and what can I do to help you?"

"*Help* me! Kill me, is what you're saying! You just want me out of the way."

"With all the bear traps you've set around Janni and Brandon, I'd say killing you would be counterproductive. I'm here to make you as comfortable as a dying man can be. You can threaten to send me back to prison, but if God wants me here—and He made that pretty clear—then nothing you—"

"God! God d—" He broke off with a spasm of coughing that touched off a spasm of pain.

Jeth held him, then eased him back and rubbed his chest. "Roll to your side again. I'll rub your back. Take shallow breaths—that's it."

Bryan groaned and looked at Janni with agonized eyes. "How long?" he asked hoarsely.

She looked at her watch. "Another half hour. We can give it to you now…"

He rolled his head back and forth.

"Can you believe!" said Janni. Sarcasm scribed her face and voice. "Doesn't want to be overmedicated. Might miss whatever's going on—something I might do to him."

"Okay, we'll ride it out. Does it hurt when I rub your chest?"

Bryan didn't answer, but neither did he grimace. Jeth worked from his chest to his arms and shoulders, and when injection time finally came, he rubbed his back until he fell asleep. Jeth leaned back. Janni started to give him a backrub, but he raised his hand and shook his head. "Ground rules." He stood up. "Any food around? Been awhile since I ate."

"I'm sorry. I should have given you something last night."

He sat at the kitchen bar while she prepared eggs and toast. "Catheter. That's a new one for me. I can see I'm going to need a full bag of tricks around here."

34

They somehow got through the next two days without bloodshed. Bryan harped on the refrain that Janni was cheating on him in his own house while he lay dying. At first, Jeth patiently assured him that he had no intention of even touching Janni. Then he noticed that the attacks came mostly right before a shot was due. From then on, he simply listened and massaged.

Brandon was less predictable. While Bryan slept, Jeth went to the boy's bedroom, almost always finding him lying on the bed. He shrugged off any touch, but as Jeth persisted with shorter, more frequent contact, he gradually came to accept it—a small but important victory.

Janni seemed always to have a glass of wine in hand. She offered one to Jeth from time to time. He took the first but not the second or any subsequent offer. One day when she came with two drinks in hand, he stood and took them both, then went to the kitchen and dumped them in the sink.

"What are you doing?" Janni screeched.

"I'm dumping wine in the sink. Seems plain enough to see."

"How dare you!" Her eyes blazed with some of their old fire.

"Good! Some gumption left, after all. Look—I need all my circuitry for this, and I'd like my right-hand man to have her brain switched on. I know you're stressed, and drinks help, but you're not doing me—or yourself—a favor. Please think about it."

Jeth called Rob just to hear his voice. "I'm holding a pressure cooker with three valves, wondering which will blow first."

"Are you getting enough sleep?"

Jeth laughed. "Sleep? What's that? At least I'm not on the floor in Brandon's room, like the first night. Janni fixed up a daybed in the sunroom, and there's a recliner in the TV room off the kitchen that we take turns on at night. He needs somebody nearby."

"Jeth—"

"It's not as bad as it sounds. This is brand-new stuff for me, and I'm feeling my way like a blind man."

"Speaking of blind…"

"I'm okay now. As I got closer here, everything started clearing up. I could see better, I felt better. I don't think it was coincidence but can't prove it. I am pretty sure that if I'd pulled a Jonah and run the other way, it would've gotten worse, and I'd be counting ribs inside of a whale. I do know I got here in the nick of time. This is a hard place, and I don't know what's really going on. A lot of dark corners I can't see yet. But it's where I need to be right now. Hey— when Bryan's pain gets bad, he actually reaches for my hand."

"Jeth, think of all you put into Dynamo and the grief he gave you in return. But you knew where you wanted him to go and put up with kicks, bites, and getting tossed. I don't know what Maybelle would say, but I see a connection here. If you're where you need to be, then Dynamo will come through."

JETH WENT TO Brandon's room one afternoon. "How about a walk, buddy?"

Brandon lay unmoving on the bed.

"Why don't you get up, and we'll go outside?"

The boy shook his head but not violently, nor did he swear, and with a little more cajoling, he dragged himself up, and they went downstairs.

Outdoors, Jeth asked, "You want to talk?"

"No!"

"That's pretty definite. We'll walk without talking for as long as—" He looked at his watch. "No, have to be back in half an hour. Sorry!"

They walked in silence, Brandon kicking twigs and pebbles as though a clean sidewalk were life's highest priority. After fifteen minutes, Jeth began to talk. "This is a hard thing we're doing, isn't it? I've never taken care of a dying person before, and I haven't the slightest idea how to spring the traps before you and Janni fall into them. And I don't know what kind of Band-Aids will stop your bleeding." He went on to tell Brandon of the day he'd heard him call—a clear, unequivocal message that came from seeing his counterpart, Devon. He told him of Dusty and how he had gotten to know Cindy and found she was a Christian and a very nice person.

Brandon stopped kicking, and his eyes sliced toward Jeth suspiciously. "You love her? Gonna marry her?"

"Huh! I've met her twice. I think I'd need a bit more time before deciding to marry someone. I like her and could possibly love her in time. But your calling out to me put everything on hold. I told Cindy I wasn't free to even consider a love relationship. You were number one on my attention pile. Cindy is on a shelf indefinitely. A lot could happen between now and when I see her again. Right now, I'm here for you."

They neared the house. Jeth put a hand on Brandon's shoulder. "What I just told you is probably as dangerous as a gun right now. You could do a lot of damage to Janni and to me. I will tell her everything I told you, but I can't do it right away. Can you give me that much?"

Brandon said nothing, and they went into the house.

As they stepped in, Janni appeared from the dining room. Brandon turned on her viciously. "Jeth's got another woman. They're an item. Did y'know that? And she's got a kid, and he gets along with him better 'n me. He's just waiting till Bryan dies, and then he'll dump us and run off with her." Then he bellowed, ran upstairs, and slammed the door five times.

Janni looked at Jeth in stark horror.

"Sheesh! Which fire do I tend to first?" Jeth looked up the stairway, then at Janni. "Whose version of this soap opera are you going to believe—his or mine? I'll tell you the straight story as soon as I can, but my guess is he's testing the fences to see if they're going to hold. We did fine till a few seconds ago, when I made the mistake of pointing out that I'd handed him a loaded gun. I don't think he would have fired if you hadn't come out just now."

From upstairs, through a wide-open bedroom door, they heard a raunchy CD at full volume.

"Yup. Testing...one, two, three. And he's hoping I'll gallop up there and throw the player out the window. I give him maybe three minutes before the noise tops his pain threshold and makes him shut it off, especially when he sees it's not working. Is Bryan awake?"

Janni pushed her hair back and returned Jeth's steady look. They had hardly turned toward Bryan's bedroom when the music stopped. They looked at each other and smiled weakly. Janni turned back and sank slowly onto the couch, a look of infinite sadness masking her face. "It helps to know he's not my child, and that I'm not responsible for what he does."

"But he's a child in desperate need, and—"

"Our baby..." She stopped and put a hand over her mouth. "Our baby would've been nine this year," she said, her voice scarcely audible.

Jeth drew ice into his lungs and stared at her. Then he dropped to his knees and bowed his head to the floor and stayed there a long time.

An hour later, Jeth got Janni to stay with Bryan while he went upstairs. As he sat down on the bed, Brandon cringed and moaned. Jeth rubbed the boy's back. After some hard, jerky breaths, Brandon whispered, "I'm sorry."

"I know you are, buddy. The bleeding got really bad out there, and you got scared. You know I love you, and I'm here for you. Janni's okay. She's tough. We haven't talked yet, but we will, maybe tonight. Why don't you get up and do something to get your mind off everything? Your room might be a good place to start. It looks and smells like the back end of a garbage truck."

35

The next day, when Bryan finally fell asleep after a particularly rough spell, Janni brought Jeth a glass of iced tea, and they both collapsed in the living room. Jeth wiped perspiration off his face. "While he sleeps, maybe we could crank up the air conditioner. I can put a blanket over him."

Janni laughed sardonically. "Our AC doesn't do cool at this temp. How about some ice in a bag?"

"Forget it. I'll live." He looked around the room. "Does Bryan really like this house? I can't imagine you ever agreeing to live here."

Again the bitter laugh. "This was Daddy's wedding present. A charming bit of real estate, don't you think? He probably couldn't off-load it anywhere else."

"And you guys just took it—gratefully."

"Oh, no. Not even Bryan was grateful, but he was earning brownie points and made it *very* clear that I was not to complain."

Jeth gnawed the side of his finger. Janni got up, dug in the coat closet, and came up with a huge, hideous palm-frond fan, which she waved over Jeth.

"Oh, stop!" He snatched it from her. "Sit down and rest. Save your strength and benevolence for Bryan."

"Benevolence! That's your corner, not mine. I'm just the relief pitcher. Not that I'm ungrateful for what you're doing," she added quickly as Jeth's face hardened. "For the first time in months, I have a tiny trace of hope. We're still in the same mess, Brandon and I, but at least I've got an ally. I can't tell you what your being here means to me."

Jeth swallowed some tea and ran his finger up the side of the glass, making a line in the condensation. "Benevolence. I like that word. He's dying, Janni, but it's too early to tag his toe. We can't just sit here, watching it happen. We've both got to stick with him, doing what we can. Brandon should, too, but he's—"

Janni got up and swirled angrily back and forth. "You can't fix Bryan, you can't fix Brandon, and don't even try to fix me! That's not what you're here for."

"I'm here for the three of you. You all need fixing."

She turned and got in his face. "*That's not your job!* At least not to fix me."

Jeth stared at her steadily until she backed off. "You need fixing perhaps most of all. You need to be able to love Bryan."

Janni spun away in exasperation and thrust her fingers through her hair. "I'm *sorry*," she rasped. "There's no way I can love Bryan." She turned back toward Jeth. "I can't do the things you're doing. Catheter, suppositories, poopy diapers… Don't ask me to!"

Jeth grinned. "You learn diapers real fast in a house with a baby!"

Janni's eyes blazed. "Well, I'm sorry about that, too. If you recall, our baby is dead!"

Jeth ignored her volley and chose his next words carefully. "Janni, listen to me. I'm asking you to care for Bryan. Care about him."

"*Care* about him! Why should I care about him? From the day we got married, he's been a monster. Never while he draws breath could I care about him."

Jeth studied her face. "Janni, Bryan is going to die, but you're dying right along with him. You've never been a mean, spiteful person…well, maybe once…but right before my eyes, you—"

"Jeth, *you don't know how much I hate him!*"

"I do know, and that's why I'm talking to you. You've got every reason to hate him, but how about taking a different route and trying to forgive him? Now, hear me out before going up in flames. Anger and hatred can only fester. It won't accomplish anything. It won't help you; it won't change Bryan. Lay it down. Set it aside. Go in there and hold his hand. *The only way he will ever change is for us to love him.*"

Janni hugged her chest, a gray, torpid smog fouling the beauty of her face.

"I didn't say it would be easy," said Jeth. "Hate dies hard, but love is way more powerful. It might even undo whatever legal trap you're in. You can best help me—and help yourself—by trying to help Bryan."

JETH CALLED MAYBELLE one Sunday afternoon. He desperately needed the balm of her voice. "Maybelle, I'm in a junkyard. Three people, totally broken. And I can't figure how the pieces go together."

"*Jeth, remember what I told you. God is in the salvage business. He's put you there with all that brokenness. Do you remember the verse that says, 'I can do all things through Christ who…'? Can you finish that verse, Jeth?*"

"That's easy.'*All things through Christ who strengthens me.*'"

"*No, that's not how it should go. 'I can do all things through Christ who weakens me.' The apostle Paul had to learn that. When he was in trouble, God said, 'My grace is sufficient for you, for my power is made perfect in weakness.'*"

"'Through Christ who weakens me.' The Revised Maybelle Version. You're something else! You got me here in one piece, you know. Did Rob tell you about my not being able to see much?"

"He did. God put blinders on you so you'd have to trust Him."

"Well, those verses you prayed at my baptism helped get me here. At first it was real bad, and I kept saying, 'Clothe me with power, clothe me with power.' And that other verse: *Jerusalem will be a city without walls…and I myself will be a wall of fire around it.'* If ever I needed that wall of fire, it's now. Will you pray it up for me, Maybelle?"

"That wall is already there, Jeth. It's done. Remember your 'tipping point'? The wall of fire went around you that day of Communion in the hospital. You didn't see it then, but God was preparing you for this very place. Here's something He may be showing you right now. Philippians says, 'I want to know Christ and experience the mighty power that raised him from the dead. I want to suffer with him, sharing in his death, so that one way or another I will experience the resurrection from the dead!' That's you, Jeth—suffering and sharing in His death. Resurrection, my dear. Don't lose sight of it."

"Okay, what translation is that? One verse you gave me took weeks to figure out where it came from."

"Let's see…it's the New Living Translation. *Do you have it?"*

"No, but—"

"You can have mine. I won't be needing it long. Do you remember—"

"Maybelle! Don't say that!"

"Do you remember that I asked God to make you a hug evangelist?"

"Huh! That's a big order. I can't touch Janni. Brandon isn't ready for hugs, and Bryan would go up in flames if I tried a hug on him."

"Oh, but you are hugging. Hugs come in many forms, you know. Everything you're doing is a hug in disguise. It's your heart that does the hugging, and with your big heart at work in all that brokenness, you just watch and see what God will do."

"If I live. They're sucking half my blood and all my heart."

"Who said anything about needing to live? One way or another—resurrection!"

"Maybelle, you're good for me. You're my angel. Hang in there for me—*please*—and I'll be okay."

PASSING URINE BECAME increasingly problematic for Bryan, and Jeth suggested that they leave the catheter in and attach a bag. "You'd be a lot more comfortable than having it put in every other day."

"No!"

"Is that *pro forma*, or do you have a reason? Think about it, and we'll talk again."

He did think and grudgingly said yes during the next catheterization.

"Good choice," said Jeth. "No more balloon bladder. But we need someone to show us what to do. The risk of infection goes—"

"No! No one here!"

Jeth sighed. Janni whispered, "Does it matter at this point?"

Later, in the kitchen, Jeth said, "Why is he so bent on not having outside help?"

Janni shrugged. "Do-it-yourself dying? Maybe he's afraid someone will put one over on him."

"If he fired his doctor, where are his pain meds coming from?"

Janni looked at him disgustedly. "With Daddy in the picture, you should need to ask?"

One morning, Jeth brought his Bible and, as Bryan came out of his drug fog, began to read, randomly at first, and then more intentionally. At first, he could read only a few minutes before restlessness set in, but gradually, as he experimented and found which types of Scripture were best tolerated, the time lengthened. Sometimes he would tuck in something from Maybelle's hymnbook, then go back to the Bible. Stories were best, from the Gospels but especially the story of David in the Old Testament. These seemed almost as effective as pain medication.

36

Meals were irregular at best, but when Janni did set the table and put out food, Jeth always called Brandon. He seldom came down, except at odd moments to grab whatever snacks he could find and take them upstairs. Jeth tolerated it for a couple of weeks, then told him that it was eat at the table when called or not at all.

Brandon chose not to remember their first McDonald's meal.

Jeth was ready for him. He said nothing but purchased padlocks to close off the food cupboards and refrigerator. And waited.

The explosion rattled the windows, but Jeth said nothing. Three hours later, while Janni was resting, Jeth himself prepared a meal and called Brandon. He came down, exhaling radioactive fumes, but sat at the table and ate.

After they finished eating, Jeth leaned back. "Buddy, we're working way too hard around here to put up with games. We'd all be happier if you'd knock off this business, but it's your choice. It's my choice whether or not to leave the locks in the kitchen."

Brandon stared at his plate.

Jeth got up and went to check on Bryan. When he came out, Brandon was rinsing dishes and loading the dishwasher. Jeth slung an arm around the boy's neck and knuckled his head.

Two days later, Brandon happened into Bryan's bedroom while Jeth was bathing him. Bryan was furious. "You *schmuk!*" he roared. "Get out of here! Nobody with a shred of decency walks in on his old man when he's naked! Are you just trying to—"

Jeth tossed the washcloth and bent over Bryan, his eyes steel blades. "You will not say that again," he said softly.

Bryan's breath came fast. "He's my son. I can say what I please!"

"He's not your son. You've never been a father. A sperm donor, yes, but never a father. There's still time, though. While you live, there's still time."

Brandon backed out of the room, but he was smiling.

THE SMILE DIDN'T last. Brandon and Janni crossed swords, and Jeth heard pitched battle in the kitchen. But when Brandon screamed *"You skank!"* he was in the kitchen within seconds and had the boy by the shoulder. "That is unacceptable. You will not say that again."

"Who's gonna stop me? You can't—not anymore."

In less than two seconds, Jeth had Brandon's arm behind his back and was leaning on him. "I learned some things in prison. That was only one. Don't try it again."

He let the boy go and, without looking at him, went back to the bedroom.

Brandon stormed upstairs. Janni went for a walk. A half hour later, Brandon came down while Jeth was folding laundry in the living room. The boy stood and fidgeted, but Jeth wouldn't look at him.

"Jeth…" But words refused to come.

Jeth pulled him to the couch and waited.

"Why is it so hard?" Brandon's voice was choked.

Jeth looked down. "Yeah, it's hard. How well I know!"

Finally, Brandon whispered, "I'm sorry."

Jeth put an arm around him. "Are we okay now?"

Brandon's face and voice threatened disarray. "Does this mean you're my real dad now?"

"Not legally, but I'm here for you like a dad would be. And a dad teaches his kid where the lines are. Janni is a lady, and you don't abuse ladies—ever. Now, if one comes at you with a knife or gun, she's no lady, and you either 'abuse' her real fast or learn how to run faster than a speeding bullet."

They sat for a minute, saying nothing. Then Jeth looked at him. "There's one more big apology, you know."

Brandon studied his bare toes. "Yeah, I know…"

Again they were silent until Janni come in. Brandon looked desperately at Jeth, who signaled Janni to sit down but did nothing more to help the boy.

He fidgeted and cleared his throat three times.

Janni looked from one to the other.

Finally, Brandon mumbled, "ImsorryJanni."

Janni's face tightened. She couldn't speak.

"Buddy," Jeth said, "you once hugged Janni for me. Do you think you could do it again?"

Brandon looked up, panic-stricken, but Janni stood with arms wide, and he had no choice. His hug was short and awkward, and he turned quickly and ran up the stairs—but the door did not slam.

37

Rob, I need to talk about something that doesn't have the smell of death on it. What's going on there? How's Jessie doing? And Dusty? Alejo still singing the horses awake in the morning?"

"*We're fine here. Dusty gets a lot of exercise. Katie loves her. She sometimes tucks Jessie in a sling and rides for an hour, or sometimes goes out just because it's fun.*"

"Is Katie doing okay? You said the other day she was on you about something."

"*She's mostly over that. Tizzies come, tizzies go, and I try to pay attention, read the tea leaves. A few ups and downs, but we're in better shape than two years ago!*"

"Time to start thinking on Kid Number Two?"

"*Huh...Kid Number Two. Now that you mention it, maybe the current batch of tizzies... Good thinking, Jeth! I'll let you know if a pregnancy test kit shows up here anytime soon.*"

"You do that! Been polishing your boy sperm?"

"*Whatever comes, we'll be happy.*"

"Tell me about Cecil and Todd."

"*The big news is Cecil getting a blue on Pixie—in an open class, no less. At Shackleton. He rode real fine and seems to be hitting his stride. And he gave Toogie his first go at show jumping, and while the colt gawked too much to get anywhere, I was impressed by his spirit and effort. He's incredible on sharp turns. You always joked about quarter-horse genes. Now I half believe it. Cecil's done well with him. Even had a guy interested in buying. Told him he's not for sale.*"

"Super! Tell Cecil I'm proud. Rob, we've helped turn a couple of youngsters—Cecil and Toogie—into men! How about that?"

"You're right! Both of them—class acts!"

"And Mama Berry? She still helping Katie?"

"Oh yes, and do we love her! Such a calming influence! Cecil was only half the gift package we got when you pushed for taking him on. Have I ever thanked you for doing that?"

"Yeah, well, you pushed for Todd. How's he doing?"

"He's doing fine. Still won't enter classes with Wingate horses, but when he does ride, he consistently gets ribbons, even some reds and a blue. No offense, but you being off the map was the best thing that could've happened to him. He's a real asset—responsible, works his tail off, and seems to love being here. He keeps coming up with new jump configurations. Remember that show with the giant butterfly wings that scared the daylights out of Nightshade? Todd rigged up colored sheets to flap in the wind, and now hardly anything fazes our guys."

"Wow! Good lad!"

"And no further legal action since our man sent a letter to Wingate's attorney."

"Does he still go to church once in a while?"

"Oh, yes. He endures, but he came two weeks in a row, which surprised me. He asks about you and says hi."

"Hi back! He's come a long way. And Rob," Jeth went on, "you were right about taking him on. I see that now. I needed a fly in my ointment right then, and I think we both grew up by rubbing off each other. And when I got…removed, shall we say, Todd was there and ready to show. Tell him to ride against Wingate. It'll put some backbone in him."

"Huh! We'll see how that goes over!"

"So you're the only one in that slot?"

"Well, yes. Pretty much. Wingate horses win more than we do, but we still get a lot of traffic. Oh! I forgot to tell you. Bought a new horse last week. Medium-sized Thoroughbred gelding with enough Arabian

thrown in to make him bright and quick, with absolutely amazing stamina. He's—"

"How old? Name?"

"He's young—six or so—dappled brown, like Woodbine. Comes with the name Sultan's Mirage. We're still arguing about what to call him."

"Huh! Sully, maybe. Put Katie on it. She comes up with good names. Who's his major trainer?"

"We haven't decided that, either. To start, I think we'll share him around and see who fits best....Changing the subject, Jeth, tell me how you're doing. Give me the buzz."

"Brandon's coming around, but it's up and down. Too much stress for a kid his age, and I don't have time to help him unpack it. We're getting some semblance of order. The boy pretty much stays within my lines now, and so does Bryan. Have to draw new ones nearly every day, but we're learning. Bryan's getting weaker. He hurts more but won't take more pain meds. His inner clock is geared to time, not the demands of pain. It's uncanny how he knows almost to the minute when it's time. Still says we're trying to kill him. No other reason I'd be there, to his thinking. I keep telling him I'm here to help all three of them, and dying trumps everything else. Then the threats... He told Janni early on that if he died before August eighth, she'd be up for murder. We're past that date, but what else she's in for I still don't know."

"What's all that about?"

"Well, she says she doesn't understand it, but her body language tells me she knows more than she's letting on. It's bad—that's clear. I keep telling Bryan that if he doesn't change his mind and his will, or whatever legal hammerlock he's cooked up, he'll just be a footnote on somebody else's gravestone. Mostly I get another harangue."

"Is he close to dying?"

"Hard to say. I've never done this before. Tell Maybelle her hymnbook soothes the dragon. It's almost the best thing I can do when the pain gets really bad, and I don't know why. Whatever works."

"*Speaking of Maybelle, she's in the hospital with pneumonia. They're concerned, of course, but she's tough. She wanted me to tell you it wasn't stopping her from praying.*"

Panic rose in Jeth's throat, and his voice went tight. "Tell her I'm counting on her. She's my angel! She can't give up on me now!"

"*Jeth, this is undoubtedly the hardest thing you've ever done. You got Dynamo ready for the main event of his life, and in the same way, God has worked you up for this trial by fire. You're hitting your stride. You are Dynamo—made to rack, Jeth.*"

"Rack. Is that 'extreme gait' or 'extreme torture'?"

Rob laughed. "*Whichever—a tough go for you.*"

"Yeah. All that stuff I couldn't figure out was just training. And now I get to see if I learned it right."

"*Jeth, try not to go down in flames this time.*"

He almost did. Bryan had gone to sleep, and Janni was cleaning bathrooms—a job long overdue. Jeth rubbed his haggard face and heard Brandon in the kitchen. The boy looked at him guiltily when Jeth came in. "Okay if I take some Doritos upstairs?"

"What do you say we go outside and play catch for a while?"

Brandon looked from him to the cupboard and back.

"In my room is a black plastic bag. Find the ball and gloves, and we'll go out and toss a few."

Brandon sighed but turned obediently.

Neither of them seemed able to handle the ball. Brandon frowned and said, "The sun's in Jetson's eyes, and he misses the ball."

Jeth smiled. "He's got it now, and here comes an easy slider to Brandovski."

But Jeth was dropping as many balls as Brandon, and when he fumbled an easy catch, Brandon scowled. "You doing this on purpose? Like, trying to make me look good?"

"Nope." Jeth shook his head. "Jetson's old injury is hanging him up. Sorry." But after another bobble, he said, "Jetson's toast. Here comes the coach...to the mound. Looks like...the pitcher is headed for the showers."

Brandon threw him a mix of anger and alarm, then slammed his glove to the ground and stalked indoors. Jeth retrieved the ball and walked slowly toward the discarded glove. He stood for a moment, staring at the screen door, then took off his own glove and laid it and the ball gently on Brandon's.

A short while later, Janni came into Bryan's bedroom and saw Jeth sprawled on the floor. "Jeth!" she shrieked, kneeling by him.

Her cry woke Jeth and Bryan and brought Brandon leaping down the stairs.

Jeth sat up groggily, rubbing his head.

"What happened?" cried Janni. "Are you all right?"

"Yeah." He looked around vaguely. "I don't know... I'm okay, though. I'm okay."

"He's not okay," bellowed Brandon. "He wasn't okay outdoors. He's not okay now."

"He's exhausted," said Janni. "Jeth, you've got to get some sleep. You were up most of the night. Go to bed—right now! Come on. I'll help you."

Jeth shook his head, then looked at Brandon's wide, panicked eyes and pulled himself up. "I'll be all right," he said, but he clearly wasn't. He turned and put a hand on Bryan's leg. "I've got to mind the boss lady, but both these guys will take good care."

Brandon steadied Jeth as he limped toward the den. Jeth collapsed on the bed, mumbling, "Gloves." Brandon looked at him, then out the window. He left, and when he came back with the gloves, Jeth was snoring softly.

BRANDON WENT TO Bryan's room and slouched against the doorjamb. Janni looked up but said nothing. With a defensive edge to his voice, Brandon mumbled, "Whadda'y wamme t' do?"

Annoyance crossed Janni's face, but her voice stayed calm. "Well, you could unload the dishwasher or maybe get the trash ready to go out tomorrow."

Brandon chose the dishes but ended up doing both.

He came back later and again stood uncertainly. "You wanna eat? I had macaroni and cheese. There's some left. I can call if he wakes up."

Janni looked at him gratefully and put a hand on his shoulder as she went out.

Bryan woke within ten minutes and began writhing in pain. His eye caught Brandon sitting beside him, and he quickly looked straight ahead. Soon, though, he was wiping his face and breathing heavily.

Brandon thought hard. He could call Janni, or he could do what Jeth would do.

"Wanna hold on?"

Bryan looked sharply at him and then, seemingly satisfied that the boy was not mocking him, raised his skeletal fingers. When Brandon took them, unsure of what he was doing, Bryan gripped hard.

JETH CAME IN the kitchen next morning, freshly showered and much improved. Janni smiled. "You won't believe that boy! He did two huge things, and on top of that, he let me hug him!"

"Huh! I haven't gotten that yet! The kid is finally getting back on track."

"Back on track," said Bryan from the bedroom. "On track for what—killing me off?"

"Right. Uppermost on our minds." Jeth laughed and looked in on him. "We were talking about your super-guy son."

Bryan said nothing and closed his eyes.

LATER THAT DAY, Bryan lay pale and panting, eyes staring. Jeth had done everything he could. The dying man refused to eat. He had drunk some juice and been bathed, oiled, massaged. There was little else Jeth could do until pain-med time. He watched him silently for a minute, then reached for Maybelle's hymnbook, paged through it, and took Bryan's hand.

> *Come, ye sinners, poor and needy,*
> *Weak and wounded, sick and sore;*
> *Jesus ready stands to save you,*
> *Full of pity, love, and pow'r.*
>
> *Come, ye weary, heavy-laden,*
> *Lost and ruined by the fall.*
> *If you tarry till you're better,*
> *You will never come at all.*
>
> *Let not conscience make you linger,*
> *Nor of fitness fondly dream;*
> *All the fitness He requireth*
> *Is to feel your need of Him.*
>
> *I will arise and go to Jesus,*
> *He will embrace me in His arms;*
> *In the arms of my dear Savior,*
> *O there are ten thousand charms.*

As he read, Jeth felt the bed tremble. He looked up to see Bryan shaking with dry, wracking sobs. He set the book aside and put his hand on the man's head. "What is it, my friend? What can I do for you?"

Bryan looked at him, eyes wide and desperate. "Help me..."

Jeth stroked his head. "You want a savior, don't you? You want the mess cleaned up. But this has to be between you and God, Bryan. I'm here with you, but I can't do it for you. Dig down in the cesspool and hold each thing up and say, 'Forgive me, God.'"

"God... Help me, Jeth."

"Can you forgive your father?" This was a shot in the dark, but it brought another spasm of grief. "Your mother? They hurt you badly, didn't they?" He waited a moment. "How about the people you've hurt or destroyed? Lay it out before God. He knows what you've done, but He wants you to say it. It hurts—God knows it hurts. I've been there. I know."

Janni had come in, and she clung to the doorjamb.

"Read...again," Bryan pleaded.

Jeth took the book and handed it to Janni. "Page one forty-seven, I think. You read it."

She started, her voice trembling. "'Hear, gracious God, a sinner's cry...'? Is that it?"

"No, but it'll do."

She tried again but broke off. "I can't..."

Jeth took the book.

Hear, gracious God, a sinner's cry,
For I have nowhere else to fly;
My hope, my only hope's in Thee,
O God, be merciful to me.

To Thee I come, a sinner poor,
And wait for mercy at Thy door;
Indeed, I've nowhere else to flee
O God, be merciful to me.

To glory bring me, Lord, at last,
And there, when all my fears are past,

With all Thy saints, then, I'll agree
God has been merciful to me.

When he finished reading, Bryan was asleep—without pain medication.

38

Bryan allowed two exceptions to the no-one-in-the-house rule. The first was Janni's father. He used a key to enter, and when Janni came out of the bedroom, he forced his way past her and into the room. Jeth was rubbing oil on Bryan's parchment skin. When he saw Wingate, his face hardened, and he moved protectively to the foot of the bed. But Bryan waved his hand. "Jeth, Janni—out. Leave us."

Jeth stood a moment, eyes grim and unyielding. Then, without a word, he angled his shoulders and slid past Wingate. The door closed firmly, followed by the even louder bang of the kitchen door.

Janni looked at Jeth. "I can't think of anything worse that could happen," she said, despair constricting her voice. "Whatever move Bryan might have made in the right direction is going out the window—right now."

Jeth went to the couch and sat, chin resting on his hands. He needed Rob. He needed Maybelle. Dusty. Someone, something, to hug... The urge was so strong that he had to bite the back of his hand. Janni was five feet away, but with her, a hug would not be the end. He knew that. His fierce hunger would consume her. What sort of twisted retribution would it be for Papa Wingate to come out and see the stable boy making love to his daughter? Jeth buried his head in his hands. Then he reached out, pulled Janni to sit beside him, and held her hand tight. He was touching her. Deliberately. What would God do to him for that? It didn't matter. Nothing mattered.

Janni looked nervously at the bedroom door. "What are they talking about in there?"

Jeth said nothing and just stared at her hand. Then, "Janni, you've got to level with me. What is going on between Bryan and your father?"

She stiffened and pulled away. "How should I know? They don't include me in their conversations. I'm just—"

"Don't play that game. There's more to this than just Papa Wingate hating me—something you're not telling—and I need to know what it is."

Janni got up and paced the room, collecting new layers of anguish with each step. "Jeth, I can't tell you," she said. "It's too hard."

Jeth stood, too. "You've got to tell me."

"It wouldn't make any difference. There's nothing you could do to make it go away. It's not your problem!"

"It is my problem, and it might make a big difference."

"No! It wouldn't help." She turned to him. "Jeth, just hold me."

"I can't hold you. I gave my word. I already—"

"Your word! Just like your father. You're your father's son. Can't bend an inch. You—"

"Would you rather I be *your* father's son? Would that make it better?"

Janni's mouth turned hard and thin, and Jeth braced against a slap that she didn't deliver. He turned away. "I'm sorry. I shouldn't have said that." He swung around sharply to face her. "Janni, you need to tell me. I probably can't do anything about it, but I need to know. I need to be able to trust you. Please...before he comes out."

The fire in Janni's eyes dampened, and she sank to the couch. "Oh, Jeth," she said, "if only we could go back...back to watching birds, going to concerts, lying in tall—"

"Janni—stop. We can't go there. No tall grass here. We're slogging through a murky hell, and you've got to show me the size and shape of it."

Janni slumped even lower and drew a quivery breath. "All right, I'll tell you, but it won't help," she said, fingers interlocked and twisting. Jeth sat beside her, but she looked straight ahead, face stony and pale. With a big breath, she began.

"The day you went to prison, I went shrieking, screaming mad. At you, mostly. I know," she said as he looked up sharply. "I just was. No amount of anger could hurt my father, but I could hurt you. And with you being out of range, I had to take it out some other way. After kicking everything in sight for who knows how long, I got in the car and drove like a crazy woman. When I finally simmered down, I was near Croswell Manor House. The place was zinging, so I decided to go in and get puking drunk. I didn't care. I wouldn't know anybody, and no one would even notice." She studied her still-twisting fingers. "Jeth, I can't…"

Jeth separated her hands. "It's okay. You're doing fine."

She drew a shaky breath. "There was this guy. He sized me up fast. Long story short, we ended up in his room. All I remember is writing a bunch of silly notes back and forth. He got onto musical terms after he discovered I knew some. He may have started it, and I picked up the thread… Can't remember. The most ridiculous, adolescent thing I ever did in my life! Jeth, I—"

"I get the picture," he said gently. "Skip the sordids."

"You don't know. That's only half. Yes, it was stupid, asinine. I was drunk, he was drunk. But the real zinger didn't come till last fall, right after your accident. Daddy laid a newspaper in front of me. At first, I hadn't a clue what he was showing me. Some operative on trial for passing classified stuff to China via Venezuela or who knows where. The headline said, 'CIA Apprehends Head of Bulcroft Spy Ring. Trial Set for'…whenever. Then I saw the guy's picture. Then my father waved a couple of those silly notes we'd written that awful night. I don't know how he got them. Out of a wastebasket—who knows? He obviously saw gold in them. Anyway, those notes—one in my handwriting, the other in the guy's—clearly linked us. 'Go to jail. Go directly to jail' was writ large in dear Daddy's eyes."

Jeth folded his arms and leaned back. "Uh, I don't think so. A note in your handwriting wouldn't put you in jail, no matter what the spy had done. Only if you had written something incriminating. What did you say that could bring the law down on you?"

Janni scoured her arm as if to erase the memory. "We split a stack of Post-Its, and he said we'd write musical terms that started with A. Any I could think of—stuff like *allegro, a cappella, aria.* Who could make the biggest list in fifteen seconds. We did a bunch of rounds that way. Then he wrote 'Arpeggio,' all alone, and showed it to me. I wrote something like, 'Arpeggio. Great word, magnificent passion, superb—oh, c'mon, guy. You know what I'm here for. I'm with you. Your move now,' or some such crappy stuff. That's my double life, Jeth, the top-secret activity I kept hidden from you all these years!" She stopped, sarcasm morphing to shame. "And it gets worse. Turns out that *Arpeggio* was code for this guy's undercover organization. Said so in the clipping. So, you see, just writing that one stupid word tied me to this guy. Sound like a bad movie? *Floozy and the Two-bit Spy.* Me, hooking up with a spy? The *last* thing I'd think of, even if I'd known he was one, which I didn't. Not hard to guess what I did have on my mind—'I'm with you. Your move now'—but there it was, my handwriting, big as life. *Arpeggio.* A 'willing collaborator,' and Daddy has it, along with the same word in the spy guy's handwriting. And Daddy—bless him—is fully capable of selling out his daughter and sending her to jail. And what then? You've been in prison. You know what it's like. Would I have it any cushier? I don't think so!"

She picked at a speck on the couch. "Brandon doesn't have the details, but he knows that his dad and mine have a tight lock on both of us. Bryan, of course, is playing it for all he's worth. Bluffing, maybe. So." She looked up bitterly. "That's what you came to rescue. What do you think of your lover now?"

She pulled away and got up to circle the living room, gnawing her knuckles.

Jeth scowled at the floor, elbows on knees, hands grabbing hair.

Janni yanked the curtain across the picture window as though it had become an enemy. "I know you despise me." Her voice quavered. "That's twice I trashed your love. I have only myself to—"

He looked up sharply. "Oh, stop! Don't think you have a corner on stupid. I don't know which of us would win that contest. I'm just trying to think a way through the mess, but it's beyond either of us. I must say, it's a mess worthy of Brandon's rage, but you said he doesn't know the details."

"No, but Bryan made it clear that if I go down, Brandon goes down, too."

"I don't see how—or why. What did he have to do with it?"

"Nothing, except his connection with you."

"C'mon! That doesn't make sense. Are you saying that Bryan is *jealous* of me? That he doesn't want me to have a better relationship with Brandon than he has?"

"I don't think it's jealousy. He lumps Brandon with you and hates you both."

Jeth leaned forward and scratched at the carpet, searching for some semblance of logic. Then he straightened. "Okay, he hates me; that I can see. But I'm trying to connect the dots between his hating me and hating you and Brandon."

"Huh! He's a hateful man, as in *full...of...hate*. He—"

"Uh-uh. You're just blowing him off. Is it because you wouldn't buy into his brand of love? Because I keep popping in and mucking up his son—is that it?"

"What does it matter? Some people don't need a reason to hate. Look at Daddy. He just plain *hates*."

Jeth shook his head. "No, he doesn't just hate. When I was a little kid, he'd give you candy and pretend he didn't have enough for me, but then he'd give me four pieces to your one."

"Well, that didn't last long, in case you've forgotten. You just learned to keep out of his way."

"Yeah, he had reason to hate me; I'll give him that. But why you? Why would your father, who doted on you not all that long ago, want to—let's face it—nuke you?"

Janni turned away, as though to examine the far edges of her universe. "Control, maybe."

"Well, *duh*! That's a safe answer. I'm just surprised he hasn't made his run for president or grand emperor of—"

"No, you don't understand. He doesn't want that. It's just his own little fiefdom that he must control absolutely. That's his life game. Daddy's the puppeteer, and any woodenhead who counters him gets tossed into the fires of hell. Mom knew that when she married him but thought her beauty would give her the tiny aesthetic space she required in life. She left when she finally realized that even death was better than slavery." With a hand to her face, Janni stood frozen in some sector that was obviously foreign to her. "I miss her." She looked at Jeth, eyes stricken. "And to think I helped drive her off..."

Then she straightened, face reconfiguring to sarcasm once again. "Well, have I connected the dots for you? Daddy hates, Bryan hates, Brandon hates—and I'm pretty sure he's had thoughts of killing his dad. And of course, I hate. I'm born and bred of hatred, and that's never going to change!" Her shoulders shook, though no tears broke through her defenses.

Jeth stood and took her hands, pulling her to the couch. "Shh," he said. "Don't go there. It won't solve anything. Bryan is dying, and I can only keep on with what I've been doing and see if the Red Sea parts."

"What?"

"Never mind." He shook his head. "Y'know, I just thought of something with your spy guy: Did you leave the hotel room first, or did he?"

"Oh, he did. I passed out, and when I woke, he was gone. I was actually surprised that my purse and keys were still there. He could've cleaned me out."

"I don't think he'd do that. Probably would have compromised him. I'm thinking he left because he realized he had the wrong pick-up. You said he sized you up fast, but maybe he made a hasty assumption. He ran *Arpeggio* by you, gave you plenty of room to respond, but then realized he had the wrong floozy and took off."

"Huh!" Janni stared through her thoughts. "Maybe so... Huh! But does it matter?"

"Maybe not, but it does makes sense." He chewed the inside of his cheek. "Y'know, there's something screwy here. I don't believe there's enough in the clipping or the notes to juice up even a first-year law student. The whole thing stinks. You mentioned 'bluff,' and you may be right. Just our raising the question might yank the fangs, like Todd standing up to the Wingate lawyer, but—"

"Todd...?"

"Long story we don't have time for now, but even trying to call their bluff puts both of us at enormous risk. That's the mess part—right there."

He took a big breath and began to pray. Out loud. There was only him and God and Janni. He didn't know what God or Janni would do, but he held her hand and poured out his heart. He wasn't making sense, but Janni seemed calmer.

Just then his cell phone rang. He pulled it from his pocket. It was Rob.

"*Jeth, I've got sad news. Maybelle died last night.*"

Jeth went white and slid off the couch onto the floor. "No! She can't die!"

"I'm sorry—for me and the rest of us, but mostly for you. Her daughter Susie told me that almost her last waking thoughts were for you, to tell you that God is still in salvage. That mean something to you?"

Tears were running down Jeth's face, and he could hardly speak. "Yes. A lot."

Just then the bedroom door opened, and Jeth heard voices filtering out. "I've got to go. Pray for me, Rob. Without Maybelle..."

He reached for Janni to pull him up, then turned her toward the dining room. "Go. Out of sight. Don't let him see you."

Wingate came from the bedroom and swept out the front door without even a glance toward Jeth. Jeth stood uncertainly, not knowing whether to go to Janni or to Bryan or to deal with the spiraling pain in his own heart. He picked Bryan.

Bryan seemed composed but exhausted. He didn't speak or even look at Jeth, just stared at a far corner of the ceiling. Jeth noticed that Bryan's private drawer on the far side of the bed was open a few inches, but he couldn't see what was in it.

"Bryan, do you want me to lock your drawer for you?"

Bryan started, then looked sharply at the drawer. "No! I can." But he couldn't. He lacked strength to even roll in that direction.

"It's all right. None of us will touch it. We'll let you do it when you can."

"No! Help me over."

Jeth positioned him so he could reach it. He had never seen the key to the drawer and didn't know what Bryan would do next.

"Go out. Shut the door."

Jeth raised his eyebrows but said nothing and left the room.

When he came back, the drawer was shut, and Bryan was gasping for breath. Jeth gave him a drink and put a hand on his head until he closed his eyes and fell asleep.

39

The second intruder was less dramatic. Bryan had been ranting about Jeth and Janni wanting to cremate him. "I don't want to be cremated. You'll cremate me just to make me suffer!"

They had said nothing about either cremation or burial, and Jeth began to wonder if some chemical imbalance was spawning paranoia. With legal action pending against Janni and Brandon, this was no time for Bryan to go off his rocker.

As Jeth pondered how to lay cremation to rest, the lamp by the bed—the room's chief source of illumination—began to flicker. In less than a minute it went out altogether. Janni said, "I'll get a bulb."

But the new bulb didn't work. Nor did another. Bryan was growing restless in the dim light. "It's okay, buddy," said Jeth. "We'll sort it out."

But screwing and unscrewing and tightening failed. Finally, Jeth unplugged the lamp and took it to a kitchen outlet. It came on. Had it been plugged in a switchable outlet, perhaps? "That couldn't be it," said Janni. "It's been working fine."

They tried a hand mixer in the outlet, and that didn't work, either. "Okay," Jeth told Bryan, "the outlet's gone. We have no light. I can't fix it, Janni can't, and Brandon…" He shrugged. We need an electrician here. Is that okay? You said you didn't want to be cremated, so I'm guessing the house burning down wouldn't sit well, either. Shall we call somebody?"

Bryan opened his mouth, then closed it and stared at the ceiling. Jeth waited, hoping he wouldn't suggest an extension cord. One more thing to trip over. Finally, Bryan nodded almost imperceptibly.

"Good lad. Got somebody in mind, or shall I run down the Yellow Pages?"

Bryan just shook his head.

Jeth called five different electricians before he found one who was able to come right away—for a price. He passed the amount by Bryan, who waved his agreement dismissively. Janni raised her eyebrows and went to hunt for a flashlight.

While they waited, Jeth studied Bryan. He was failing and needing less pain medication. But it was Jeth who felt troubled and restless. Finally, he leaned forward and spoke. "Bryan, I have a confession to make. Yesterday when Wingate was here, and Janni and I went out of the room, I did what I said I wouldn't do. I held her hand—deliberately. She was upset by her dad's coming, and so was I. I wanted to hold her whole body—for my comfort as much as hers—but I didn't. We talked awhile, and then I prayed. That makes it sound better than it really was. I was just too tired to be in control. I promised you and I failed. I'm sorry. Will you forgive me?"

At first, Bryan seemed about to laugh, but his eyes studied Jeth's face. He looked away—and back—and away again. A tear trickled down his cheekbone. He didn't answer, but Jeth whispered, "Thank you."

The electrician came shortly—Prichard and Son Electric Service. Jeth considered asking if the man was Prichard Junior or Senior, but he was too tired. They had to move the bed a little to make room to work, and after Mr. Prichard had turned off the current downstairs, he laid out his tools and unscrewed the outlet cover.

Bryan raised his hand to Jeth. "You...Janni...go out...shut... door. Go...pray again." This time, a tiny smile lifted one corner of his mouth.

Jeth smiled back. "I'll be good—I promise."

The job took longer than Jeth had expected. Mr. Prichard came out once to go to his truck and looked curiously at Jeth and Janni. Finally, the job was done and the current turned back on. The lamp blazed brightly once more. "Good thing you called when you did," Prichard said. "The wire was bare—looked chewed. Old wiring. Mice, maybe. You might want to check all the wiring one of these days." He said good-bye, again peering at them inquiringly, and went his way.

40

As Bryan sank lower, the strain carved gullies in both Jeth and Janni. He was no longer railing at them, no longer fighting, but neither had the situation been resolved. Jeth spoke even more directly that Bryan might want to think about his wife and what would become of her after he died, but all he would say was, "I've taken care of *her*." Neither would he talk about how he stood with God. Jeth continued to pray and sing and read Scripture, but Bryan had sunk too low to respond.

Finally, Jeth sat back and rubbed his head. "I think you'd better get Brandon, and yes, he does need to be here."

The boy came, looking less than comfortable. "This man is your father," said Jeth. "He gave you life, and he's going to die very soon. Have you been able to forgive him in your heart?"

Brandon frowned and kicked at the leg of the bed.

Suddenly, Bryan opened his eyes and looked at Janni. Their hearts leaped with hope, and they all leaned forward. But, just as suddenly, he lost focus and was gone, eyes blank and fixed.

The three stared at him, then looked at one another in utter shock. Jeth took deep breaths, trying to keep control while flashing back to his rehab days. "Stokie reincarnated?" he muttered petulantly. *God, why do You do this? Why Stokie then? Why Bryan now?*

Brandon grabbed his arm and shook him. "You lied!" he shrieked. "You said God would make it come out all right, and it didn't!" He turned away savagely. "He's not ever going to heaven.

271

He's in hell—right now—and *you can go there, too!*" He kicked a hole in the drywall for emphasis.

Jeth stood and stepped toward him, but his eyes glazed as he crumpled to the floor.

Janni screamed, and Brandon went white. "What'd I do?" he cried. "I killed him!" He dropped down and bent, sobbing, over Jeth's head. "I'm sorry! I'm sorry! Oh God, don't let him die!"

Janni put her ear to his chest. "His heart's beating. His eyes are open, but… Jeth, say something! Can you hear me?"

Brandon blubbered and rubbed Jeth's face. "Please, Jeth. I'm sorry! I didn't mean it. I forgive my dad. Really I do. Please say something!"

Janni put a hand on his shoulder. "He won't hold it against you. You know that."

"I don't want him to die…" He bowed low and wept.

"Go call nine-one-one. Tell them what happened and to come as quick as they can."

Brandon gave Jeth one last pat, then ran to the kitchen phone, shouting words that were scarcely intelligible.

PARAMEDICS WERE AT the door within minutes. They took in the situation—one body on the bed, another on the floor. "My husband is dead, but Jeth is alive," Janni explained. "I just don't know what's wrong."

The two paramedics looked at each other, then checked both bodies. "How long has he been dead?" asked one, bending over Bryan. "Not long, I'd say."

"Ten—fifteen minutes? However long it took you to get here."

"What'd he die of?"

"Cancer!" Janni almost shouted. "But it's Jeth that needs help!"

"He your boyfriend?"

Janni turned away, eyes closed, hand on her head, trying to gain control.

They asked the usual questions: Heart problems? Hit his head? Epilepsy? His blood pressure was low, and he wasn't responding to stimuli. "We'll take him in, but we have to call the police."

Janni nodded. "I'll call the police as soon as we get Jeth taken care of. Bryan can wait. I can't help him anymore."

Janni and Brandon got in the car and rode behind the ambulance, but at the hospital, they were not allowed to stay with Jeth.

"Please, can you look in his pocket for his cell phone?" Janni asked. "I need to call someone, and he has the number programmed."

They brought it to her, and she quickly found Rob's number and explained that Bryan had died and Jeth had crashed. "His blood pressure's low," she said, "but that's all they can find. He's exhausted. We all are, but him especially."

"*Whoosh! That's so Jeth! This happens, Janni—way too often. There's no explanation. He'll come out of it, if it's like the other times. You've all been in a cooker, trying to make a miracle happen. Did it happen, by the way?*"

"No...it didn't. I think that's what pushed him over the edge. He tried so hard..."

"*Janni, we'll do whatever we can for you. Would it help if we came?*"

"Rob, I met you only once." Her voice was trembling. "But I feel like I've known... I can't begin to say..." She couldn't go on.

"*We're here, and we're praying. This whole thing makes me think of Dynamo. The night he won that class, his leg had to have been hurting before he started that final turn around the ring. But he poured out every last ounce of strength and never let on. For you and for Bryan, Jeth gave everything he had and went down like Dynamo, but he's going to be okay. I feel sure of that. I don't know what else to tell you, except to watch out for God. Every time this has happened, it's been an in-your-face thing. And a friendly word of warning: Don't ever stand between God and Jeth. Not safe."*

"Huh!" Janni bit her lip. "I learned that three years ago. On purpose, I stepped between him and God, and *wham!* My loving husband started smacking me down—literally."

Rob didn't reply right away. *"I'm sorry. I hadn't thought of that. You know, then. It's been hard for us to learn. Jeth wears different glasses, and I still haven't got him—or God—figured out. The big question is, what's next? Give me a call when you know something."*

Janni reported the little that Rob had told her to the emergency staff. A nurse looked at her. "Are you all right?"

Janni ran fingers nervously through her hair. "No. My husband is dead at home, and I haven't even reported it."

"You mean, *dead*, dead? Honey, you go straight home. I'm sorry about your husband."

Janni could manage only a weak twitch for a smile.

"They'll do tests," said the nurse, "so it'll be a while. And they'll keep him overnight, pretty sure. You go home, take care of your husband, and get some rest. This your boy?" She turned to Brandon.

"My husband's son, but yes, he is my boy." She smiled shyly at Brandon.

"You go on home now. We'll take care of your friend."

Janni thanked her silently for not asking about Jeth's relation to her. She couldn't have explained that right now.

41

When they got home, Janni forced herself into the bedroom. Brandon, to her surprise, followed. She stood a long time, looking at Bryan—the man who had begun tormenting her as soon as they'd gotten home from their honeymoon. For a month after that, she had tried to please him, and then the full enormity of slapping Jeth had settled in. She sighed. That dinner and the walk by the river—how many centuries ago? She had thrown it all away. Jeth had every right to turn his back, but he had come in her hour of need—first taking Brandon, and now... But what had he actually done? Yes, he had lifted her burden of care. He had poured out his life for her—and yes, for Bryan—but in the end, he had not been able to prevent the day of reckoning. Doomsday was now, the only question being just when and how calamity would hit.

Janni felt some of the anger that had made Brandon lash out at Jeth. Jeth had collapsed, leaving her alone to face her father. He would come, and soon. He was probably checking death notices daily, even before they hit the newspapers. He could well have arranged for someone to call him as soon as his "dear daughter" reported her husband's death. She had no strength left to stand up to him. And yet...and yet... She looked at this man who had been her husband. Something was different. She no longer detested him as she once had. Her situation had not changed, but something in her—something in him... "We didn't even close his eyes." Gently, she bent and ran her hand over his eyelids. Then she clutched her chest against the laceration within and felt Brandon's arm go around her. Knowing full well how costly it might prove, she turned to him and wept.

The doorbell rang. Janni pulled away to answer it, trying to repair her face. The policeman apologized for intruding. "I have a few questions, if you don't mind."

Janni closed her eyes for a moment. "May I ask why?"

"Just routine. Seems the parameds had some concerns about how your husband died and why the other man—" He consulted his notebook. "Jeth Cavendish—that's J-e-t-h?"

"Cavanaugh." She closed her eyes again, this time in relief. At least her father was not behind this visit from the police. "My husband died of cancer. He lived two weeks beyond the date given him. Jeth is an old friend from way back who served as a surrogate father to Bryan's son, and he was here to help us. We were all exhausted, Jeth especially, and when Bryan died, Jeth collapsed. You can look over Bryan's medications." After this quick summary, she led him to the bedroom, where she pointed toward the nightstand and its clutter of a half-filled water glass, skin oil, mouth swabs, tissues, and Jeth's watch and water bottle. "If you have questions about Jeth, you could check at the police station. He's been there two or three times to keep...Sgt. Reye, I think he said—to keep you people abreast of what's been going on. He's been very careful. Didn't want anybody getting the wrong idea."

The officer's only response was a miniscule lift of an eyebrow and a glance at Bryan's body. Then he bent over the drawer to rummage through pain packs and latex gloves.

"He needed hardly any pain meds for nearly a week. You can do an autopsy to check..." Janni rubbed her forehead.

"Anybody pronounce him dead?"

She snorted. "We did. I guess that wasn't too hard."

"What time?"

Janni looked at Brandon. "Five o'clock?"

Brandon shrugged. "Yeah. I guess."

"Well, we'll need to get the coroner here."

The policeman moved to the far side of the bed and examined the contents of that nightstand, then walked through the other rooms on the ground floor. He came back and shrugged. "Those guys been watchin' too many forensic shows. Sorry to bother you. Who's his doctor?"

"He gave up on doctors. Fired them, is what he said. A single round of chemo turned him off, and after that, he wouldn't let anybody in. That's why it was so hard and I needed help. Jeth even figured out how to do a catheter."

"What funeral home you usin'? An autopsy isn't out of the question, but we'll see what the coroner says."

"Labrec Funeral. Bryan was very specific. He didn't want to be cremated, and they know that. I haven't had a chance to call yet. Will they come tonight and take his body, or…"

The man nodded. "I'll call the coroner; you call the funeral. They'll come."

They did come, first the coroner, then the "funeral"—efficient, suave, condescending. "We'll need to sit down with you, perhaps tomorrow or whenever you feel able to talk."

Janni closed her eyes. *Professional death. Oily, smooth…* "Yes, maybe tomorrow. I'll call."

The policeman waited until the men went out with the body, then he too left, leaving Brandon and Janni staring at each other. Brandon turned suddenly and lunged toward the bedroom. "Did you see what he did?"

"Who—the policeman? The other guys? What do you mean?"

"The cop! He looked in the locked drawer!"

Brandon pulled the drawer completely out and set it on the bed. He picked up a sheet of lined paper and scrunched his eyes, trying to make it out. Shaking his head, he set it down and searched through the rest of the drawer. "Phone book…here's his checkbook. Wow! If his scribble's right, he paid the electrician a wad! What else? A pad—same paper." He compared it with the loose sheet.

"Let me see that." Janni picked up the sheet. "It's Bryan's writing—so bad, he must've done it recently." She looked at it closely. "That's my name up top. I'm sure of it. A note for me? Looks like a signature at the bottom—two, actually. This one's Bryan's. And the other is…" She squinted. "A bunch of *l*'s with squiggly lines? Then *P-r* and more squiggles." She shook her head. "Can't make it out."

"Lemme see." He looked over her shoulder. "*P-r*—huh. I dunno."

She shook her head. "It's almost like a legal document, signed and dated. A will? Can't read it! Makes no sense." She threw the paper down and clutched her hair.

Brandon picked up the paper and took it to the kitchen, turning on all the lights. "Sort of like chat talk—letters standing for words. Come help me. Right after your name. *R gnt gt NVLP…* something *bx*. Then big letters, *BRN*."

"Would that be 'Brandon'? No…'Burn,' maybe. Burn what?"

"Dunno. Not this, you'd think. Something in the drawer—the checkbook, maybe?"

Janni took it from him and thumbed through it, then shook her head.

"This *bx* and *pswd*," said Brandon. "And this big *GRNDL* in front of them. A line by itself. Seems important. Caps seem to mean something."

"Yeah, seems so. Something really big. My name didn't even rate a big *j*." She put her hands to her face. "Brandon, we're not *getting* this."

"Jeth would know."

"Yes. Dynamo… He'd know. But it's the middle of the night. The hospital would never let us in, and we don't even know if he's— Wait! If we tell them about Bryan being dead and that we didn't get a chance to see Jeth after— Brandon, let's try it! Be sure to bring the paper. I'll get the checkbook and pad—everything out of that drawer. My father's got a key to the house!"

She had hardly spoken the words when they heard the doorbell and the sound of a key in the lock.

Janni froze. She turned and thrust the checkbook and pad at Brandon. "Quick! Take everything somewhere and hide it!" She put her hands over her face and tried to calm her pounding heart.

The door opened, and Mr. Wingate came through. He pushed it shut with his foot, his pouched eyes glaring at Janni. "Bryan's dead," he said, shoving past her into the bedroom. Within seconds, he came out with the empty drawer in hand. "Where is it?" he demanded. "What did you do with it?"

"What did I do with what? What are you looking—"

"Don't play games! You know what I'm talking about. What did you do with it?"

"I did nothing with anything! The drawer's empty; you can see that. I took it out to see if something was in back or under—ow!" She cried out as he grabbed her arm and shoved her over the arm of the sofa.

"Tell me, or I'll turn you to pulp!" He yanked her upright and slapped her to the floor.

Just then Brandon came down the stairs, speaking loudly into a phone in his hand. "I'm at five-five-seven-three Maple Avenue. My stepmother's father came in the house, and he's hitting her. She's down on the floor. Please—" His voice was trembling. "Please come as quick as you can."

Mr. Wingate looked up sharply and moved toward the stairs.

"Hurry!" cried Brandon into the phone. He ran back upstairs, slammed the door of his room, and shoved furniture against it.

Wingate stopped at the foot of the stairs. "*You...scumbag!*" he hurled upward, and with a powerless "Ehhhrr!" he turned and banged out of the front door.

Janni lay crying in the silence, then called out with shaking voice, "He's gone."

Brandon moved aside enough of the pile to get out of his room and descended the stairs cautiously, phone still in hand.

"It's okay," Janni said. "I heard the car start and tires squeal, but check out the window."

"Yeah, he's gone. Should I call the police?"

"You just did."

Brandon grinned and tossed the phone toward her. "That thing's been wasted for light-years. The only one I could find upstairs."

Janni stared at him stupidly, then began laughing hysterically. Brandon laughed, too, until Janni's laughter turned to sobs. He stood uncertainly, then bent down. "It's okay now. He's gone."

She sat up and wiped her nose. "He's gone but not done. He's a viper. He won't leave us alone."

"Okay, then we gotta go see Dynamo."

Janni half laughed, half cried. "Brandon, what would I do without you?"

42

They had no trouble getting in to see Jeth. He had been awake for some time and was asking for them—urgently, repeatedly. He looked terrible, face pasty and deeply etched. He had an IV in his arm and oxygen tubes in his nose, and Janni hoped he wouldn't see her battered face. She smiled brightly. "You're awake. Rob was right. He said you'd be okay after scaring everybody to death."

"Bryan's dead."

"Yes. And we called the funeral home. That part is taken care of."

"But he left you in a swamp full of crocodiles."

She shifted uncomfortably and glanced at Brandon. "We don't know. He—"

"I blew it." Jeth closed his eyes. "I—"

"Shh. No. You didn't blow it. We just don't know yet. He wrote something we can't figure out. His handwriting is crappy, but then he used some sort of shorthand."

"He wrote something?" Jeth struggled to sit up.

"Let me raise the bed, and we'll show you. Brandon's got the letter."

She pushed the button and adjusted his pillow, then handed him the paper. "It's written to me—that much we figured out."

"I can't read it. Can you turn up the light?"

Brandon went to the doorway and fiddled the lights full-on.

"We think it might be a legal document. He signed it, and there's another signature beneath his, but it's just initials and squiggles. Like four *l*'s with squiggles in between, then *P-r* something. He says a lot in the middle, but we can't make sense of any of it. I don't want to get you stirred up, but maybe you can…" She tried to appear calm.

Brandon leaned over and pointed. "Capital letters—see? Didn't use many. Like here—*R gnt* and *BRN NVLP*. We think that's 'Burn'…something."

"Urgent burn envelope?" Jeth suggested.

"'*Urgent*'—yes, that's it!" said Janni. "And 'envelope.' Why couldn't we see that? But what envelope? This paper? It wasn't in an envelope."

"Well, don't burn anything till we figure it out," said Jeth. He drew a shaky breath. "Keep going."

A nurse came into the room. "You'll have to make this a short visit. He needs rest."

Jeth sat up straight and raised his hand. Janni captured the hand and pushed him back, then ushered the nurse to the corridor. "This is critical in so many ways, and we need some time. If I were to leave now, Jeth would be in such a state, he'd probably check himself out of the hospital. Please—will you guard us? I promise to keep him as calm as I can. It's more like a puzzle we need to figure out, a puzzle with enormous consequences. Give us at least a half hour. If you shut the door, maybe no one will notice the light on."

The nurse's lips pursed ominously, but she turned, and Janni came back in. "Okay. I bought some time. But you, my man—keep cool, hear?" She smiled.

Jeth, not smiling, put a trembling finger on the paper. "*Bx* has to be 'box,' and *pswd*…'password'? But the *GRNDL* before 'box'…" He thought a moment, then shook his head. "Let's go on to the small print."

"*Wsh treetd b-t-r Brndn to lat. Nt to lte.* Kind of messed up. *Cpy this*, and here's the 'urgent burn envelope' part. *Gt wtns to brn.*"

"Get witness to burn, maybe," said Jeth. "*Dnt let W get. Hoosh!*" He scratched his head. "Wingate?" He looked at Janni, his eyes narrowing. "What happened to your face?"

"Never mind that. We don't have time. I'm okay. Just focus."

He stared at the *GRNDL* and rubbed his ear. "I can't figure it out. 'Grand' something?"

They tossed around whatever words came to mind—grand, ground, grind. "How about 'groaned'?" asked Brandon. "I'm doing that. But what's the *L*?"

The nurse returned. "I'm sorry, but you've got to go. My supervisor says you have to leave—now."

Janni put her hands to her face, her breath coming in gasps. But she looked at Jeth and knew the nurse was right. They did have to get out so he could rest. "I'm sorry…" She took his hand and held it as she pulled away, stretching as far as she could. "We'll be back as soon as they'll let us in." She turned quickly so he wouldn't see her dismay.

JETH, EYES DESPERATE, watched them disappear, paying no attention to the nurse's attempts to calm him. Suddenly, he sat up straight, even though she had lowered the bed. "Grundel!" he exclaimed. "The Grundel box! Janni! Come back!"

"What?" The nurse looked at him, perplexed.

"You've got to get them!" he cried. "Grab them down the hall. Get them back here!"

"You need to—"

"Go!" he thundered. "It's life-and-death. *Run!*"

She looked at him uncertainly, then turned and ran. Jeth closed his eyes but continued to sit upright, breathing heavily into the pulsing silence of a hospital night.

After in interminable interval, the nurse returned. "I tried," she said, "but—"

Jeth threw himself back on the pillow, his hands over his face.

"I'm sorry," she said. "The elevator door was closing when I turned the corner. I called, but I don't think they heard me. She did say they'd be back soon."

"She doesn't have it. The key information, the missing piece of the puzzle."

The nurse said nothing helpful and instead hovered, fluffed his pillow, pulled the blanket straight.

Jeth yanked the oxygen tube from his nose. "Get rid of this thing. And just go. I'm all right."

She stood uncertainly a moment. Then, as she turned to shut off the oxygen, rapid footsteps sounded in the hallway. Janni appeared at the door. "What happened? What's wrong?" she asked the nurse. "Somebody called. Was it you? We tried to get the elevator to stop and go back up, but it kept going all the way down, and then a lot of stops on the way up. I'm sorry!"

Jeth sat up and reached for her hand. "It's Grundel—the Grundel box! That's the password!"

"Grundel? My *grandfather*?"

"Yes! Years ago, your grandfather saved the honor of some electrician your father hired to replace an electrical panel. Wingate tried to tell him how to do his job, and if the instructions had been followed, the stable would've been toast and the electrician in court. Your grandfather sized things up, gave his own instructions, and it all worked out. The 'Grundel box' was a standing joke after that—out of your father's hearing, of course. One of the stable guys must've told Bryan the story. I don't think he was around when it happened." Jeth's hands were trembling. "The electrician—what was his name?"

"Who? At the stable?"

"No. The house. The outlet."

"Oh, him!" Janni thought a moment. "I can see the truck out front. Somebody and Son."

"P-r..." said Brandon, looking at the paper. "Wait! I got the checkbook!"

"Orchard—something like that?" said Janni.

"Hard to read...*l*'s and *y*'s...can't make it out the first name. Last name...*P-r-c-h-n-d*? Or maybe *r-d*...Prichard!" declared Brandon triumphantly. "I remember!"

"Prichard and Son—you're right!" Jeth exclaimed. "What's the date by the signature on the paper?"

"August twenty-third. And that's the checkbook date—I think." Brandon pulled it close to his nose. "His handwriting..."

"We'll go with it," said Jeth. "Go find Prichard, run the password by him, and see what he can tell you. If he has the envelope, he could probably witness the burning. But get a piece of paper and write what you're doing. Get him to sign it legibly and print out his name. But if it's just extra running around, get whoever's handy and trustworthy. Don't take chances. You got enough to go on. Just go."

"There's more on the paper," said Brandon. "Something about you."

"No time. Wingate owns the house. He won't wait till things are neat and tidy here. Go!"

Janni leaned over with a quick kiss. "At least this time we have something to go on. You'll pray for us? And be calm. Stop hyperventilating. You make me nervous."

ONE MIGHT HAVE as effectively invoked calmness on the rapids of the Amazon River. Jeth lay on the bed, heart pounding. He couldn't find his watch. The only time he had asked, it had been around one in the morning, and he didn't know how much time had passed since then. Tied to the intravenous drip, his toss-and-turn was limited. Finally, after what seemed like a whole day, he pulled the bedside table close enough to reach the phone.

"Rob. I woke you up. I'm sorry. I don't know what time it is, but I'm terrified. I had to do something. I had to call. I'm sorry."

Rob cleared his throat. *"Jeth. Where are you? No—dumb question—sorry. You're in the hospital."*

"Yes. What time is it?"

"Uh…three-o-seven. Do you need a nurse to come in?"

"That won't help. Rob, I can't pray, I can't think. I've never felt so weak in my whole life. God has left me, Rob. The glo—"

"Stop. God hasn't left you, Jeth. And no, His glory hasn't departed. He said—He promised—He would never leave you. He meant it then; He means it now. What's going on? Where are Janni and Brandon?"

Jeth took a big breath. "Bryan left a note that looks like some sort of signed, legal document. Hard to decipher, but I think we got the important part. They went out to follow up on it. But Wingate's closing in, and it could all go up in flames. They haven't been to bed, haven't eaten…"

"Jeth—"

"It's the middle of the night. Who are they going to find to help them? I don't know what the actual arrangement was between Wingate and Bryan—I don't think Janni knows, either—but—"

"Jeth, stop talking. Listen to me. Do you remember the day we bought Woodbine? He was scared, didn't want to go over the jumps. You took him over low jumps in easy steps. Remember where you've been, Jeth, where God helped you. The time you couldn't ride worth beans, but Woodbine came through and won the class for you. We both agreed it had to be God. You drove to Janni's when you could hardly see. Had to have been God. He hasn't left you. You've got gremlins under your bed right now, and they're making a lot of noise. Jeth, you're exhausted. You need to sleep. I'll see if I can get somebody on that. Sleep, Jeth. Rest. I think you'll find out tomorrow that God is still alive and in business."

"In business… Maybelle…"

"Yeah, Maybelle. Salvage business, wasn't it? Remember what she said at your baptism? *You will be clothed in power from on high.* We've seen that, again and again. Hang on to it, Jeth. Hang on to Maybelle."

43

Sun slanted across Jeth as he lay asleep. Janni and Brandon whispered back and forth. The nurses had needed to give him a shot to settle him down, they said. Sleep was what he needed most, they said. But for Janni and Brandon, other matters loomed equally large. While they debated, Jeth convulsed with a sharp cry and a wild, frightened look. Janni leaned over and cradled his head. "It's all right, Jeth. I'm here. It's all right."

His breath came in spasms. "I was riding...Dynamo...at Candlewood, only the horse was Wingate...ears flat against his head. The trophy was you, and I...I couldn't stop him. He was winning, his finest form, but...his heart...a molten lump of evil. The judges couldn't see that part. Saw only his dazzling conformation, his long, wavy mane and tail. I couldn't stop him, Janni!"

"Shh. The nightmare is over." She stroked his head. "You're awake now. I'm right here. Brandon's here."

Jeth closed his eyes, then opened them abruptly. "Did he win?" His voice croaked.

Janni frowned, trying to catch his drift, then smiled. "No, he didn't get the trophy. He's got the house. That was his to start with, but he doesn't have me." She looked around, then picked up a glass from the tray table. "Think about food for a minute. They left you some breakfast. Take a sip of juice."

He took a few swallows, but his eyes didn't leave her face.

"Let's see what they fixed." She lifted the lid from the tray. "Cereal, toast, a poached—"

"What time is it?"

"Nearly ten. Better eat this quick. Brandon's drooling from both sides of his mouth."

"Let him have it."

"No, we had a little food. You need this. Come on. I'll help you. And while you eat, I'll tell our story."

"I wanna raise the bed." Brandon grinned and pushed the button. "Say when."

Jeth smiled weakly and waved his hand when it reached the right angle.

"I learned from you that the police station was the best place to start," Janni began. "I told them how you'd talked to Sgt. What's-His-Name, and sure enough, they found all of us on the computer. They made photocopies of the letter and kept one. They looked up the Prichard address for me—Llewellyn—those multiple L squiggles—and off we went, trembling in our boots. Well…Brandon wasn't scared. I was." She nudged the boy with her elbow.

"We rang the bell and knocked a long time before anyone came, and then finally Lew opened the door a crack. I didn't even apologize. Just asked if 'Grundel box' meant anything. His eyes went wide and then the door. No, he didn't have the envelope, but he knew where it was—at the house." She reached over and replaced the bedsheet Jeth had thrown off. "While he dressed, the police came. Turned out he'd called them before answering the door. I explained what was going on. Anyway, we got a police escort to the house, and I was glad for that."

Jeth looked at her. "Does being 'glad' have anything to do with Daddy messing with your face?"

"Still shows, hm? I tried powder, but wrong color. Anyway, we went to the bedroom. Lew had Brandon go downstairs and shut off the electricity, and with the cop holding a flashlight, he unscrewed the outlet plate and the box. The envelope was there, inside the wall! Bryan's idea. I don't think Daddy ever would have found it."

Jeth shook his head in amazement. "What was in it?"

"The agreement he and Bryan had worked out, and it was awful. Your dream about my beloved father wasn't far off the mark. So bad, I wanted to take it to a lawyer before burning it, to get his take on it and to see if we had cause for legal action, but Brandon insisted we get rid of it ASAP. The cop didn't actually say he agreed, but you could tell he did. We went out back, dug a hole in one of the flower beds, and torched it. Oh! Let me tell you what else was in there, and I have no idea how Bryan got hold of them. Those stupid notes I wrote to whatever his name was. They were there, and you can't believe how good it felt to see them burn! I'm thinking maybe Bryan threatened to scratch the agreement unless he had those notes in hand." She thought a moment. "The newspaper clipping wasn't there, but without the notes, it wouldn't mean anything."

"Maybe Bryan got the notes the last time your father came?"

Janni looked off. "Maybe something happened inside Bryan, after all," she said wistfully. "Anyway…" She looked back at Jeth. "We still had the pad, so I dated a sheet and wrote down exactly what we did, and we all signed it. Don't know if anyone but Llewellyn Prichard's signature proves legal, but we did what seemed best. I can't begin to tell you exactly what the agreement was, but it put everything—including Brandon—in Daddy's hands, and just wrap your mind around what that would have meant for our guy here." She looked sideways with a grin and a nudge. "I would, of course, get nothing from the estate, and the threat the note posed for me would have effectively kept you out of the way. Any attempt by you to wiggle around it would have sent me straight to prison."

Jeth's eyes widened, but Janni hurried on. "The agreement did say clearly, though, that the copy signed by Bryan had to be presented for the deal to go through." She stopped and stared at the steady drip of the IV bag.

"We talked to my lawyer briefly—a miracle appointment in itself—and I think...I *think* there will be some money for me from Bryan's estate, but knowing how much he hated me, I'm not counting on it. The attorney was short on time. It was a mess, he said, that he'd have to sort through, but he confirmed that destroying the agreement was a good thing. He's going to get a court order so we can get our stuff out of the house." She took a big breath. "So, I'm homeless but not in prison and not in the gutter, as both of them wanted." She smiled and reached toward the tray. "Here. Take a bite of toast. I know—cold toast is nasty."

Jeth chewed, then grinned impishly. "We'll have to talk about the house part. I have an idea or two. Think she'd like the trailer, Brandon?"

"Hey, I'd like it!" he said. "You dudes go somewhere else."

"You said there was more to the letter," said Jeth.

"Oh, yes! Almost forgot that part. Where is it, Brandon?"

The boy pulled it from his pocket and spread it on Jeth's lap.

"Okay," said Janni. "This first line. Couldn't figure it out. *Wsh treetd btr Brndn to lat nt to lte*—is the next word 'rescind'? Kind of messed up. *Cpy this*, then the 'urgent burn envelope' part and 'get witness to burn.'"

Brandon went back to the first line. "That's my name. Does it say what I...?"

"I think so, buddy," said Jeth. "He wished he had treated you better, but it was too late. And the rest must be 'not too late to rescind.' And then he goes into the urgent business."

"Sounds right," said Janni.

"Hey," said Brandon, "this is crazy cool!"

"Yeah, it is," said Janni. "And we're all in it. Here's the line about Jeth: *Jeth say sry me. I sry hm Gd b mcfl.* That one I can't make out. Something about God. Is that 'sorry'? It doesn't make sense. 'Jeth say "sorry me."'"

Tears were running down Jeth's face. "'God, be merciful to me.' That hymn you started to read." For a moment, Jeth couldn't talk. Then he went on. "After your dad left, I apologized to Bryan for breaking my word and holding your hand."

"You didn't!"

"I had to tell him. There in the living room with you, my head was R-rated, but I did manage to keep it down to hand holding. Just the telling shook him—I could see that—but it did something, and I'm almost positive he forgave me. I think right then, *everything came together.* This note…" His breath came in gasps.

Janni's face collapsed. "Oh, Jeth! It did happen! We just didn't know."

Brandon gripped his head. "Stop it, guys!" He spun away, fighting for control.

"Come over here," Jeth ordered. "I need my son to hug me. And remember—if you ever need to be catheterized, I got that down pretty good!"

Brandon started to laugh, then fell on the bed, crying. "I'm sorry, Jeth. I thought I killed you. And you were right about God. God…I'm sorry…I'm *sorry.*"

A nurse came through the doorway and saw the tangled cluster on the bed. "Oh!" she exclaimed. "Should I be worried about this or not?"

"Not," said Jeth, looking up and laughing weakly. "Definitely not. This is a gorgeously wonderful, extraordinary day. God saves sinners, God saved us—from more than any of us will ever know."

The nurse raised her eyebrows beyond high. "Well…if you need me…" She beat a hasty retreat.

Jeth watched her leave, his face turning somber. "God saves sinners…but the naked truth?" He continued staring at the door. "I'm the one who caused this huge, snarly mess. I touched off the clash between you and your dad. I came between Rob and Katie. If I hadn't come into your life, everything would've been different."

His voice took on energy. "Daddy and Bryan hated you only because of me. If I hadn't been in the picture, you'd still be Daddy's girl, and Bryan the last person you'd ever think of marrying. You'd be rich and happy with whoever else you chose, and—"

Brandon glanced anxiously at Janni, and she quickly put her hand over Jeth's mouth. "Shh. You're tired. You're not thinking straight. You need rest."

He closed his eyes, but gloom remained heavy on him.

"Stop and think," said Janni. "Could I possibly be happy without you? Sure, we fought and scrapped from our playpens on, but always, always, our hearts were one. I see that now. And if anyone's to blame, it's me. Number one: My anger over you going to prison drove me smack into that spy mess. Number two: I whacked you by the river and made that terrible vow—which I soon broke, you may have noticed. Number—"

Laughter broke through Jeth's angst. "C'mon! You can't possibly outdo me. I won't let you!"

Janni gripped his arm and hitched toward him. "Here's something else to think about: Without all this, we wouldn't have Brandon." She beamed. "He's *our* boy now. And Jeth, I see other things, too." She laughed, but her eyes, wide and glistening, looked past him. "A lot of connections. Hidden stuff I never knew. You tried to tell me, but I wouldn't hear you. But now, like you said, *everything* has come together. Everything. If only I had listened that night by the river…"

"Yeah," Jeth said softly, putting his hand over hers. "That slap… It changed our lives and sent us both down long, dark tunnels. Not exactly what we were hoping for, but God's light might never have appeared—for either of us—any other way."

Janni squeezed his arm, then pulled away and dug Jeth's phone from her purse. She scrolled through his contacts, punched her selection, and pushed *Call*. "Rob!" she cried. "Dynamo lives! You told me to watch out for God, and you were right. You won't believe the story we have to tell!"

She told it in brief and then said she'd call back with more details. She listened to Rob for a moment, and the smile left her face. She took the phone from her ear and handed it to Jeth. "Rob wants to talk to you," she said softly.

"Rob—what's wrong? What happened?" His voice was tight. "Katie? Jessie?"

"Jeth, we're okay—all of us. I just got back from Maybelle's funeral. One of the most powerful and moving services I've ever been to. She was an extraordinary woman, that angel of yours."

"She came through for me, Rob, right to the end."

"She did. And you were mentioned more than once in the service. You were very special to her, and everyone knew it. And I wanted you to know."

Jeth could not finish the conversation and handed the phone to Janni. She talked a bit more, then put the phone back in her purse and reached across the breakfast tray for a tissue to wipe his face. "Here we are, brimming with joy, and you haven't had a minute to grieve. My dearest, I wish I'd known this special lady of yours." She turned on the bed, took him in her arms, and rocked. "Someday, though, O best beloved, you will again be as happy as I can make you."

Jeth settled back. "I am happy—even for Maybelle. And now," he added with a weak grin, "I can hug you with my arms and not just my heart." He touched her face. "Almost as though the past has been erased and we can start over. Almost as though..." He stopped, his face tightening again.

Brandon came close and put his hand awkwardly on Jeth's head. He cleared his throat and shut his eyes tight. "God. Help Jeth. And thanks for helping us." He opened his eyes, then closed them again. "And I'm sorry for what I did. Did You hear me say that before?"

Janni reached out and gripped Brandon's arm. "God, I say amen to all that! And P.S., God—I'm a Wingate. Does that put me off Your charts? If not, I'd much rather line up behind Jeth than behind my father. And a double amen for that one."

As she leaned to kiss Jeth, the nurse came through the doorway with starch in her step. "And I say, God. Send them out of here so that man can get some sleep!"

They laughed and separated. After assuring Jeth that they would return later, Janni kissed him one last time and then pulled away.

Jeth watched as they waved out of sight down the hallway, then lay back, eyes closed. One last kiss. How different this one from that final kiss in the motel parking lot years ago! That one had left him cold, withered, hopeless. Although this kiss lasted no longer and packed no more passion, he felt warm, filled, whole. Filled with Janni's love, yes, but God was hugging his soul, and that made all the difference. Dynamo was dead, Maybelle was dead, Bryan was dead, but God had dredged new life out of these deaths, and the three now rode with Jeth on a victory lap that would end in an incredibly beautiful and unfading blaze of glory.

GLOSSARY

American Saddlebred: A horse breed developed in Kentucky by plantation owners, now used largely for showing. These horses can be trained as three-gaited or five-gaited. (See **Gait**.)

Colors

> **Bay:** A horse coloration ranging from tan to reddish-brown, with black mane, tail, and lower legs.
>
> **Chestnut:** A horse coloration in which the body, mane, and tail are uniform shades of brown. A liver chestnut, sometimes referred to as a brown, has brown legs, not black as a bay would have. Lighter shades are sometimes called sorrel.
>
> **Gray:** A horse coloration involving black skin, with hair a mix of black and white, growing increasingly lighter with age. A white horse has pink skin.
>
> **Dapple:** A horse coloration distinguished by round spots of a different shade or tone, giving it a mottled appearance, most commonly seen on the horse's rump, although gray horses can be entirely dappled.

Currycomb: A device made of metal, plastic, or rubber, with small teeth for deep-cleaning a horse.

English: Referring to riding with English tack (including an English saddle, which is flat and has no horn) and appropriate attire.

Farrier: A skilled horseshoer.

Faults: Type of mistake factored into the judging of horse shows. A knockdown or refusal incurs four faults. Every four seconds over the time allowance results in one fault. Placings are based on the lowest number of points, or "faults," accumulated. A clear round means no jumping faults or penalty points. Tied entries usually jump over a raised and shortened course; if entries are tied on faults, the fastest time wins.

Gait: A specific pattern of foot movement, such as the walk, trot, or canter. Walk is a four-beat, flat-footed gait; trot is a two-beat, diagonal gait; canter is a three-beat gait with the right or left foot leading. A gallop is a fast canter. Five-gaited is a progression: Walk, trot, slow gait (a fast, smooth walk), rack (a fast slow gait), canter. (See **Rack.**)

Gelding: A male horse that has been castrated (had its testicles removed).

Girth: A wide strap beneath a horse's belly that holds the saddle in place.

Grand Prix: Top-caliber classes in dressage and show jumping, often offering large cash prizes.

Heat: The time in the mare's breeding cycle when she is "hot," or receptive to the stallion.

Jumps: A series of obstacles in stadium-jumping classes that must be negotiated, usually within a certain time frame. Included are verticals, spreads, double and triple combinations, with factors including distance between jumps, type and order of jumps, and height. Jumps may have simple or complex wings that direct the horse to the jump itself. Some specific jumps:

>**Oxer:** A pair of rail jumps positioned closely, both of which must be cleared. The rails can be arranged in assorted patterns.
>
>**Water fence** in various configurations.
>
>**Brush fence:** A solid base with brush placed on top.
>
>**Faux stone wall** with blocks on top that can be knocked off.

Lungeing: A training method in which the horse moves in a circle, roughly 60 feet in diameter, at various gaits around the handler, limited by either a long line and long whip, or by a roundpen with whip alone.

Mare: A female horse four years old and over.

Open: Competition available to anyone: professionals, amateurs, youth.

Paddock: A small enclosure for exercise or pasture.

Paint: A breed of horse whose coat features large blocks of white and black or brown.

Rack: See **Gait**. The faster a horse can rack while staying in good form, the better, though speed without proper form is unacceptable.

Rein: A long strap, passing from the bit to the rider's hands, by which the rider maintains control of the horse. A horse is normally mounted from the left, or near, side of a horse. Thus, an "off rein" refers to the rein on the right, or "off," side of a horse. Keeping a tight off rein prevents a rider from being bitten by the horse.

Roundpen: A round enclosure roughly 60 feet in diameter, formed by sections of pipe fencing positioned in a circle and used for lungeing.

Shying: An instinctive reaction of a horse that has been startled by a sudden noise or movement.

Stadium jumping: Competitive show jumping events within a ring or arena in which the horse's performance is the sole deciding factor.

Stallion: A male horse four years and older that has not been gelded.

Stirrup: A light frame or ring that holds the foot of a rider, attached to a saddle by a strap often called a stirrup leather.

Tack: Equipment used on a horse (saddle, halter, bridle, etc.).

DISCUSSION QUESTIONS

1. What did you like or dislike about the story plot? What characters were especially appealing to you? Did you find that you identified closely with any of them?

2. Does the horse theme serve a larger purpose?

3. Jeth had unusual experiences with God. What were some of them? Measuring them against the God who is revealed in the Bible, are they believable? Have you had events in your life that you thought odd or uncomfortable? What unusual experiences are happening in today's world?

4. Jeth felt at home with Old Testament prophets. Can you name any prophets who had experiences similar to Jeth's?

5. Maybelle served as an anchoring "angel" for Jeth, helping him interpret the events of his life. In what instances were her words frightening to Jeth?

6. Rob and Katie had an up-and-down relationship. Did baby Jessie fix it totally? Why or why not? (Perhaps your own experiences will help you respond.)

7. Relational tensions among characters are sometimes hard on readers. What can be learned from the way these characters reacted to each other, positively and negatively?

8. Do you think Rob handled Jeth well? If you were in his shoes, how would you have reacted to Jeth's personality and to his odd experiences?

9. After Jeth's win on Jo Jo and Wingate's offer to buy him, he experienced a "burning bush" encounter. Did you see other evidences in the scene that back that up?

10. In your opinion, is Dynamo the main character of the story? Why or why not?

11. In light of Katie's statement that Jeth was born to ride Dynamo, did the horse become an idol in his life, or was the stallion a tool in God's hands?

12. Janni says at the end, "Dynamo lives!" What did she mean by that?

13. What are Janni's strengths and weaknesses? Assuming she and Jeth marry, what problems do you see arising in their marriage?

14. Brandon did turn around. How, specifically, did Jeth help make this happen? Would this work with children in real life?

15. "Love your enemies" may be the most radical words that Jesus spoke. Henri Nouwen comments that "these words reveal to us most clearly the kind of love proclaimed by Jesus. In these words we have the clearest expression of what it means to be a disciple of Jesus. Love for one's enemy is the touchstone of being a Christian."* Apply this to Jeth's situation.

16. Comment on Maybelle's statement that many Christians are "starving" at a banquet table because they are simply not hungry for the Word of God.

---

* Henri Nouwen, *Show Me the Way* (New York: Crossroad Publishing, 1994).

17. What was the significance of the private Communion service in the hospital?

18. Maybelle spoke of a "tipping point" in Jeth's life. What was this event, and do you agree with her? Do you see other moments that one might identify as "tipping points"?

19. For some readers, Jeth and Janni may not be likable characters. Does God "improve" them or simply use their personalities?

20. What is the takeaway message of this story for you?

ABOUT THE AUTHOR

Eleanor K. Gustafson began thinking up stories when she was five or six. When she started to read, God drew her to Himself with—yes—a story. Her fascination with story continued, but after reading her early attempts at writing, friends and even her mother told her straight-out to stick to music as a career. She pushed manfully along, however, and began publishing both fiction and nonfiction in 1978. *Dynamo* is her fifth novel and builds off her lifelong love of horses. Her previous title with Whitaker House is *The Stones*, a novel of the life of King David.

A graduate of Wheaton College in Illinois, Eleanor has been actively involved in church life as a minister's wife, teacher, musician, writer, and encourager. Additional experiences (besides horses) include gardening, house construction, tree farming, and parenting—all of which have helped bring color and humor to her fiction. One of her major writing goals has been to make scriptural principles understandable and relevant for today's readers through the undeniable power of story.

Readers can find out more about Eleanor on her Web site, www.eleanorgustafson.com.